"I didn't gamble my horses away,"

Sage said finally. Did it matter how much he told her or what she thought? He would do almost anything to get what he wanted. "I sold the stock off, one by one, each sale like cutting off a piece of my own skin."

Sage glanced down at Carly, who was listening to him with compassion on her sweet face. He swallowed. Damn, but he hated this. If he managed to pull himself back up, he swore he would never be vulnerable to anyone else again.

"Why did you have to do that?" Carly asked when he didn't continue.

"There's not that much to tell." Again he swallowed a lump of pride. He didn't want help, especially not hers! He wanted to take, not ask, and to give her back something to remember, the passion that sang in his veins whenever she was near.

Dear Reader,

Welcome to Silhouette **Special Edition** . . . welcome to romance. Each month, Silhouette **Special Edition** publishes six novels with you in mind—stories of love and life, tales that you can identify with—romance with that little "something special" added in.

And this month has some wonderful stories in store for you. Lindsay McKenna's *One Man's War* continues her saga that is set in Vietnam during the sixties—MOMENTS OF GLORY. These powerful tales will capture you from the first page until the last! And we have an exciting debut this month—Debbie Macomber begins her new series, THOSE MANNING MEN. Don't miss the first book—*Marriage of Inconvenience*—Rich and Jamie's story.

Rounding out March are more stories by some of your favorite authors: Mary Curtis, Erica Spindler, Pamela Toth and Pat Warren. It's a wonderful month for love!

In each Silhouette **Special Edition** novel, we're dedicated to bringing you the romances that you dream about—stories that will delight as well as bring a tear to the eye. And that's what Silhouette **Special Edition** is all about—special books by special authors for special readers!

I hope you enjoy this book and all of the stories to come!

Sincerely,

Tara Gavin
Senior Editor
Silhouette Books

PAMELA TOTH
Two Sets of Footprints

Silhouette Special Edition

Published by Silhouette Books New York

America's Publisher of Contemporary Romance

This book is dedicated
to the memory of Jonas W. Patterson,
for all the lives he touched with love

 SILHOUETTE BOOKS
300 East 42nd St., New York, N.Y. 10017

TWO SETS OF FOOTPRINTS

Copyright © 1992 by Pamela Toth

ISBN: 0-373-09729-8

First Silhouette Books printing March 1992

All the characters in this book have no existence outside the
imagination of the author and have no relation whatsoever to
anyone bearing the same name or names. They are not even
distantly inspired by any individual known or unknown to the
author, and all incidents are pure invention.

®: Trademark used under license and registered in the United
States Patent and Trademark Office and in other countries.

Printed in the U.S.A.

Books by Pamela Toth

Silhouette Special Edition

Thunderstruck #411
Dark Angel #515
Old Enough to Know Better #624
Two Sets of Footprints #729

Silhouette Romance

Kissing Games #500
The Ladybug Lady #595

PAMELA TOTH

was born in Wisconsin, but grew up in Seattle, where she attended the University of Washington and majored in art. She still lives in the Pacific Northwest with her husband, two teenaged daughters, a boxer named Jackson, two Siamese cats and several tanks of tropical fish. Relationships have always fascinated her, especially relationships between parent and child; friends and lovers; husband and wife. Writing romances gives her the chance to explore the courtship between men and women, and the potential for love that exists in all of us. When she isn't sitting at her computer, she likes to read, travel and spend time with her family and pets.

OKLAHOMA

ARK.

NEW MEXICO

Dallas

The Rolling Gold ●
● ● Fort Worth

LA.

TEXAS

Austin
★

Houston
●

N

MEXICO

Gulf of Mexico

All underlined places are fictitious.

Chapter One

A horse's shrill whinny pierced the heavy air, and the stablehand's body crashed against the inside wall of the barn with a solid thud. The young man's moan of pain was all but drowned by the overhead rumble of thunder, and the horse reared, almost pulling Carly Golden off her feet.

"Damn it, Ben! Help me get Sky Walker back into his stall, then see to Joey!" she shouted over the fury of the storm, holding with all her strength on to the rope that threatened to snake through her palms. They never should have waited until the storm began.

Ben was an old man who moved slowly, but for once Carly was unable to be patient.

"Hurry!" she implored as Joey groaned and the panic stricken horse screamed again.

Before Ben could grasp the free end of the other rope, a figure in black came through the doorway and pushed past him.

"Hold open the stall door," the stranger said harshly to Ben. "And stay the hell out of the way."

Carly was too grateful for the help to ask questions, even though she wondered where the man had come from. He seemed to have appeared out of the very night itself. Only when Sky Walker was safely back in his stall and Ben was bent over Joey, did she take time to really look at the stranger.

A battered cowboy hat shadowed most of the face, above a black work shirt and faded jeans that were spattered with raindrops from the storm. Scuffed Western boots completed the picture.

"Seen enough?" The man swept the hat from his head with one hand, raking the other through his straight black hair. His eyes were glittering slits in a deeply tanned face.

Before Carly could speak or even react to his abrupt question, Joey groaned yet again, drawing her attention. She brushed past the stranger to peer anxiously at her youngest groom.

"Arm's broke," Ben announced curtly. "He needs a doctor."

"Of course." Carly's mind began to work almost automatically as she rapped out orders. "Bring the pickup around while I get the first-aid kit. We'll splint the arm and then you'll have to take him to town." She pushed back a strand of blond hair that had worked loose from its single braid and fallen across her cheek. That would leave only Tony and herself to attend to the evening chores, but there was no help for it. Since she'd fired Artie the week before for drinking in the broodmare barn, they'd been shorthanded. Now Joey's injury made them even more so. At least Sky Walker had calmed down as soon as his stall door was shut. The muscular colt now stood with his head hanging, each new rumble of thunder sending a shiver over his chestnut coat.

"Tell Tony where you're going," she told Ben. "He and I will have to get started here alone."

"I could help with him if you want," said a rough voice. Carly turned, reminded of the stranger's presence, and stared at him. "I've put on splints before," he continued.

His compelling face held Carly's gaze. "I, uh, we'd appreciate that," she said, realizing she hadn't yet thanked him for helping with the horse. "I don't have a lot of experience with first aid myself." She tried a smile.

His set expression never wavered, nor did the direct gaze of the narrowed gray eyes above the thin, arrogant nose. If those eyes hadn't been such a light color, she would have guessed from his straight dark hair and bronzed skin that he had Indian blood. Carly studied the planes of his face, then went hot as she suddenly realized that she was staring again and he knew it.

Her smile faded as Joey groaned once again. "I'll get the first-aid kit," she said, turning on her heel.

When she came back moments later, the man was bent over Joey, who was sitting with his back against the wall, cradling his injured arm. His young face was white beneath his freckles. Carly knelt on the concrete floor, and offered him the water she'd brought in a paper cup.

"Take these," she instructed him, opening a pill bottle. "They're only aspirin, but they might help with the pain." She realized her own hands were beginning to sting from the rope.

"Whiskey'd work better," the stranger remarked. His deep, rough voice played across her nerves, and the truth of what he said annoyed her unreasonably.

Carly remembered how well stocked the bar had been when her father ran the ranch. "We don't have whiskey here." She didn't spare him a glance, preferring to watch Joey swallow the pills and water.

"Thanks," the young man muttered; she touched a hand to his uninjured shoulder and straightened. As she did so, Ben walked back into the barn.

"Pickup's outside," he said before turning to the stranger, who was still squatting by Joey. "That your rig?" Ben asked him.

"Yeah." Busy with the first-aid kit, he didn't look up.

"Do you really know what you're doing?" Carly asked.

He tipped back his head, those cold eyes sending shivers across her skin. "Yeah."

A man of few words, she thought, crossing to look out the open barn door. A muddy, dented truck with faded red paint sat in the rain, a two-horse trailer in equally decrepit condition hitched behind it. The truck's front bumper bore an Oklahoma license plate. As a fork of lightning lighted the sky, Carly heard a piercing whinny from the trailer, and restless hooves drumming against its floor. The cab was empty.

She turned, waiting for the stranger to finish with Joey's arm. When he rose again, she held out her hand.

"Carly Golden," she said. "I run this ranch."

He gazed at her outstretched palm for so long, she thought he was going to ignore it. Then his own hand swallowed hers in an iron grip. Carly was aware of leashed strength in that hard, callused palm, and the touch sent a sizzle all the way to her elbow. She tried to pull away and their eyes locked in a clash of wills. He was letting her know she would be freed when he chose to release her.

Carly's brows arched and her chin went up. She thought she saw an answering gleam of amusement in the depths of the stranger's silver eyes before his grip relaxed. She barely resisted the urge to wipe her hand against the leg of her jeans in a purely defiant reaction.

"Your name?" she asked coolly when he remained silent.

His full lips twitched. "Sage Edwards."

"Sage?" she echoed before she could stop herself.

His nod was abrupt. "That's right."

"I'm taking Joey to town," Ben said, breaking the tension. His old eyes strayed to the man with Carly, then back to her. "You be okay?" he asked.

"Of course." Carly smiled at the hired hand she had known since before she could walk. "Thanks, Ben. Tell Doc Drury to put it on my tab." She patted Joey on the back as he moved past her. "Sorry, pal."

He glanced up, trying to smile.

Sage stood aside until Ben and Joey were in the ranch pickup, headed back down the long drive. When the woman named Carly walked them out, he watched her go. She was as slim and long legged as a filly, but moved with the grace of a show horse. Then she turned back to him, and he had a chance to study her from the front. Her oversize Western shirt was loose across her breasts, leaving him to guess at her shape. A Western hat shaded her eyes and hid the hair that wasn't caught in the braid that fell down her back. Her chin was pointed like a Siamese cat's and her throat rose from the collar of her cotton shirt as smoothly as a sweep of porcelain. She didn't look much like a ranch manager to him.

He had been listening to the gentle rise and fall of her voice as she talked to Ben. It was low and rich, vibrant with life. She'd colored with embarrassment when she'd reacted to hearing Sage's name, but hadn't shifted her gaze. And she'd been all business when they had maneuvered that crazy horse back into his stall, ignoring what Sage was sure the rope had done to her bare palms. The one she'd held out to him was an angry red. The lady had guts, at least, even if she did look too soft to be in charge. Now he was about to discover if she had any of the more charitable virtues.

When she turned away from the sight of the ranch truck's taillights, Sage grabbed her other hand and held it palm up. Her gasp and the way her delicate fingers curled to protect the raw skin sent a whisper of pity stabbing through him.

"You should have been wearing gloves. This needs salve."

Carly pulled away. "There wasn't time for gloves. The storm hit fast, and Sky Walker spooks at thunder."

Behind them the horse whinnied shrilly, one hoof kicking out against the wall as if to emphasize her point. Carly put her hands behind her back in an unconsciously protective gesture. "I'll tend to this when I have the time."

Sage walked to the first-aid kit and bent over it, searching until he found the tube he wanted. Then he crossed back to her and again took her hand. This time she didn't struggle. After he'd squeezed out the cream and massaged it gently into both injured palms, he raised his head.

She was watching, her face expressionless. Only her eyes, a deep, pure blue, reflected the same awareness he felt seeping through himself like liquid heat. He'd probably live to regret what he was about to suggest.

"Does the boy's injury leave you shorthanded?" he asked.

Carly answered with a wry smile. "The groom I canned last week left us shorthanded. What happened to Joey today only makes things worse."

"Then I guess you're the one I need to talk to," Sage drawled, ignoring the warning his well-developed sense of self-preservation was sending out. "I'm lookin' for a job."

Sudden interest flared in the woman's eyes, and she pulled the hat from her head, revealing thick, golden hair that sprang into stubborn curls around her face. Sage only hoped she didn't hear his indrawn breath.

Carly was too busy pushing the heavy, damp hair off her forehead to notice the expression on his lean face. Self-consciously she flipped the braid behind her shoulder, wishing suddenly that she wasn't such a mess. Swallowing, she looked up.

"Is that how you happened to show up just when we needed you?" she asked. "Because you're looking for a job?" Warmth flooded her cheeks when he continued to stare at her hair. His own, she could see, hung straight to his collar. The sides were shorter. A tiny silver earring pierced one lobe.

Sage's face had a pagan beauty to it with those penetrating gray eyes, high cheekbones above intriguing hollows, and a mouth whose grim line hinted at a more sensual fullness if it ever relaxed. His features were stamped with an arrogance that set her teeth on edge as he returned her stare without expression.

"Yeah," he said finally. "I've had a lot of experience with horses. Palominos, mostly."

"Palominos are mostly what we've got." Carly waited for him to volunteer more, but it became apparent that he didn't intend to add anything else.

"Where's the last place you worked?" she asked when he remained silent.

"My own spread in Oklahoma." His tone was grim, discouraging further inquiries.

Carly had seen the way he handled Sky Walker and was desperate enough not to require references. If she could put up with his arrogance, it might work out.

"I have two horses I'd need to board if I stayed," he added before she could speak. "Take it out of my pay."

"I will. And the pay's not much, but the food's good. Rosa, my cook, sees to that." Carly named a wage that she knew was lower than what some were paying. Perhaps, since he was here and the job was open, he'd just take it instead of looking further. Either way his horses would need attention that night.

"What kind of horses?" she thought to ask.

He glanced toward his rig. "Palomino mares. Both in foal."

"Where did you get them?" As soon as the words were out, Carly bit her tongue at the way they'd sounded.

Sage's eyes narrowed, cutting lines into his cheeks. "They're mine," he said evenly, his expression closed. "I won them back in a poker game. Fair and square."

Leaving her to deal with that last bit of information and wonder what he meant by "winning them back," he turned on one heel without waiting for an answer, grabbed his hat and moved silently outside. When he stuck his head back into the open doorway a moment later, he said, "I'll take the job. Where shall I put my mares?"

She walked past him into the rain. "I'll show you."

By the time Sage had settled his horses and taken his shaving kit and duffel bag into the bunkhouse, dropping them onto an empty bunk, it was almost time for the dinner Carly had told him would be served at the main house. He ran a hand over his chin, deciding on a shave and shower before he presented himself at the kitchen door.

While he was toweling off, he tried to think of his new boss as "Miss Golden," but his brain refused to cooperate. If he wasn't careful, he'd be calling her Carly to her face.

Combing back his wet hair, he shrugged into a clean shirt and a fresh pair of worn, tight jeans. Then he bent to wipe the mud off his boots with a bandanna-print handkerchief before he glanced around. The sight of his meager belongings on the bunk brought a bitter smile to his mouth. Once he'd had big dreams, and for a while it had seemed as if he and Mac, his partner, were going to attain them. Now, except for the two mares he'd managed to get back in that card game and the land that awaited him back home, he was closer to having nothing than he'd been in a long time.

Serves you right for thinking big, you dumb half-breed, he thought as he left the bunkhouse. He was mildly curious about the setup here and the people. Then he reminded himself that he'd come for one thing and one thing only. How he felt about Carly Golden or anyone else here was immaterial to his purpose.

Carly changed into a dry shirt and cotton slacks before going back downstairs for dinner. She hesitated for a moment in front of the mirror in the small bedroom that had always been hers. There would be more room if she moved into the master suite, the one her father had shared with his second wife, but Carly didn't plan on staying long enough to make the switch worthwhile. Her life was in Houston.

As she loosened her damp braid, spreading the long crimped strands of golden hair across her shoulders so they would dry, her thoughts returned to Sage Edwards. Carly sensed with a shiver that more than one secret lurked behind those bleak eyes.

When she descended the curving staircase to the front hallway, she could hear Ben's voice coming from the kitchen. He and Rosa, the housekeeper, were good friends. Carly wondered how poor Joey was feeling and what the doctor had said about his arm.

"Carly! Carly, wait for me!" piped an anxious voice behind her.

She stopped and turned, watching the stairs above for the sight of her blond half sister, Mollie. In seconds the tiny figure appeared at the top of the stairs and hurtled down toward Carly, curls bouncing.

"Whoa!" she exclaimed, reaching out to catch the four-year-old before she could trip and hurt herself. "How many times have I told you not to run in the house?"

To Carly's dismay, the round face crumpled and the big blue eyes filled with tears.

Instantly contrite, Carly swiftly knelt next to Mollie's sturdy little body, bringing their faces level. "I'm sorry, punkin. I didn't mean to make you cry."

Mollie sniffled and jammed small fists into her eyes, rubbing vigorously. "Okay." She dispensed forgiveness with her usual unfailing generosity and blinked the tears away; her mouth curved into a shy smile.

Carly still wasn't used to being around a young child, but she was learning. She tucked Mollie's hand into her own and descended the remainder of the stairs at a sedate pace. "Are you ready for dinner?" she asked.

"We're having fried chicken," Mollie said. "That's one of my very favorites." She'd said the same thing about almost every meal that Rosa had fixed since Carly's arrival a month ago, but she still had to be coaxed to eat.

When they got to the bottom of the stairs, Carly caught herself listening for her father's booming voice before she remembered with a crushing sense of loss that she would never hear that voice again. After the accident, Carly had been summoned home to attend the funeral and take over the running of the ranch. Apologizing to her boss, she had packed and flown back to the ranch she had once sworn she would never be involved in again, all her unresolved feelings for her father frozen in shock and grief.

A stunned and fearful Mollie had latched onto Carly, who hadn't seen her since she was a baby, with all the pent-up love in her tiny soul. Although Ben and Rosa clearly adored her and showered her with affection, Mollie's eyes remained shadowed and her chatter subdued except for the time she spent with her big sister. Carly grieved for Mollie's loss as well as her own, but what she would do with a young child when the ranch was sold, she hadn't yet worked out.

They walked into the dining room together and Mollie came to a halt, pulling her hand free from Carly's grip and ducking behind her. Puzzled, Carly glanced around to see what had caused Mollie's acute shyness.

Standing in the doorway was the new employee. He had changed clothes and was now wearing a faded but obviously clean red plaid shirt with fresh jeans that fitted his lean body just as snugly as the last pair had. Tearing her gaze away, Carly put a hand on Mollie's shoulder and urged her forward.

"It's okay," she said coaxingly. "Don't you want to meet our new helper? He brought two beautiful horses with him."

The temptation was a strong one, as Carly knew it would be. Mollie loved the golden horses best. She peered upward, head bent back as she studied Sage. "He did?"

"Two lovely palomino mares," Carly said, remembering her surprise when he'd led first one and then the other from the battered trailer into stalls she had directed him to at the far end of the broodmare barn. A dozen questions had crowded Carly's tongue at the sight of the obviously well-bred pair, but one glance at Sage's closed expression had kept her quiet. It was clear from the way his thick, straight brows were drawn together and the hard line of his jaw that he wasn't in the mood to satisfy her curiosity.

Ben came in from the kitchen and glanced at the new hand, raising his grizzled eyebrows when he looked at Carly. Before she could explain, Sage approached slowly and squatted before Mollie.

"Would you like to meet my girls after dinner?" he asked in a warm voice, one far removed from the one he had used earlier. "They're almost the same color as your hair."

Mollie hesitated, looking to Carly for guidance.

She nodded, giving Mollie's hand a squeeze.

After a moment the little girl released her clasp on Carly's fingers and stepped closer to Sage, who had been waiting patiently. "Could I?" she asked.

Carly was staring, fascinated by the changes his smile brought to his face.

"Sure," he said. "If it's okay with your mom."

Mollie scuffed one foot against the rug. "My mom's dead," she told him. "She and my daddy crashed in their plane."

"I'm sorry." Sage glanced at Carly, gaze questioning.

"Mollie's my half sister," she explained, "from my father's second marriage."

"What's your name?" Mollie demanded.

Sage turned his attention back to the little girl who regarded him with none of the animosity or distrust he was so used to seeing on other people's faces. "You can call me Sage."

"That's a funny name."

For once the comment didn't bother him. "I know. You haven't told me yours yet."

"It's Mollie Golden."

Sage straightened, holding out his hand. When Mollie slid hers into it, he closed his fingers. "I'm glad to meet you, Mollie Golden."

To his surprise she giggled. "I'm glad to meet you, Mr. Sage."

"Just Sage," he said, releasing her hand.

"Are you an Indian?"

Carly gasped at Mollie's bluntness. She glanced at Sage, but before she could intervene, he answered Mollie himself.

"Only half. My mother was Comanche, but my father was a white man."

"Then how come—?"

"Mollie, that's enough questions for now. Supper must be almost ready." Carly shifted, uncomfortably aware of the tall man standing so close.

Mollie bobbed her head in agreement. "Okay. Can I sit by Sage at the table?"

Sage felt Carly's eyes on him and turned with lazy slowness to meet her gaze. He'd noticed when the two sisters walked in that Carly's hair was now loose. A shade darker than Mollie's, its burnished color reminded him of sunlight. Absently rubbing his fingers together, he wondered if the strands would feel as silky as they looked.

Carly's expression was questioning. "Would it be okay if she sits by you?" she asked.

This time Sage tried to hide his surprise. "Sure."

"Thank you." The husky voice slipped beneath his indifference, provoking his senses.

Carly nodded to Mollie, who was waiting expectantly. "Okay, punkin. Just don't talk Mr. Edwards's ear off."

Too late she remembered that Mollie didn't talk much to anyone these days except her.

"I won't," Mollie said, then ducked around the adults to go see Rosa in the kitchen.

"Thank you," Carly told Sage quietly. "This last month has been hard on her."

Sage wanted to ask how long it had been since the accident and whether the time had been hard for Carly, too. Before he could debate with himself the wisdom of questioning her, she had shifted her gaze to Joey, who had just walked in, sporting a cast on his arm.

"How are you doing?" she asked.

Joey's face was still pale. "Okay, boss."

"Good." She looked at Ben. "Thank you for taking him."

The old man shrugged. "No problem."

"I've hired Sage to help with the horses," she continued. "He has two pregnant mares in the broodmare barn and he's already settled in the bunkhouse. You can show him what else he needs to know."

"Okay." Ben's glance narrowed as he looked from Carly to Sage, but he didn't add anything. Carly knew he had been relieved when she came back and took over. Ben was more comfortable with direction than responsibility. He and Rosa were aware that Carly planned to sell the ranch and they both intended to retire when that happened.

On her way to the kitchen to help Rosa with last-minute preparations, Carly moved around Sage's imposing frame with care. He stepped back, but his presence still unsettled her.

In the doorway she made herself turn slowly. "Please sit down," she told the men. "I'll be right back." She would have to learn to relax around the new hand. Something told her he would be deeply offended if he saw her tension, and honesty compelled her to admit—if only to herself—that it wasn't distrust that made her stiffen when he was around.

Rosa was bent over the open oven door. Taking out a platter of chicken, she said, "Everything's ready. Please bring the potatoes."

Carly took the bowl of mashed potatoes from the counter and turned to follow her cook into the dining room, smiling when she saw Mollie carefully pick up a dish of black olives in both hands.

"The chicken smells delicious," Carly told Rosa. Her stepmother had hired the woman after Carly moved to Houston. Rosa was a wonderful cook and an adequate housekeeper, and seemed to appreciate what little help Carly had found time to give her around the house.

"Thank you," Rosa replied, a polite smile appearing on her lined face. "Fried chicken's one of Ben's favorites. Might as well put it on the table before it gets cold."

As soon as they took their seats, everyone began passing dishes. Carly couldn't help but notice that Sage hesitated, watching the others. Then, when Ben handed him the platter of chicken, he asked Mollie what she wanted before serving himself. Thanking him for the drumstick, Mollie took the dish of olives and set two up on the edge of Sage's plate, then took one for herself.

Carly was distracted when Ben passed her the biscuits. By the time she'd served herself, everyone else had dug in, including Mollie. Sage ate quietly, apparently oblivious to the talk going on around him. Carly noticed there was nothing wrong with his appetite. Rosa must have noticed, too, because she kept urging more food upon him.

"Don't forget that Homer Bryson's coming out to look at a horse for his daughter tomorrow," Ben said between mouthfuls. "Do you want me to show them Spun Gold and Lucky Penny?"

"What about Spangles or Bright Star?" Carly asked. They were two fine sorrel mares. "Either one would make a good horse for a young girl."

"She wants a palomino," Ben said.

Carly shrugged, toying with her food. He didn't really approve of her plans to sell the operation as soon as she could untangle the finances and get the place fixed up, and he was bound to object to her selling off breeding stock. She had been shocked to see how run-down her father had allowed everything to get over the last couple of years, but at least the horses were still in top shape.

"Remember," Ben added, "when Golden Gamble covers the mares you mentioned, they usually deliver gold." He was referring to the fact that palominos didn't always breed true colorwise. The best combination to ensure success was a palomino-sorrel cross. Golden Gamble, one of their champion studs, had an excellent record of fathering golden colts when he was bred to sorrel mares.

"If the girl wants a palomino, her daddy will have to pay for one," Carly said. "What about Gold Dust?"

"She's on the feisty side," Ben told her. "But I'll bring her out, too."

Carly nodded, her glance briefly meeting Sage's; she turned her attention back to her plate. If he had any comments he kept them to himself, speaking only to answer a direct question.

Finally everyone had finished. Carly pushed her chair back to help Rosa clear the table and serve dessert. Ben and Joey were half-done with theirs when Carly came back to the table. She was about to ask Sage if he didn't care for peach, but as soon as she and Rosa were seated he dug in.

Realizing that he was merely being polite, and slightly shaken by the admission that she hadn't expected him to have decent manners, Carly took a bite of her own pie, barely tasting it as she chewed. If she wasn't careful, the first thing she'd need to do when she got back to Houston, next to getting a good manicure, would be to go on a crash diet. Rosa was too good a cook.

"Great pie," Sage said when Carly was almost done.

She raised her head to meet his gaze. How long had he been watching her and what was he thinking?

Later that evening Carly finished some of the paperwork she had been struggling through and glanced at the clock, wondering what Mollie was doing. It was almost her bedtime.

"I think she said she was going to the barn to see Sage's mares," Rosa said when Carly asked her. "I hope that was okay."

"Sure. As long as she doesn't make a pest of herself."

Rosa frowned. Obviously, Mollie could never be a pest to her. "Shall I put her to bed?"

"No, I will. Go on up, if you'd like. I know you start breakfast early."

"Thank you," Rosa said. "Good night."

Carly returned the wish and glanced at herself in the hallway mirror. Her hair had dried in waves. Ignoring the urge to run a brush through it before going to the barn, she went in search of Mollie.

The thunderstorm had passed, leaving the air still and humid. Carly looked around as she walked down the gravel driveway. Once her father had expected her to run this ranch with him. But they had never gotten along well, and after she'd graduated from college, Carly had made a different choice, visiting the ranch that had once been a major part of her life only occasionally over the last six years. Now it was hers and Mollie's. Her father had willed her fifty-one percent to Mollie's forty-nine—but the will didn't prevent her from selling. That was what she intended to do, and she would insure Mollie's future by starting a healthy trust fund with the child's share of the proceeds.

When Carly entered the barn she heard Mollie's high voice coming from the direction of the stalls assigned to Sage's mares. The answering rumble of his deep voice told Carly that he wasn't far away, either.

Mollie stood outside one of the stalls, but Carly didn't immediately see Sage.

"Hi," she greeted her sister. "What do you think of these ladies? Aren't they beautiful?" She reached out a hand to the mare who was hanging her head over the stall door. The horse sniffed curiously as Carly rubbed her velvety skin.

Before Mollie could answer, the other stall door swung open and Sage backed out, murmuring in hypnotic tones to the horse inside. He turned slowly, and Carly's mouth went dry. No doubt responding to the muggy atmosphere, he'd let his shirt hang open, and the light from the overhead bulb made his damp skin gleam. The bronze beauty of his muscular chest was marred only by a thin scar that slanted across it, disappearing into his low-slung jeans.

He slammed the stall door shut, and Carly's cheeks flamed. She forced her attention to his face. His expression was one of chiseled stone, but to her utter stupefaction, the light gray eyes that bored into hers were burning with a fury that was savage in its intensity.

Chapter Two

Carly found herself unable to move as she stared into Sage's silver eyes, now molten with anger. Before she could speak, he turned away, removing his hat to draw a dark hand over his face and into his straight hair, pushing it off his forehead. When he settled the hat onto his head and turned back to her the emotion was gone, replaced by a distant air. Blinking, Carly wasn't sure if she'd really seen the fury on his face or only imagined it.

"I'm keeping Sage company while he takes care of Princess and Lady," Mollie said importantly.

"Is this Princess?" Carly asked, glad the tension-filled silence was broken.

Sage's face relaxed its harsh lines and he glanced back at the mare who was lipping his shoulder. Patting her neck, he said, "This is Comanche Lady. Comanche Princess is in the next stall."

Carly heard the pride in his voice, surely more than was warranted by winning the pair in a card game. "They're beautiful," she said, stepping closer. "Did you raise them?"

Sage was looking at his mares, not at her. "Yes," he said absently. "And they're both in foal to my best stud."

There were a lot of questions Carly wanted to ask him, but they would have to wait. It was time for Mollie's bath and bedtime story. Glancing down at the little girl, Carly could see shadows of fatigue under her eyes.

"If you have everything you need for tonight, I better get *this* little filly to bed," she said.

Sage turned his attention back to her, their gazes locked, and awareness held her in an ironclad grip.

"Yeah, thanks," he said, breaking the spell. "We're fine."

It was a fraction of a heartbeat before his words penetrated. All thought had been wiped from Carly's mind when his silver eyes had met hers. "Good," she said, recovering quickly. "I'll see you in the morning, then. Breakfast is at five-thirty."

"I'll be there." Not that he was likely to see her at that unholy hour, Sage thought. She might help serve dinner, but there was definitely a "lady of the manor" attitude to Carly Golden. She probably slept until noon.

He remembered to wish Mollie good-night, then stood and watched her and Carly as they left the broodmare barn, hands linked. A playful shove from Comanche Lady distracted him. When he looked back, the two golden-haired figures were gone.

He'd have to keep himself under better control, he thought. Carefully closing the stall door, he went in to check on the other mare. Carly's bold appraisal had made him feel like one of his own studs led out for approval, but

he'd let her see how it affected him and that wasn't smart.
For now, at least, Sage needed to stay on her good side,
and losing control of his temper wasn't the way to do it.
Neither was lusting after her, so that was another thing
that would have to stop. All Carly Golden was or could be
to a bastard half-breed like him was a means to an end, and
life would be one hell of a lot simpler if he remembered
that.

"How come Sage brought his horses here to have their
babies?" Mollie asked as Carly dried her off from her bath
and helped her into a flowered nightie.

"I don't know, punkin. He was looking for work, so I
guess he had to bring them with him, so he could take care
of them." Carly combed out Mollie's wet hair, working
carefully through a snarl in the back. Privately she wondered about him, too. Why *had* he showed up with his
horses? Where was he from, and if he'd had a ranch where
he had raised palominos, what had happened to it?

"Doesn't he have a home of his own?"

"I guess this is his home for now," Carly replied absently, switching on the hair dryer. When she was done, she
followed Mollie to her pink and white bedroom, waiting
while the little girl selected a book from the crowded shelf.

"This one is about cowboys and Indians," Mollie said.
"Do you think Sage would tell me a story if I asked him?"

Carly was happy that her sister was beginning to be more
talkative, but wasn't sure how she felt about Mollie's interest in the new hand. After all, what did Carly know
about him? Next to nothing.

"Sage will be pretty busy with the horses," she told
Mollie. "Why don't you wait and see?" That would give
Carly time to find out more about him, which she deter-

mined to do, the first chance she got. The man did work for her; surely she was entitled to ask a few questions?

When Sage followed Ben and Tony into the dining room at the main house the next morning, he was surprised to see Carly there. She looked freshly scrubbed and even more attractive than he had remembered in a chambray shirt and faded jeans that hugged her slim hips, and was setting the table as Rosa brought plates of eggs, biscuits and sausage from the kitchen. The other hands sat down and began helping themselves to coffee and juice, so Sage did the same. There was a general exchange of greetings, and then silence fell as everyone began to eat. Sage noticed that Carly sat down and joined them, but Rosa went back to the kitchen.

"What are your plans for today?" Carly asked Ben, biting into a piece of toast.

"Sage is helping me work some of the yearlings this morning so I can see how he does with them. Tony's going into town for a few things. Later we'll see if either of Wilson's mares are ready for the boss."

"The boss?" Sage echoed, holding the forkful of eggs he'd been about to eat.

Ben grinned. "Red Rocket, one of our studs. Both ladies have dates with him sometime this month."

Sage nodded his understanding. Apparently Wilson's mares were at the farm to be bred to the quarter horse stallion. Red Rocket was the stud Sage hoped to persuade Carly to let cover his mares after they'd dropped the foals they were now carrying. They would be in season again soon after delivery.

The stallion had fathered a record number of golden foals for palomino mares, and Sage was hoping to leave the ranch with a future champion planted in each of his mares' bellies. It might not be the fastest way to restock his own ranch, but it was one of his few remaining options.

"He's a sorrel, isn't he?" Sage asked innocently.

Ben nodded. "Has great conformation and the sweetest temperament you'd ever want to see. Usually passes it on, too. And he's a real ladies' man, if you know what I mean. Doesn't have to cover many mares twice." He glanced at Carly, then at his full plate, as if the talk of breeding and virility suddenly made him uncomfortable.

"I wish Sky Walker had inherited some of that sweetness," she said dryly, looking at Sage. "You met him yesterday."

"The horse who doesn't like storms."

"Or much else," Carly added. "We got some beautiful foals from him last year, but he's such a pain to handle, I'm thinking about having him gelded."

"That would be a real shame," Sage observed. "I'll have a look at him later."

Carly's brows rose. "Thanks," she muttered, but somehow he didn't think she meant it.

"Just watch yourself around him," Ben said. "He can get real ugly."

Sage didn't bother to explain he had dealt with horses that made what he'd seen of Sky Walker's temper seem like Sunday school behavior by comparison. He'd spend some time with the feisty young stallion and then he'd do something about the problem of personality.

Success was something that Sage didn't trouble himself over when it came to horses. He and the big animals understood each other. He glanced at Carly, who hastily lowered her gaze. Too bad a gift that almost amounted to telepathy didn't quite take in leggy blondes, he thought grimly.

* * *

Sage was mucking out stalls in the broodmare barn when the sound of approaching footsteps made him glance around. The rhythm was wrong for Ben, and Tony had already left for town.

He stopped what he was doing and watched Carly come down the wide center aisle. The same Western hat she'd worn the day before shaded her eyes, and he noticed that leather work gloves now covered her hands.

As she got closer to the open stall door, Carly slowed her steps, making a pretext of checking out the horse nearest her. The bay mare shifted her weight awkwardly and blew out a stream of air.

"Sorry, sweetie," Carly crooned, scratching between the mare's black ears. "Pretty soon you'll have a baby to show for all this discomfort."

She could feel Sage's eyes on her and took her time in acknowledging his presence. "I thought Ben would be here."

Sage wiped a sleeve across his forehead. "He went to get something from the other barn. He'll be right back."

Carly had no choice but to wait, so maybe now was the time to ask Sage about his background. Before she could formulate her first question, however, he leaned the shovel he'd been using against the stall's wall and grabbed her hand.

"What are you doing?" Carly's breath was trapped in her throat, her voice thin as she felt his warm skin against her wrist.

"Checking out the raw places." He stripped off the glove, and his callused fingers skimmed her sensitive palm, making her hand curl protectively. She felt his touch all the way up her arm. When she pulled away, he looked into her face. "Other hand okay?"

"Yes, thank you. The cream you put on them helped a lot."

His mouth relaxed into the semblance of a smile. "Good."

Carly groped for poise, finally calm enough to begin her interrogation. "You're from Oklahoma?" she asked, trying to remain unaffected by his presence. The mingled aroma of horse, hay and the musky scent of a hardworking man teased her nostrils.

"That's right." He wasn't going to make this easy.

"You mentioned that you raised your mares and they were bred to your own stud. Did you have a spread?"

His nod was abrupt, as if it caused him pain. "Yeah."

Carly felt as if she were trying to get a stray nail out of a horse's hoof. "What happened?"

His eyes narrowed. "A lot of things."

Irritation colored her tone, "Like what?"

Sage took the shovel and turned his back, bending to scoop up dirty straw and manure. His action was pure dismissal, and Carly's temper stirred. She was his boss, for heaven's sake, not some prying stranger. She had a right to ask.

Circling him determinedly, she tried again.

"Look," he said, straightening abruptly when she stopped in front of him. "You needed a hand and I needed a job. I know what I'm doing with horses. I'll give you a day's work for a day's pay, but I won't share my soul with you." His eyes were bleak. "If that isn't enough, I can be gone this afternoon."

Carly held his gaze stubbornly, refusing to look away. She could hear Ben's footsteps approaching, and something inside her wanted this settled before he arrived.

"You've got one hell of a chip on your shoulder."

He shrugged, a take-it-or-leave-it gesture.

"Don't be so quick to quit," she said, still irritated. "I'm asking nothing I don't have a right to know." She glanced down the aisle, then back at the tall man who stood so still he could have been a statue. Finally she sighed. "I'll need the answers to a few basic questions," she told him. "But I guess I don't need them right now."

Without giving Sage a chance to reply, she directed her attention to Ben. "Bryson called. He and his daughter will be here at two to look at mounts for her."

"We'll be ready." Ben nodded toward Sage. "He thinks he can work out Sky Walker's kinks."

Carly raised her chin. "Is that so? Mind if I ask how?"

Sage wondered why he felt so compelled to give her a hard time. Perhaps it was because she tempted him, and he would be a fool to give in to that temptation. If he touched her, put one bronzed finger upon that silky skin, she would scream the place down.

"Trade secret," he said curtly. One look at the hurt in her expression and he softened slightly. "But you can watch if you want." The force of her soft blue gaze hit him like a punch to the gut. "Just don't get in the way."

Carly's brows climbed higher as she looked for Ben's reaction to the rude remark. He rolled his eyes. Maybe the simplest thing for the time being would be to ignore it, as well as the involuntary response she was beginning to feel whenever she was around the new hand. That response she was determined to subdue. "I'm going to take Dancer out and check the far pasture."

Ben nodded his approval. "Good idea. You need the break."

Carly refused to let her gaze slide back to Sage. The man was impossible. He didn't know how lucky he was that she'd been desperate for help, she told herself, or he and his mares would have been down the road before he'd even had a chance to apologize. But something told her that if he had been staked out on an anthill, she wouldn't have gotten an apology from that set mouth.

Riding along the fence of one of the far pastures, letting the sun soak into her shoulders and melt their tightness, Carly thought again of the new hand and his prickly personality. She told herself it was for Mollie's sake that she needed to understand him better. She couldn't allow an innocent four-year-old be exposed to someone whose background was a complete mystery.

Carly shifted in the saddle as Dancer tugged impatiently on the bit. He wanted to run.

"Be patient, old boy," Carly told him, reaching forward to pat his neck. Dancer was the palomino gelding her father had given her before she left. On her return, she had been surprised and pleased to discover that Dancer hadn't been sold in her absence. Instead he'd been worked and cared for; his golden coat was shining, his creamy mane and tail were long and silken, while white stockings and the blaze on his face made a stunning contrast to the richness of his coat and the chocolate brown of his eyes.

Dancer shook his head, but kept up the sedate pace Carly had set as her thoughts returned to Sage. She wanted to be there when he took on Sky Walker. That would be an interesting contest of wills. She sensed that when he chose to, Sage Edwards could be even more stubborn than any horse.

Carly came to a part of the land that she especially loved, a rolling section of pasture that ambled along a stream and wound below stately shade trees. Murmuring to Dancer, whose ears had swiveled to catch her voice, she gave him his head.

He leveled out into a dead run and Carly clung to his back, the wind whipping her loose hair behind her as her hat blew off her head, prevented from sailing away only by the rawhide strap that anchored it around her neck. While Dancer's powerful body raced beneath her, she allowed her concerns about the ranch, Mollie and Sage to be temporarily swept away; it was as if she and her golden horse could outrun all her problems.

Only moments later, it seemed, she was turning Dancer, slowing him to a more sensible gait, allowing him to cool down before they reached the stable yard. Though Carly missed the activity and pulsating energy of Houston, she was well aware of the spell of Rolling Gold Ranch. Silently she reminded herself that her life was elsewhere now, not at the ranch that had once claimed her heart.

This stay was only temporary, until she could undo the neglect her father had allowed and prepare the entire operation for sale. Even Dancer would have to go; Carly needed no more ties to her past.

Sage was crossing the yard when she rode up. He stopped in front of her, eyeing her mount.

"Been riding him hard," he said.

Carly bristled at the criticism she heard in his tone. Some devil made her kick loose the stirrups and slide from Dancer's back so she almost brushed against Sage when she landed on the ground next to him. She tossed him the reins.

"Put him up for me, would you? He needs cooling down." Without waiting for a reply, she headed toward the house. Almost instantly she regretted her high-handed attitude. She was usually free of such airs, but Sage brought out the worst in her.

"Yes, ma'am," he drawled behind her retreating back, a smile twisting his lips. It was when she acted like this that he could tell himself he had been right all along; she was a coldhearted bitch used to tossing out orders. Somehow it made him more comfortable to see her in that light. It was certainly less dangerous than picturing her warm and willing, wrapped around him tighter than his jeans. That was the way he'd been dreaming of her when he woke this morning, rock hard and ready. His hormones might want a woman, but the last thing he needed was one like Carly Golden, more trouble than a bag of snakes with a hole in it.

Even as he turned, clucking softly to the horse that followed him, his body reacted with predictable discomfort to the remembrance of the hazy dream. Swearing under his breath, Sage vowed to keep his distance, even if he had to do it with rudeness. Somehow he had to find a balance between the utter futility of his attraction to his boss and the need to persuade her to let her prize stud cover his mares. There had to be a way, and he had to find it quickly before he did something stupid, like he'd been tempted to do when she'd come down from her horse almost on top of him. His hands had already been reaching when he'd managed to jam them into his pockets. Another temptation like that, and he was liable to swarm all over her like bees on the flowers her subtle scent reminded him of. Not for the first time, he wondered what a classy woman like Carly was really doing on a ranch like this one. She didn't belong there any more than he did.

"I know I'm putting you in an impossible position," Carly said over the phone to the woman who was filling in for her, "but I had no idea when I first came up here for the funeral how run-down the ranch would be. It's going to take me a couple of months at least to get it in shape to sell. The paperwork's a nightmare and there's so much else to do.''

She paused, listening to Lisa Canfield's well-modulated voice. Lisa rarely sounded anything less than calm. She was a pro when it came to picking up loose ends at the shipping company where she and Carly both worked.

''I'll do the best I can, dear, but you must realize that Mr. Bass will only put up with your absence for so long. He can hardly function without his executive assistant, you know.''

''I'll appreciate anything you can do to appease him,'' Carly said quickly. ''I realize I'm being unfair, not telling you when I'll be back, but I can't cheat my half sister out of her inheritance and let Rolling Gold go for peanuts. I'll be calling Mr. Bass myself when he gets back from New Orleans.''

''Well, as long as I can call you if I need to,'' Lisa said. ''I'll do the best I can. Everyone misses you.''

After a few more moments Carly thanked her again and hung up, relieved that she didn't have to confront her boss for several more days. Ever since he had promoted her four years ago and she had figured out that his bark was worse than his bite, she had enjoyed working for him. Still, his reaction to her prolonged absence was guaranteed not to be a pleasant one. It was a good thing that family was so important to him; she only hoped that he would understand.

How ironic it would be if, in death, her father managed to destroy the career he had disapproved of so much while he was alive. Still, she couldn't let him down in this last undertaking. She had to stay until his estate was put right and disposed of. When the thought intervened that by selling the ranch she was hardly fulfilling his wishes, Carly thrust it aside.

* * *

Homer Bryson stuck out his hand as his daughter fidgeted excitedly beside him. "Much obliged for your time," he said to Carly. "I'm sure that my girl here and Lucky Penny will be a winning combination." He glanced in the direction of the trailer where Ben and Sage had already loaded the horse.

Carly returned the firm pressure of his hand. "We appreciate your coming to us, Mr. Bryson. If there's anything else we can do for you, please don't hesitate to let us know."

"Call me Homer," he suggested, giving Carly a grin that revealed a gleaming set of expensive dentures. Homer, a neighboring rancher and widower, considered himself a bit of a ladies' man despite his advancing years and expanding belly. His gaze raked over Carly's slim form in what he no doubt considered an appreciative manner. It made her skin crawl and her temper rise.

Her attention flickered and moved to Ben and Sage, who were still standing by. Ben was doing his best to hide his annoyance, but Sage's expression was one of outright contempt, his mouth twisted into a cynical smile. Carly allowed her own gaze to freeze on his, then turned her attention back to the man who still maintained a death grip on her hand.

"Very well, Homer," she said, pulling away. She smiled at his daughter. "I'll bet that you and Penny are going to win a lot of ribbons together."

The girl beamed, obviously pleased with her choice of mounts. It was easy to get what you wanted when price was no object, Carly reflected.

"I love her already," the youngster said. "I can't wait to get home and ride."

Carly was still watching as Bryson's shiny truck drove in a wide circle, towing a matching horse trailer, and headed back down the long driveway. She had made a handsome profit on the sale. Most of the money would be used to help restore Rolling Gold to its former glory, so that it, too, could be sold at a profit. Money to insure Mollie's future, Carly reminded herself, as she turned away.

"That's a man who'd benefit from gelding," Ben said dryly.

Carly stifled a gasp. "I'm sure that Homer Bryson's harmless," she replied, her words also meant for Sage's benefit, although she wasn't sure why his opinion mattered. Just who the hell did he think he was to sit in judgment?

Ben shrugged. "I remember Bryson's wife," he added. "Pretty thing, but frail. There was talk about Homer even when she was alive."

Carly pressed her lips together. "I don't have time to stand around and gossip," she said more sharply than she had intended. "I wouldn't think you did, either."

Ben's manner became purposely subservient. "No, ma'am." He dipped his head, both hands gripping his battered hat.

Carly was tempted to laugh. She and Ben both knew he didn't follow her orders; he agreed to do what she wanted if he thought it was a good idea. Only Sage's expression stopped her from making the retort she had intended.

"Very good, then," she said instead, including the younger man in her imperious gaze. She saw a spark of something she couldn't identify in his silver eyes, but he turned wordlessly and followed Ben to the barn.

Damn, she had done it again; she'd let him bring out the worst in her without uttering a word.

* * *

The next day threatened early to bring its own share of problems. A load of feed was delayed, a prospective buyer for two palomino yearlings called to cancel his appointment later that week, and Mollie woke with a fever and a runny nose.

Carly was doing paperwork in her father's office, attempting to wade through the stack of mail that had been sitting since his death. Little by little the intimidating pile was shrinking. She did her best to ignore the sparkle of sunshine and the beckoning nicker of horses through the window, even though she would have much rather been riding Dancer or spending time in the stables instead of being cooped up in the house.

A knock sounded against the open door and she looked up. Tony, one of the hands, was standing there, a frown on his face. He shifted his weight from one foot to the other.

"I need to talk to you," he burst out before Carly could do so much as say hello.

"Of course," she said, pushing the papers to one side. "Come in and sit down. How's everything going?"

Her question seemed to open the floodgates of Tony's resentment. "It's that Indian!" he exclaimed.

Carly's brows rose halfway to her hairline. "Do you mean Sage?" she asked, her tone cooler.

Tony must not have noticed the chill in her voice. "Yeah, the half-breed. You'd think he owned the place the way he acts, throwing his weight around." He sucked in a breath, gaining momentum. "Mosta the time, when I tell him to do something, he ignores me like he didn't even understand English and does something else."

Carly folded her hands on the desk pad. "Maybe he just has his own way of doing things."

Tony's frown grew darker. "How much do you know about him?" he demanded, leaning forward. "I don't know if we should trust him. He could steal us blind when our backs were turned."

Thoroughly irritated by Tony's attitude, Carly bent forward in her chair, chin thrust out. Tony immediately scooted back.

"I know enough," she said in a mild tone lined with steel. "The man has a special gift with horses. We need him, especially while Joey's laid up. And there's not much around here for him to steal except the stock. He could hardly hide those in his pockets."

Tony uttered a deprecating snort. "He wears an earring, for God's sake. And he ought to either braid or cut that hair, one or t'other."

"I can't imagine why you would be giving him orders in the first place," Carly continued. "After all, you're both ranch hands and you're both accountable to Ben."

Tony's face turned red. He opened his mouth as if to speak, but Carly didn't give him the chance. The last thing she needed right now was squabbles among the help.

"From what I've observed, Sage knows what he's doing. You don't have to like him to work with him." She shifted gears abruptly, well aware that she couldn't afford to lose Tony, either.

"You're a valued employee, and we couldn't manage without you. Sage may be difficult, but I know you can get along if you try." She gave Tony what she hoped was an encouraging smile. "Maybe you need to back off a little, let him do his job and you do yours. That way, if he does screw up, he'll have no one to blame but himself."

Tony rose, obviously struggling to keep his temper in check. "I can get along with anyone if I've a mind to, even an Indian," he growled.

Carly's hands clenched at his bulldog-stubborn tone, but she kept the smile pinned to her face, rose and walked him to the door. Resisting the urge to lace into him, she said instead, "Come and talk to me anytime, Tony. I'd appreciate knowing how things are going. We'll have to all pull together to get this place back to the way it used to be."

Not for anything would she stoop to interrogating the help as to why her father had let the ranch run down. Ben was the only one whose opinion she valued on the matter, and Ben had nothing to say on the subject. Despite his disapproval of her plans to dispose of her and Mollie's inheritance, he and the housekeeper had both agreed to keep mum on the subject until Carly herself was willing for it to become general knowledge. She'd probably have to say something soon, before Tony and Joey began to wonder what was going on.

Carly thanked Tony for coming in and shut the office door behind him. She walked back to the desk and glanced through the open window that was covered only by a sheer lace panel.

Outside, leaning against the fence, arms folded across his broad chest, stood Sage. It was perfectly clear that he must have heard everything that had been said about him. It was equally clear from the rigid set of his body that he was less than pleased. Was it Tony's tactless remarks that had brought that arrogant, closed-off expression to his bronzed face, or her own defense of him? After a second glance at his narrowed gaze and the grimly set jaw, Carly wasn't sure she wanted to find out.

Unwilling to hang out the window and try to smooth over the incident, she went back to the chair behind her father's desk.

She had no more than begun to pick up the next piece of mail when there was a sound at the window. Carly glanced up, just as Sage vaulted over the sill like a graceful cat; he swept aside the panel of lace to stand before her. He wasn't even breathing hard, but Carly found her own breath was choked off as she jumped to her feet to protest his unorthodox method of entry.

"Just what the hell were you trying to prove a few minutes ago, lady?" he asked. His eyes raked over her with contempt. "If I ever needed a skirt to hide behind, it sure wouldn't be yours."

Chapter Three

"You were eavesdropping!" Carly felt guilty until she realized that *she* wasn't the one in the wrong.

"I was headed for the kitchen to get a thermos of iced tea." Sage's voice was low, the words bitten off. The iron control in his tone made Carly shiver. If he ever lost that formidable temper...

She lifted her chin, her gaze passing his jaw, lurching at his mouth, finally locking with his narrowed eyes. "I didn't say anything I'm ashamed of. My talk with another employee is really none of your business."

Sage turned away, yanking off the bandanna that was tied around his head. He raked one hand through his hair. Carly watched in fascination as the longer strands in back shimmered like black silk against his collar.

"I don't need you defending me," he growled, blotting the sweat from his neck. "I've been doing it just fine all my life."

"Where did you get the name Sage?" she challenged him, trying to turn the tables. "Is it Indian? Did you choose it yourself or was it given to you?"

He moved slowly, unable to keep the reluctant grin from his mouth. The woman was quick, he'd give her that. And she was either very brave or foolhardy to the extreme. Grown men hesitated to provoke him.

"People usually call me 'breed or half breed. My real name hardly matters most of the time."

Carly's expression remained steady, and if it held even a trace of pity, he couldn't see it.

"Edwards is after the church that took me in when I was little," he admitted, surprising himself. "Saint Edward's. My first name was all my mother left me with, that and the clothes I was wearing."

Carly blinked and looked away, as if what he'd told her was too much to deal with. "It sounds like you had a difficult childhood," she said carefully.

Her words snapped him back to reality. He didn't want her feeling sorry for him. "I survived. And I'll go on surviving, despite men like Tony." He frowned, jamming the bandanna into his back pocket. "And do-gooders like you."

Leaving her standing there with hurt on her face, he turned away, wrenching open the door. Maybe he'd been too tough on her. It wasn't Carly's fault that he'd blurted out more of his past than he had told anyone but Mac before. Then he shook his head. Why was he worrying about *her* feelings? It was his own butt he'd better be guarding. Sage shut the door firmly behind him.

Still surprised by the whole conversation, Carly glanced down at the papers she had been shuffling. After staring for a long while without absorbing a single word, she decided it was time to check on Mollie, who'd been confined to the house all day because of her cold. She put the papers neatly away. Then, without a backward glance, and doing her best to banish Sage from her mind, she ran lightly down the hall.

"So the little boy asked his brother the wolf to lead him through the snow back to his camp," said a deep voice from the living room.

"And were his mommy and daddy glad to see him?"

Carly remained frozen in the hallway, listening to the rich, husky voice as it replied. "His mommy and daddy fed him venison stew and wrapped him in warm furs. And every winter after that, his daddy put out food for the wolf's family when the snow was deep."

"That's a neat story," Mollie said as Carly moved into the doorway. "Please would you tell me another one?"

Sage was sitting in a chair next to the couch where Mollie lay beneath a quilt and a pile of books and dolls. He rose when he saw Carly.

"Sage *did* have time to tell me a story," Mollie said. "And it was a good one, too."

Carly smiled down at her sister's overbright eyes and flushed cheeks. "That's nice," she said, resting her hand against Mollie's warm forehead. "But now it's time for a nap."

Mollie's smile turned upside down. "I've *been* napping," she grumbled. "Being sick is bo-ring."

"I know, punkin. But you need rest to get better." She glanced at Sage, meaning to tell him that she was sorry she had interrupted.

"Rosa said it would be all right to come in here." His head was thrown back, tone defensive. The light from the lamp on the carved oak end table threw his high cheekbones into sharp relief.

"I appreciate you taking the time to visit," Carly told him. "I just came to check on Mollie myself."

"Rosa didn't have the iced tea ready, so I thought I'd stick my head in while I was waiting." For someone who rarely explained himself, Sage was really going on.

It occurred to Carly that he might think he was in trouble. For venturing past the dining room? For wasting precious work time? Then it came to her. He was afraid she would be angry that he was with Mollie. She forced her gaze back to the figure on the couch, noticing that Mollie's expression had become anxious as she picked up on Sage's tension.

Carly gave her a reassuring grin. "We both appreciate your visit, don't we, punkin?"

Mollie bobbed her head, making her curls dance. "Sage knows lots of stories," she said. "All about Comanche Indians and wild animals."

Carly turned to him. He had edged closer to the doorway. "I know how boring it can be for a child to be sick," she said. "Thank you for being so thoughtful."

For a moment his eyes searched hers, then he nodded abruptly. His earring winked in the light. "I'd better see about the tea." He glanced down at Mollie. "I hope you feel better soon, *mah-tao-yo.*"

"What did you call me?" Mollie's eyes were wide.

"That's Comanche for 'little one.'" His gaze swung warily toward Carly.

Before either she or Mollie could speak again, he was gone. Carly listened for the sound of his footsteps on the hardwood floor, but even in boots his tread was silent.

"So," she resumed, sitting down on the edge of the couch. "What story did Sage tell you?"

The rest of the week was as uneventful as foaling season gets on a horse ranch, with Mollie finally over her cold without passing it on to anyone else, Joey visiting the doctor to hear that his arm was healing nicely, and the renovation of the ranch proceeding at what Carly felt was a snail's pace.

Two mares foaled, both without complications, several more that had delivered earlier were bred, and a yearling sold for a little less than Carly had hoped to obtain for the promising chestnut filly. She spent another hour with the accountant and finally began to feel she was making sense out of the ranch's financial position. Perhaps she would get back to Houston before everyone there forgot her, after all.

"I know the timing's awful," Ben confessed, standing before her in the stallion barn early one afternoon, "but Emma's my only sister and she's always been healthy. This surgery's got her spooked and she wants me to be there. If I leave right away and everything goes as scheduled, I'll be back by tomorrow evening or the next morning."

Carly looked into his lined face. She knew he wouldn't even have brought the trip up if he hadn't felt it absolutely necessary. It *was* foaling season and, unlike cattle, horses needed careful observation, even assistance in bringing their young into the world. And Ben was the most experienced midwife on the place.

"Of course you can go," she told him, injecting her voice with confidence. She forced aside the images that crowded her mind. "Joey's on duty at night, none of the mares are acting restless today, and if anything happens I'll call the vet in plenty of time."

Neither she nor Ben voiced the possibility that the vet might be off delivering someone else's future champion. Ben had never mentioned the one foaling Carly had witnessed as a child and neither had she, preferring not to think about it. Since then, she had always managed to be somewhere else whenever birth took place.

"Tony's useless," Ben observed. "Faints at the first sign of blood. Joey doesn't have the experience to be much help yet when things start to happen, especially with his broken wing. But Sage should be able to handle whatever comes up."

Ben paused a moment, his expression thoughtful. Carly knew that he and Sage had assisted at the recent births. Ben took his duties seriously.

"Sage knows almost as much about foaling as I do. And that's saying some." Ben grinned and Carly stretched her lips in reply.

It took an effort to keep that smile in place. The birth she had watched had ended in disaster, the foal born deformed and lifeless, the mother, Carly's first horse, too damaged internally to breed again. Carly could still see that poor little creature in her mind and remember the seemingly heartless way the vet had described the mare's injuries after he had finally arrived to examine her. And Carly's father had been too preoccupied with losing a valuable foal and the future offspring of a promising filly to give a thought to the daughter who'd stood in the shadows, sensitive heart breaking for her pet and its baby.

Carly hoped desperately that the rest of the mothers-to-be would wait for Ben's return!

"Don't worry about a thing," she said, patting his slightly stooped shoulder. "Give your sister my regards, and don't come back until you feel right about leaving her."

Ben's smile was worth all the doubts and fears she'd forced herself to swallow. "Thank you," he said softly. "I'll call you tomorrow."

* * *

Carly was finishing evening chores when she decided to check the broodmare barn before going in. This time of year the expectant mares were never left alone for long. Joey, on light duty until his arm healed, watched over them each night, grabbing what sleep he could in the bunkhouse during the day. Carly found him mixing up the warm mash that was part of the pregnant mares' evening meals.

"Remember," she told him after she had asked about his arm, "if anything unusual happens during the night while Ben's gone, come to the house and wake me. Upstairs, second door on the left." She had no idea what she would do then, besides calling the vet and making sure Sage was there to take control.

"Okay," Joey said agreeably. "But so far everything looks pretty routine." Carly was about to breathe a sigh of relief when he added, "Never can tell about horses, though. Sometimes it happens pretty fast."

Carly gave him a rueful smile, then walked the length of the stable, stopping to glance in at the equine ladies-in-waiting. They returned her curious stare, some ambling over to thrust a muzzle at her in search of a treat. None of them appeared unduly restless, had swollen udders or any of the other signs of impending labor.

Sage was in the end stall with one of his horses, talking softly and stroking her full side while she ate, but he glanced over his shoulder when Carly approached. She had thought her steps nearly silent, but obviously his hearing was finely tuned.

"Everything okay?" he asked, turning his attention back to the horse Carly now knew as Comanche Princess. "Ben told me he'd be gone at least until late tomorrow."

"It seems quiet," she said, "but I'm not that experienced with four-legged pregnant ladies. You'll probably want to look them over yourself."

"If I don't have my hands full right here," he said dryly.

Carly tensed. "You don't mean . . . ?"

"Yeah," he drawled. "This is one female who doesn't intend to still be pregnant in the morning."

"Oh, God!" Carly heard the panic in her tone and pressed her lips together. "Have you called the vet, or do you want me to?"

Sage straightened abruptly. "Easy, now. We have plenty of time." His voice held a soothing note Carly found mesmerizing. No wonder he was so good with the horses. "We've got hours before we need to call," he said. "I just wish Ben was here. I had to turn her last colt, as well as pulling it."

Carly swallowed, praying for calm. "You know how to do everything, don't you?" she asked, seeking reassurance.

"Yeah, but it might take two." His gaze burned into hers. "How steady are your nerves?"

Carly curled her hand behind her until the nails bit into her palm. It was past time she faced her fears. If her father had ever taken a few moments to discuss what she'd witnessed before, she might have faced them years ago. "My nerves are steady enough, I guess."

"Good girl."

She warmed to the approval in his tone.

"I may need your help," he continued. "Not squeamish, are you?"

She ignored the sudden impulse to cross the fingers that were hidden from his view. "Of course not."

He raised one dark brow, and she fought the reaction that raced through her. "It wouldn't be my first foaling," she said. "I grew up here, remember?"

"That's right. I guess I wasn't thinking." He moved closer, wiping his hands down his jeans. "But you just came back, didn't you? Back from where?"

The direct question surprised her and she studied him for a moment before answering. He opened the stall door, gave Princess a last caress and murmured something Carly couldn't hear.

"I've been living in Houston," she told him.

He had shut the door behind him and was watching her expectantly.

"How long were you away?" He was standing too close and Carly steeled herself against retreating. He would take it wrong and be insulted. She didn't stop to analyze her desire to keep him talking for a few more minutes.

"I've been there for over six years."

He cocked his head to the side. "And you like it, living in a city?" His expression held disbelief that anyone really could.

"I love it. How long since you've had your own spread?" she asked daringly.

For a moment his gaze strayed to a point beyond her shoulder and his eyes clouded. "Too long." The words were uttered softly, and there was such loneliness in them that Carly felt an immense sadness for him. A man like Sage should be free, his own boss. Then he blinked, as if coming back from a long way off.

"I still have the land," he said, a muscle in his cheek twitching. "It was the stock and most of the equipment I had to sell off."

"Why?" As soon as the question was out, she realized how personal it was. "Don't answer if you don't want to," she said quickly, flushing at the long look he gave her.

"I wasn't going to." He turned away and opened the door to the next stall. Comanche Lady whickered softly.

Carly watched Sage's wide shoulders flex beneath the soft fabric of his worn shirt. She felt foolish, waiting to see if he intended to say anything else. Then she began to grow angry and twisted away abruptly.

"Carly," he called over his shoulder. "I'll let you know if I need your help tonight."

She didn't realize until she was in the house that he had used her first name.

Something woke her later and she lay perfectly still, wondering for a moment if she was still alone in the darkened bedroom. Telling Joey to wake her if he needed her was one thing; finding Sage standing silently over her would be another matter entirely.

Holding her breath for a moment, eyes staring into the darkness, she decided that no one else was there. Still, she couldn't shake the feeling of urgency that gripped her; if Sage needed help, he might not be able to leave the barn. She almost jumped up, out of bed, then reminded herself that he could always send Joey.

She flopped over, trying to go back to sleep. She willed herself to relax, but her mind was too busy. Outside all seemed quiet. In the house no one stirred.

Carly had checked Mollie one last time before going to bed herself, and had been pleased to find the child sound asleep. She seemed to be starting to adapt to the shock of her parents' sudden death, although Carly knew it would be years, if ever, before the healing process was complete. For either of them.

She forced her eyes shut and snuggled under the covers, sighing. Suddenly her eyelids snapped back open and she sat up. Had she heard something?

She listened again, straining her ears. No, the sound must have been inside her head.

This was ridiculous. Carly glanced at the clock. One-thirty. Swinging aside the covers, she switched on her bedside lamp and reached for the clothes she had left out, just in case. The only way to get any sleep was to go to the barn herself and make sure that everything was all right.

The light was on at the near end of the long building and she could hear Sage's voice, low and encouraging, before she saw him. Hurrying, she came up to Princess's stall and peered over.

The mare was down and Sage was urging her to rise. "Come on, girl. Trust me." He added some words in a language Carly didn't understand. Blowing noisily, the horse got to her feet. Her tail was already bandaged to keep it out of the way, and her bag was dripping milk.

"Good girl," Sage murmured. "Perhaps your foal will turn by itself."

Carly trembled, watching him stroke the mare's neck as if nothing on earth was wrong. "Can I help?"

"Yeah," he said without glancing in her direction. "Some coffee would be welcome. In the thermos outside the door." His hand shifted to caress the horse's distended belly. He was still wearing the clothes he'd had on earlier, and Carly wondered if he had gotten any sleep.

She found herself speculating about his touch as his hand slid over the mare, and turned swiftly to look for the thermos. Schooling her thoughts, she filled the cup and handed it to him over the door, their fingers brushing as he murmured his thanks. Sage's silver eyes glittered between thick lashes, then he turned back to the restless animal.

"Come on in here," he told Carly. "Find a corner and stay still."

Moving slowly, she opened the door, careful not to disturb the mare, who let out a groan.

"Is she in pain?"

"Just trying to get comfortable," Sage said. "She wants to lie down, but I'm afraid the foal's turned wrong, and sometimes making her get up will shift it around."

Settling down quietly to wait, Carly took the opportunity to study Sage as he concentrated on his horse. He swallowed a mouthful of coffee and she watched the muscles of his throat ripple. Then he set the cup aside and began again to stroke the swollen belly, talking softly all the while.

Carly realized that his soothing voice was calming *her* fears as well. "Will she be okay?"

Sage's sensitive fingers continued to probe and stroke. Then, when the mare attempted once again to lie down, he squatted beside her. "I hope so," he muttered.

Some of Carly's new found confidence ebbed away. For the first time she noticed the rubber gloves on the floor of the stall and the sweat stains on Sage's tan shirt. "Have you called the vet?"

His brow furrowed as he stroked the horse's shoulder. "He's not available."

The words hit Carly like ice water. Frantically she tried to think of someone else to call, but couldn't. How she wished Ben were here! "What are you going to do?"

He gave the horse a final pat and rose to stand over Carly. The light behind him made his form appear menacing for an instant, then he dropped down beside her and sighed heavily, resting his back against the wall. When he turned, there was a smile on his lips but his eyes were solemn.

"I'm going to deliver a foal, and you're going to help me," he said, reaching out his hand. Without hesitation, Carly put hers into it. His skin was warm. "And then when it's here, alive and healthy, perhaps you'll grant me another favor."

"What's that?" she asked curiously as he released her hand.

"We'll talk about it later," he said, looking away. "First we have a job to do."

The minutes crept by, and Carly kept sneaking looks at Sage, trying to read something from his grave expression. At one point he brought the supplies he'd gathered into the stall and put them into a corner. Then he went back out to wash his hands at the sink in the tack room. When he returned, Joey was with him.

"All quiet down there," Joey said after greeting Carly. "One night last year we had two mares deliver, one right after the other."

"I hope that doesn't happen tonight," Carly replied, tensing. Sage's first loyalty would have to be to his own horse.

Joey shook his head knowledgeably. "Nobody even close." He left to renew his vigil. "Holler if you need me," he called softly.

Sage stood over Princess, his expression tender. Carly wondered what it would be like to have him look at her that way. Dismayed by the direction of her thoughts, she shifted her gaze, following the powerful lines of his body until she realized what she was staring at. Shaken, she rose hastily to her feet. The night and the strain of waiting were getting to her.

"Easy," Sage murmured as another shuddering contraction went through the mare.

Carly wasn't sure if he was speaking to the horse or to her. Then Princess's water broke, sending out a rush of fluid. Carly knew they were down to serious business.

"Won't be long now," Sage said as Princess settled onto her side, legs outstretched.

Carly steeled herself to do whatever he needed. The barn was warm but she felt chilled, remembering. More than once in the long moments that followed, Sage's gaze found hers. A faint smile would twist his lips, but Carly could feel his tension.

"Is Carly short for something?" he asked once.

"Caroline. It was my mother's name."

He nodded abruptly, but made no comment. The silence stretched on, except for the noises Princess made and the low drone of Sage's voice as he encouraged her.

Finally he bent over her, and watched as one tiny front hoof appeared and then the other, still enclosed in the grayish-white amniotic sac. He looked at Carly, who had moved closer, and gave her the first genuine smile she had seen him direct at anyone other than Mollie.

"The foal's in the right position," he said, relief in his voice. "We got lucky."

Even as he spoke, while Carly was trying to tell herself that the flood of warmth she felt was a perfectly natural reaction, the foal's head appeared.

"Oh!" Carly gasped when she saw that the tiny creature was alive. Emotional tears sprang to her eyes and her throat closed.

Sage sighed deeply. "It's always a miracle," he said.

Carly couldn't speak; she merely nodded.

Princess took a short rest from her exertions, and Sage got a pair of scissors to slit the sac, peeling it back. Then, working quickly, he cleared the foal's nostrils.

The little head looked perfect to Carly, wet and matted but exquisite. She blinked away her tears, feeling foolish and sentimental. Her father had often accused her of being weak when she let her emotions show. But there was something about witnessing a new life entering the world that made everything else pale by comparison.

She glanced up; Sage was watching her. For a timeless moment their gazes locked. Then another contraction rippled through Princess. They looked on in silence, and the foal tumbled onto the straw.

"It's a filly," Sage exclaimed, "and as gold as a newly minted coin!" This was the color standard by which palominos were judged.

He rubbed the leggy body with towels that Carly kept handing him from the pile of supplies. Then he curled the foal close to its mother, carefully holding the umbilical cord in his hand. Carly knew that it was important to let every bit of life-giving blood pulse through to the newborn. After that it was all right for the cord to break.

Sage set it down gently and rose, taking Carly's arm and urging her from the stall. Joey was standing outside, his expression reflecting the wonder and excitement she felt. They exchanged grins, then watched over the door as Sage dealt with the mother and her new filly.

Finally both mare and foal were on their feet. Princess nuzzled her daughter with maternal pride as it wobbled precariously beside her. Four white stockings adorned the spindly legs and a wide blaze marked its head. When the newborn's steps grew less shaky and it finally began to nurse, Sage left the stall and joined Carly and Joey.

Joey wiped his eyes. "Always gets to me," he said brusquely. Then he stuck out his hand. "Congratulations, man. I'm glad they're both okay."

Sage grasped it firmly. "Thank you," he said solemnly.

Carly thought she heard fatigue in his voice. Her own eyes felt gritty, but she was much too excited to be tired.

Bidding her good-night, Joey turned and slowly walked away, stopping at each stall to check its dozing occupant.

Carly wasn't sure how long she stood there beside Sage as they watched the new baby take its first meal. After a while he shifted his weight and his arm grazed Carly's shoulder. She leaned closer, not really knowing why.

To her utter surprise, Sage raised his arm and let it casually encircle her. His muscular imprint burned her through the layers of clothing. Afraid he would pull away if she moved, Carly stood perfectly still, barely breathing as she absorbed his strength.

Together they watched the filly's antics, while Sage silently questioned his judgment. What was he thinking of? Even though they had shared something special, he was surely pushing his luck, even though she hadn't jumped away. He was still surprised at that when Carly broke the silence.

"What are you going to name her?" she asked.

Sage dropped his arm. "She's going to be a beauty, like her mother," he said, voice slightly rough. "Perhaps I'll name her Promise."

He looked into Carly's blue eyes, liking the steady way she returned his gaze. Her hair was in its familiar braid, but tendrils had escaped all around her face, framing it with a softly curling halo. A thicker strand slanted across her forehead, almost falling into one eye. He reached to push it aside, then realized what he was doing and let his hand fall back his side.

A flicker of disappointment sparked her eyes and disappeared. Had she wanted him to touch her? Perhaps the attraction he felt was returned in some measure.

"I like that name," she said, smiling at the pair in the stall. "She looks perfect to me. A promise for the future." She glanced up hastily, as if afraid she'd said something she shouldn't have.

"Yes," Sage found himself agreeing, "I like that, too." He returned Carly's stare, the sudden emotional pull he felt surprising him. He would have sworn he was immune to the kind of feelings she raised in him with no effort.

Powerless to fight their overwhelming force, he dipped his head, trying to tell himself his judgment was blurred by fatigue. Carly didn't move as he bent closer, but her eyes widened. Finally they drifted shut with a flutter of her lashes, as if she felt as powerless as he. Sage's lips settled lightly upon hers.

He almost gasped at her softness. Her hand touched his neck as gently as a butterfly, her fingers tangling in his hair. His hands clamped around her waist and drew her closer, his lips pressed hers more firmly. His head was spinning, her sweet taste seeping into him like honey. He shifted his mouth to deepen the kiss.... A high, shrill whinny made them jump guiltily apart.

Carly couldn't look at Sage. Instead, she stared over the side of the stall, concentrating on the awkward foal; it whinnied again and began to explore its new home. Her lips were tingling, her body on fire, and she felt as if something infinitely precious had been snatched from her arms.

She heard the sound of the stable door opening and saw the glow of early-morning light. Sage turned away as Tony approached and asked him something. Sage answered. Carly barely heard them, for she was still caught in the sensual spell she and Sage had woven together.

It was easy enough to explain how the kiss had happened, she decided finally. They had shared something moving, something special that had affected them deeply. That had translated itself into an outpouring of emotion. Simple, she thought, convinced by her logic. The kiss was nothing more than the response to the scene they had both witnessed.

Why, then, did a tremor shake her when she turned and saw Sage staring down at her, his silver eyes unreadable?

"You'd better get some sleep," he said gruffly. "You've been up most of the night."

Carly took fierce control of her scattered wits. "I'll be fine. You must be tired, too."

He shook his head. "I'm used to going without sleep. Thanks for your help."

She couldn't stop the smile that curved her lips. She had faced her fears and dealt with them. "I didn't really do much."

His expression changed, giving her a glimpse of his feelings, but he recovered swiftly. "You were here," he said quietly. "That was enough."

Before Carly could ask him what he meant, Tony shouted from a stall farther down the row.

"I'd better see what he wants." Sage's gaze dropped to Carly's mouth, searing her tender flesh as hotly as any brand. Then he turned away, leaving her to wonder if she had seen what she thought she had in his narrowed eyes, or merely what she wanted to be there. If she wasn't careful, Sage was going to become a complication she didn't need, couldn't allow herself to want, and sure as hell wasn't equipped to handle.

Suddenly she remembered that he had said he had a favor to ask, but he was already deep in conversation with Tony. Whatever it was, it would have to wait.

Chapter Four

The next day, Carly overslept and missed breakfast, then spent the morning and most of the afternoon on the telephone in her father's office. She had to deal firmly with the painting contractor, who was trying to postpone the date his crew was coming to redo the house and the outbuildings. By the time he'd finally agreed to stick with his original schedule, she was grateful for all her experience at Dwyer Shipping with reluctant suppliers, indecisive shippers and uncooperative government officials. *Now* she was free to escape from the confines of the house, and she headed to the broodmare barn to check on Promise and her dam as well as the other horses.

Part of her was just as anxious to see Sage as the new filly whose birth she had witnessed the night before. How would he react when he saw her, after the kiss they had shared? Would he pretend that nothing had happened? What else could he do? Although she doubted their boss-employee relationship would daunt a man of Sage's arrogance, he did seem to need the job at Rolling Gold. For the smallest second, Carly wished that things could be different. She discarded the thought hastily. He could only be a serious complication to her life. Any kind of relationship with a drifter like Sage, no matter how brief, was a short, straight road to disaster. And that was all.

So how was she going to act toward him?

An answer still eluded her as she went into the barn and stopped at the door to Princess's stall. The new mother whinnied softly, Carly crooned to her, and the apprehensive filly tried to hide behind her dam's long legs, twitching her fluffy tail like a feather duster.

"That's okay, precious," Carly murmured. "You'll learn all about people soon enough. Take a day to get used to life first, if you want."

Tony walked into the stable and stopped beside her. "How are you?" he asked. "Didn't get much sleep last night, did you?"

Carly managed a smile, but kept her gaze on the horses. "I wasn't the only one," she said. "Sage and Joey were both up longer than I was. Besides, I slept for a couple of hours. I feel just fine."

"Glad to hear it." Tony reached out a hand to Princess, who investigated it briefly, then turned her attention back to the foal who had begun to nurse. "Good-looking filly," he said.

"Yes," Carly replied. "I'd love to see her sire." She wanted to ask where Sage was, but refrained. He would show up sooner or later.

"So would I. And I'd like to know how a man like Edwards had access," Tony commented with a sneer, working the plug of chaw in his cheek from one side to the other. "He claims to have won the mares in a poker game."

Carly kept silent, remembering the hand's animosity toward Sage.

"I'd better get to work," he resumed. "Can't shirk just because Ben's away." He grinned ingratiatingly, and Carly suddenly realized that she didn't care much for the man, even though he had been at the ranch for years. Perhaps it was merely a lingering bad taste from their earlier conversation about her newest employee.

Tony had disappeared into the tack room when Carly heard a familiar sound from somewhere outside. Tensing, she walked to the open doorway between the rows of stalls. Sky Walker was in one of the training paddocks, dancing at the end of a long lead. Sage held the other end and Carly could hear the deep rumble of his voice as he talked to the nervous horse, whose ears were pricked toward the sound. Joey sat perched on the fence.

Carly's first impulse was to join Joey. She would have liked to see Sage in action. Then she remembered the chores she had to do while Ben was gone; there were several horses to be groomed, and the show tack still had to be inventoried. She stood in the doorway for a few more minutes while Sage moved with a masculine grace that made her sigh with longing. Quickly she turned away.

It would be better to face him over the dinner table. In front of the others she would be forced to maintain control.

Carly shrugged away her tension, picked up a currycomb and a hoof pick, then opened a stall door. She had been so tired when she finally fell into bed early this morning that she had dropped into an immediate, dreamless sleep. Only when she woke later had the memory of Sage's kiss returned to provoke her. She had liked the touch of his mouth too much, that and the way he'd made her feel as he held her close to his hard, masculine body. His tenderness had been a surprise, but the fiery passion she had sensed simmering beneath the enigmatic surface had surprised her even more.

Sage's attention was divided between the balky Sky Walker and the spot in the open stable doorway where he had glimpsed a feminine silhouette. He wondered if she had been deliberately avoiding him. Maybe he should be grateful she hadn't fired him after the way he'd come on to her. It had to be one of the dumbest things he'd ever done.

"Sky's beginning to trust you," Joey said from his perch on the fence.

Sage shifted his thoughts back to the job at hand. "Can't do anything with a horse until you have his trust," he drawled. Or a woman, either.

What would it take to earn Carly's trust, and why did he care? He wasn't planning to stick around long enough to find out. Sage's gaze cut to the other barn again.

Sky Walker appeared to sense that he wasn't paying strict attention. The horse lunged, teeth bared, but Sage's reflexes were quick. Expertly he stepped out of the way, speaking to Sky Walker in the same low, even voice he'd been using all along. He resisted the urge to yell at the mule-headed nag for being so stubborn, the urge to forget what he was doing and find Carly. Then he remembered that he still had to ask the favor he needed from her. That was the reason he was here. The *only* reason.

"That's enough for one day," he said both to Sky Walker and to Joey. "I've got two more horses to work before dinner, and I bet you've got chores of your own to do."

Joey grinned sheepishly. "Yeah, I do," he said. "But I sure enjoy watching you work a horse."

Sage returned the younger man's grin. "Ben will have both our hides if the chores aren't done when he gets back."

Putting up Sky Walker, he thought about going to the other barn to see if Carly was still there. He told himself that he had too much to do, but even as he led a docile yearling from its stall, he knew the real reason he didn't cross the dusty yard was because Tony was also in the broodmare barn. The last thing Sage needed was another run-in with the other groom, who liked to throw his weight around when Ben wasn't there to curb him.

One day Tony would go too far, say too much, but until then Sage planned to avoid what could only be a nasty confrontation. If it also meant avoiding Carly for the rest of the afternoon, that couldn't be helped. It was probably even a good idea, would give him more time to get his hormones under control. At some point, though, and damned soon, Sage would have to face her. What he needed to ask wouldn't wait much longer.

As she changed for dinner, Carly told herself that the reason she chose to wear a navy-blue skirt and a sleeveless blouse striped in shades of blue and lavender was because she was tired of jeans, but her innate honesty wouldn't let her get away with it. She might be playing with fire, but it was more than she could do to stop. Sometime soon she would have to get her attraction to Sage under control. Sometime soon, but not tonight. Tonight she would sit across from him at the dinner table, enjoy his presence and the occasional sound of his deep voice.

"You look pretty," Mollie said when Carly ducked into her room to see if she was ready to go downstairs.

"Thanks, so do you. Did you remember to wash your hands?"

"Yes." Mollie held them up for inspection. She was wearing a plaid shirt in pastel colors, and pink denim overalls with pink and white athletic shoes. Her hair hung in loose curls around her face and her eyes sparkled with excitement.

"I'm lots better," she said. "Rosa told me I could eat with everyone else if I wanted." She picked up the coloring books she'd spread across the miniature table that sat with its four matching chairs in front of the window framed with ruffled priscillas, and stacked them on a built-in shelf on one wall. While Carly looked around, admiring once again the way her stepmother had redone the bedroom with deep rose carpeting, pink print wallpaper and white furniture, Mollie put the crayons back into their box and set it next to the books.

"Tomorrow I can go outside," she added. "If that's okay with you." Her blue eyes were anxious.

"We'll see, honey. I don't want you to overdo it."

"We could go riding," Mollie suggested wistfully. "No one has had time to go with me for days and days." Their father had bought Mollie a black-and-white pony named Polka Dot last year, but she wasn't allowed to ride alone.

Carly made a mental note to spend some time with her sister the next day, then held out a hand. "All ready?"

Mollie nodded, dimples flashing, and linked her fingers with Carly's. "Maybe Sage could go with us," she suggested as they went down the stairs.

Carly took the coward's way out. "He has a lot of chores to do, but you and I might find the time to go."

They entered the dining room together, and she released the breath she was suddenly aware she'd been holding. The room was empty. Rosa was rattling pans in the kitchen. Mollie let go of Carly's hand and raced ahead.

"What's for dinner?" Carly heard her ask.

Before she could cross the room and join them, the outside door opened and Joey came in, followed by Tony and Sage. Carly greeted each of them in turn.

"No sign of Ben yet?" she asked.

"Not yet," Tony said. "Did he call?"

Carly nodded. "A couple of hours ago. His sister came through the surgery fine, and he was heading back pretty soon." She didn't want to face another night without him here to supervise any more equine births that might take place.

Joey and Tony were more interested in the promise of food than conversation and found their chairs right away. Sage, however, seemed to slow as his gaze met hers. Carly could read nothing on his face, but his eyes lingered briefly on her mouth as he returned her greeting. A wave of dizziness threatened her equilibrium.

Glancing at his clean, worn jeans and work shirt, Carly thought of the men she knew in Houston. Despite their custom-tailored suits and imported ties, their expensively cut and styled hair, not one of them managed half the sex appeal Sage exuded without effort. She turned away, breath caught again in her throat, and Mollie came into the room carrying a bowl of grated parmesan cheese.

"We're having lasagna," she said importantly. "Rosa needs you in the kitchen."

Grateful for the interruption, Carly hurried away, conscious of Sage's stare. As she picked up the huge wooden bowl of green salad that sat on the tiled counter, she wondered how she was going to get through the next forty-five minutes with her poise intact. Contrary to what she had thought earlier, enjoying Sage's presence calmly wasn't going to be easy.

The meal was finally over. Sage was impatient for the other two men to thank Rosa and file out the door. Mollie had left to watch a television program, Rosa had gone into the kitchen with a stack of dirty dishes, and Carly was gathering up the used silverware.

Sage stopped beside her and waited until she looked up. For a moment he was afraid he wouldn't be able to stifle the impulse to pull her into his arms, then regained his control. If he wasn't careful, she might stick him with one of the forks she held in her hand.

"I'd like to talk to you later, if you have some time," he said quietly.

Carly's eyes seemed to grow bluer, and a flush of color stained her cheeks. "Of course," she replied. "In my office? When will you be finished working?"

Sage shrugged. "By seven, I suppose."

Carly frowned, considering. "I really won't have any time until after I get Mollie ready for bed. That would be a little after eight."

He thought for a moment and then gave in to a sudden impulse. "You know that spot where the creek takes a sharp curve? I like to walk down there in the evening. It reminds me of a place I used to go back home. Would you mind coming down there?"

"That's a good idea. I'll see you then."

Sage forced himself to turn away. "Thanks," he remembered to say over his shoulder. Now all he had to do was figure out how to persuade her to go along with what he wanted. Even though that had been his intention all along, he was finding it surprisingly difficult to ask Carly for such a big favor. His pride balked. He had to remind himself that the only thing he could count on was his land. To save it he would do almost anything. And while he was choking on his pride, he had to keep his hands to himself. He wondered which was going to prove harder.

Carly's eyes had adjusted themselves to the dimness by the time she found her way down the sloping pasture to the spot by the creek Sage had mentioned. It had been one of her own favorite places when she was growing up. The bank was grassy and shaded, the creek itself wide and shallow, an ideal place to wade and to dream with her dolls or a book for company. Later on it had turned out to be a soothing retreat after one of her frequent arguments with her father.

She hadn't changed out of the skirt she had worn to dinner, and the slight breeze that had come up felt good against her bare legs and arms. Her hair had been pulled back in a clip all day, so she had taken the time to brush it out and apply fresh lip gloss.

She really should give up trying to make excuses; she wanted Sage to be attracted to her. What she might do if he was she hadn't a clue, but at least she was honest enough to admit to herself that the man intrigued her. Curiosity quickened her steps. She had deliberately waited a few extra moments back at the house, but now she was eager to discover what he wanted to discuss.

When she got to the creek bank, disappointment stabbed her. The wide log she used to sit on was empty, as was the area around it. Perhaps he had already left.

Then Sage straightened from where he had been leaning against a large tree and came toward her. A smile curved her lips.

"You're here," she said inanely. She glanced around; except for a couple of curious horses on the other side of the fence, they were alone. The slope she had walked down almost completely hid them from the outbuildings.

For a moment Carly thought Sage was going to kiss her again and her heart began to race. Then he stopped a few feet away, pushing one deeply tanned hand through his black hair, and she realized how much she wanted to be in his arms. Perhaps agreeing to meet him here hadn't been wise.

"Well," she said to cut short the silence, "what did you want to talk to me about? A raise?" She tried to laugh, but he didn't return her smile.

Feeling painfully awkward, she studied the creek and the night sounds beyond its far bank. She should have insisted they meet in her office. Her father's office, she silently corrected herself. She had never intended to make it, or any other part of the ranch, her own.

"It wasn't an accident that I came here that first night," Sage said, surprising her; she turned to stare. "I drove all the way from Oklahoma to do just that."

Carly didn't know how to respond. She had thought him a drifter looking for a job, any job. "Does all this have something to do with the favor you want?" she guessed.

He rubbed one finger along the side of his nose, and she realized that his usual icy control had melted a little.

Impulsively she stepped forward and put a hand upon his forearm. "What is it?" she asked, concerned. The heat of his skin seared her palm and she immediately let go, but before she could retreat, Sage's hands whipped out to capture her shoulders.

"You're right," he said in a husky voice, "it has everything to do with the favor I need." His gray eyes bored into hers, then he released her and took a step back. "Damn," he muttered to himself, bracing his hands on his hips.

His gaze roamed everywhere but where she stood, and Carly had trouble holding back both her impatience and curiosity.

He began speaking again, his words fast, his tone clipped. "Comanche Lady is going to drop her foal any day. When she and Princess come in heat again, I want to breed them to Red Rocket. That's why I came here. It's the best way to rebuild my stock."

Carly tried to sort through what he had just told her. "You came here to breed your horses?" she asked. "With no booking, no stud fee?"

It was Sage's turn to look away. "That's right," he said grimly. "With no money, with no rights at all. The only thing I have to offer is myself. I'll work it off."

Carly could see pride in the stiff set of his shoulders and the angle of his head. He was braced for rejection, whether he realized it or not.

"You'd work here for nothing?" she asked.

"Room and board," he replied.

"For how long?" she persisted. She needed him to stay until she sold the ranch.

He shrugged. "How long you got in mind?"

She considered a moment. If she told him the truth, that none of them would be there for too much longer, his pride might keep him from accepting. And she wanted him to accept. For herself and for him. "Six months?" she asked.

He looked relieved. "You put a high price on my skills."

She ignored the way his smile made her feel. "I have a feeling you're worth it."

"Deal." He put out his hand.

"Wait," Carly said hastily. "Before we agree, I want something else."

His silvery gaze bored into hers, and one corner of his mouth quirked. Lord, what was he thinking? He shifted, jamming the extended hand into his back pocket. "Oh, yeah? What's that?"

"Tell me how you lost your horses and how you won those mares back in a card game. I can't believe you gambled it all away." She didn't want to believe it.

Sage's laugh was a blade that sliced through the peaceful music of encroaching evening. "Life's a gamble," he said. "Sometimes you get dealt a bad hand."

"What do you mean?" Carly asked.

For a long, awkward moment Sage remained silent. "I didn't gamble my horses away," he said finally. Did it matter how much he told her or what she thought? He would do almost anything to get what he wanted. "I sold the stock off, one by one, and each sale was like cutting away a piece of my own skin." He remembered the sensation of parting with each of the horses he and Mac had either bred themselves or bought after careful consideration. And despite the pain and the desperation, nothing he'd done had helped Mac.

Sage glanced down at Carly, who was listening to him with compassion on her sweet face. He swallowed. Damn, but he hated this. If he managed to pull himself back up, he swore on the memory of his mother that he would never again be vulnerable to anyone else's whim.

"Why did you have to do that?" Carly asked when he didn't continue. Her eyes were full of emotions he was too impatient to read.

Sage released a sigh that felt as if it came from the depths of his soul. Even now it was difficult to think about the man who had been his closest friend. "There's not that much to tell."

Again he swallowed a lump of pride. He didn't want help, especially not hers! He wanted to take, not ask, and to give her back something to remember, the passion that sang along his veins, taunting him whenever she was near.

Instead he forced himself to go on. "I met Mac in the army. We were in the special forces together. We started out as enemies, but ended up saving each other's butts so many times, we lost count of which one owed the other." He paused, remembering the deep bond of trust he had forged with the big black man in the steaming hellholes of Southeast Asia.

"Mac was from Chicago, the roughest part, tough as an army boot and as trusting as a snake in a mongoose cage. I was surprised that he wanted the same thing I did when we got out, a spread somewhere with horses. Eventually we decided to pool the pay we'd saved and combine our efforts. I always knew I wanted palominos. Did you know my ancestors, the Comanches, used to breed them?"

Sage didn't wait for an answer; he forced himself to go on in an emotionless voice. "It was no problem convincing Mac to come back to Oklahoma with me. He had no real home anymore, no family left."

Sage paused, taking a long breath.

"My father used to say that people who breed palominos get gold fever, just like prospectors," Carly said. "One look at them spoils a man for anything else."

Sage studied her bright blue eyes, that sweet-tasting mouth and sassy, pointed chin. It wasn't the horses that gave him gold fever, he thought. It was Carly. The first time he'd seen her standing up to Sky Walker, she had fired his blood. And he knew what it would take to quench the flames. More than he could afford to risk.

"When I got out, I started scouting around. When Mac was discharged six months later, we took our pay and bought Comanche Creek," he continued. "After five years of hard work we were doing okay." He almost laughed at the understatement. Things had been going better than okay. His throat closed on the bitterness that flooded it. Just a taste was all they'd had. A taste of succeeding at something they'd both wanted with such hunger. Of having something that was *theirs*.

"What happened?" Carly asked softly when he remained silent.

"Mac got sick. I finally dragged him to the doctor." Sage's voice was gruff. "He went in the hospital and he never came home."

Carly gasped, hand flying to her mouth. "Oh, no!" she exclaimed.

Sage forced himself to go on. "Mac died of the cancer that had spread all through him, and I sold the rest of the stock to pay his medical bills."

"But what about Princess and Lady?" Carly asked, deeply moved. "You weren't kidding when you said you won them back, were you?"

He shook his head. "No. That's another story. I think I've told you enough." His tone was harsh, but he couldn't help it. So much to hold inside, but he couldn't lose control, not around her. "So," he said impatiently, "what's your answer? Does Red Rocket cover them or not?"

Sage stood unmoving while Carly's beautiful eyes searched his face. He couldn't tell what she was thinking. After a moment a small, uncertain smile tugged at her lips. "We'll breed Red Rocket to your mares whenever they're ready," she said quietly. "I'll tell Ben."

Sage turned away abruptly and felt himself sag with relief. "Thanks."

His voice was still so emotionless that Carly hesitated, wanting to add something more. He didn't look at her, though, and after a moment she had little choice but to start back to the house, leaving him alone to deal with whatever memories his reluctant words had reawakened. She could only hope that when she told Ben what she had done, he wouldn't ask too many questions about the bizarre deal she had made.

When Carly got back to the house, she noticed a sheriff's car pulled up in the driveway. Curious, she hurried inside.

"Hello, Caroline. It's been a long time, but I heard you were back."

The deputy who was standing in the front hall with Rosa, his muscular body clad in a khaki uniform only shades lighter than his curly hair, had never been as important to Carly as she'd been to him. Grady Harper was one person from her past whom she had hoped to avoid while she was home.

"Hello," she said, briefly clasping the callused hand he held out to her. "It's nice to see you again." She tried to mean the words, but couldn't.

"Excuse me." Rosa brandished a wooden spoon. "I have things to do in the kitchen."

As soon as the housekeeper was gone, Grady moved closer. "I'm sorry about your father," he said. "I wanted to go to the funeral, but I was on duty."

"That's okay. I understand." Carly wondered why he was here now. Their last parting had been less than friendly; Grady had refused to believe that she didn't care more than she had.

His brown eyes narrowed. "At least it brought you home. You look good," he said warmly. "I was surprised to hear you're still single."

"Too busy with my career, I guess," Carly told him. She had heard that he'd married and divorced, but didn't comment.

"Oh, yeah, you're working for some big outfit in Houston. I guess our little part of Texas is pretty boring after the big city."

"No," she denied, surprised to realize that it was true. "I've enjoyed being back."

"Yeah, I guess." His expression was impatient. "Could I take you out to dinner, for old times?"

Carly shook her head without hesitating. "I don't think seeing each other like that would be a good idea." She had no intention of getting involved with Grady again.

"Aw, come on," he coaxed. "What harm would it do?"

Carly remembered that he could be mule stubborn. She held her ground. "There's no point. It's better we leave things as they were."

Grady tried to grin, but she could see the beginnings of temper in his dark eyes. "Maybe I'm not happy with the way things were."

Carly raised her hands, palms out, partly in frustration, partly in a defensive gesture. "I'm sorry," she said. "I'm swamped with work here. I've got no time for anything else, even if I wanted it."

"And you don't want it."

For a moment she got a glimpse of the younger man she had genuinely liked so many years ago. She didn't care to hurt his feelings.

"Give me another chance," he pleaded. "Let me spend some time with you. We were good together, remember?"

She was becoming more and more uncomfortable. "No. I'm sorry," she repeated, not knowing what else to say. A movement from outside distracted her, but when she looked, there was nothing there.

Suddenly Grady's hand snaked out to grab her wrist, his grip hard enough to leave bruises. "Come on," he wheedled. "What have you got to lose?"

Carly tugged at her imprisoned wrist, exasperation edging her voice. "Let me go! I want you to leave."

"And maybe I'm not ready to go." His hold didn't slacken, and she twisted angrily. His fierce determination was starting to frighten her.

"Let me go!" she repeated. "You're hurting me."

Footsteps pounded up the porch steps. Sage burst in, and Grady released her abruptly.

"What the hell is going on?" Sage demanded. "Are you okay?"

Carly rubbed her wrist. "Yes, I'm all right."

Sage's eyes were silver slits, his bronze face set. Grady stared. Sage was clearly ready, his lean body braced to take on the heavier man.

Before anything could happen, Carly said, "Really, everything's okay." Sage didn't need to tangle with the law on her account.

Her heart seemed to freeze until Grady relaxed. "This buck your new watchdog?" He jabbed a thumb in Sage's direction.

"He works for the ranch." Carly glanced at Sage, who was watching Grady with an unwavering gaze. "Thank you," she said. Under the circumstances, introductions seemed ludicrous, but she made them, anyway. The men eyed each other warily, neither extending a hand.

"Watch yourself, Indian," Grady said. He glanced at Carly quickly, as if afraid to turn his back on Sage for even a second. "I'll see you later."

She wanted to say something, but Grady was out the door and down the front steps before she could open her mouth. Damn, she thought, embarrassed by his attitude. Then she looked into Sage's smoky gaze, and thoughts of Grady Harper went right out of her head.

Chapter Five

Sage's gray eyes were opaque, his feelings hidden. Carly expected him to ask about Grady, but instead saw him study her intently.

"What's that guy to you?" he asked when the silence had stretched to an unbearable length.

"Someone I used to know." Now that the ugly scene was over, she realized that reaction was setting in. She needed to be alone. "Thanks for the help."

"Anything else?" Sage was acting as if he'd done nothing out of the ordinary. Carly wished he would just leave, so she could collect her scattered wits in peace.

"What's going on?" Rosa demanded from the hallway. "I thought I heard shouting, but I was in the laundry room." She pinned Sage with an accusing gaze, then looked at Carly. "You all right?"

"Yes, I'm fine." Poor Sage. First he came to her rescue yet again, and now Rosa was watching him as if she were planning her next menu around him. Carly saw that his body was still braced, as if he wasn't sure which direction the next assault was coming from. "Thank you again," she said to him. "There won't be anything else."

"Yes, ma'am." His tone mocking; he touched two fingers to the brim of his hat and slipped out the door.

Too late Carly thought to ask what he'd been doing at the front of the house. Just as well. He would probably take her question wrong, anyway. She glanced at Rosa, who was still waiting expectantly.

"Grady Harper let his temper get the best of him, I'm afraid. Sage thought I was in some kind of danger, but everything's fine now." Carly realized that her smile was shaky around the edges. "I have some paperwork to do."

"Hmm." Rosa sounded disbelieving. "That Grady Harper's a hothead. Fine thing when we have to be protected from those sworn to protect us."

"I don't think Grady's going to be a problem," Carly said.

Rosa just gave her a look, then went back down the hallway, shaking her head and muttering.

Carly crossed to the living room and sank into the nearest chair. Good Lord, what next? All she wanted to do was to get the ranch in shape to sell, so she could return to Houston while she still had a job there. She was beginning to wonder if she was going to succeed with her sanity intact. Not if she didn't get her attraction toward Sage under control, that was for sure.

Was his coming to her rescue the way he had just the typical reaction of a gallant male? Or did his concern for her go deeper? No, he had heard the angry voices and acted like any decent man would. That was undoubtedly it. He had only done what Ben or Tony would have under the same circumstances.

Carly pushed her bangs back from her face. She would be a fool to read anything into the situation that wasn't there. Uttering a tired sigh, she got to her feet. Despite the extra sleep she had gotten that morning, her long night in the barn was still taking its toll. But there was work to finish in the office before she turned in. A dip in the small swimming pool behind the house would have been refreshing, but she didn't have the time. Nor did she have time to waste thinking about Sage.

"Why can't Tony go to town?" she asked Ben several days later, after Sage had come into the tack room to get the keys to the pickup and left again.

"Tony has work to do here. What's wrong with sending Edwards? He can probably find the vet's office okay, and the grocery store. Rosa wanted a few things for the pantry, since he was going anyway." Carly saw Ben studying her curiously.

She knew she shouldn't object without a good reason, but couldn't help worrying that Sage would run into Grady Harper. If anything happened, even a speeding ticket, it would be her fault.

"I'm going with him," she announced suddenly, ignoring the surprise on Ben's face and her own inner reservations. So much for staying away from the man. "I have some errands to run myself, and this will save me the drive tomorrow."

"You didn't say anything about errands," Ben said. "But Sage can probably do them for you."

"Uh, no." She thought fast. "I need a few personal things. I'll just ride along."

"Better hurry," Ben told her, turning away. "I think I just heard the truck start."

Carly ran outside, determined to stop Sage before he drove away. It was lucky she'd put on a good shirt and clean jeans that morning. Once she caught up with him, she didn't want Sage to have to wait for her. There would only be time to grab her purse and tell Rosa not to expect her for lunch.

Sage was backing the truck around when he heard a shout. To his surprise he saw Carly in the rearview mirror, waving her arms. Suppressing a grin at the idea of her chasing him, he braked and rolled down the window. Ben must have forgotten something.

"I'm glad I caught you," she said. "I'm going, too. If you'd wait at the house, I'll only be a minute."

Her words were the last thing Sage had expected to hear. He didn't want her company, especially in the close confines of the truck. "Why are you coming?" he demanded. "Do you think I'm going to run off with the ranch pickup or something?"

Answering fire sparked in Carly's eyes at his unexpected attack. "Not while your horses are still here," she snapped back at him. "But I suppose if they were bred and you were towing a trailer I'd really be sweating it."

Sage looked away. "Sorry," he said briefly. "Guess I'm in a touchy mood today."

If his apology surprised her she gave no sign of it. "Fine," she said briskly. "I'll meet you out front."

He watched her as she strode toward the house, hips swaying in the snug jeans. Shifting into low gear, he drove toward the big white ranch house, trying not to raise any dust as he followed her. Her braid was bouncing and her long legs ate up the ground. If her clenched hands were any indication, she was in a blazing temper, and he was more than likely the cause of it.

Suddenly he found himself relishing the idea of an argument with her. Maybe it would release some of the pent-up feelings that had been churning around in his gut since he'd found that sheriff's deputy with her the other day.

When Carly hustled out of the house moments later, he thought briefly about getting out and opening the passenger door, but before he came to a decision she was climbing in beside him. A breath of some flowery perfume wafted under his nose, teasing his senses.

Swallowing a curse, he hit the gas pedal with his foot and the truck surged forward, spraying gravel.

"Whoa!" Carly exclaimed, bracing herself. "Let me get my seat belt on, at least."

"I'm in a hurry," he told her, deliberately forgetting that she was the boss. "Ben needs some stuff from the vet's and I have to pick up groceries for Rosa. Why *are* you going?"

She sniffed and looked out the window. "I have some errands of my own," she said, turning the radio on to a country station. "You don't mind, do you?"

Sage glanced at the radio, then back at her, cocking an eyebrow. "No, ma'am," he drawled.

Lightning flashed in her blue eyes, and he swallowed a grin. She all but bristled when he called her that.

"Besides," she said defensively, stretching her legs in front of her, "I haven't been off the ranch for ages. I needed to get away for a little while."

Secretly pleased that she wanted to get away with him, Sage turned onto the main road and accelerated, resigning himself to keeping his ever-growing desire under strict control until they were back at the ranch and he could breathe freely again without inhaling her scent with every lungful of air.

When they reached the outskirts of the nearest small town, Hamlin, he slowed the truck. "Where do you want me to drop you? We can meet again after we're both finished."

"Oh, that's okay," Carly replied airily, as she glanced up and down the street. "I'll just stay with you, and then you can drive me where I need to go."

Sage released an exasperated sigh. "Better my way," he growled. "You don't want anyone here to get the wrong idea."

Carly's gaze slammed into his. "What exactly do you mean?"

He sighed again and looked away. How the hell was he going to warn her about being seen with him? She'd think he was a crazy, conceited jackass. Even if they had shared a somewhat emotional kiss, it didn't mean she was interested in him that way. Not really. She must have more sense than that. She had probably left half a dozen boyfriends back in Houston. Even the local version of the law was hot on her trail.

She was still waiting for an answer. "Don't want anyone to think you're, uh, with me, if you get my drift," he mumbled uneasily. "They might not realize I just drove you into town if you stick with me the whole time."

Carly's eyes widened. She studied him for a long moment while the heat crawled up his neck. He hadn't felt this stupid since the time he'd tried to get friendly with a redhead at the Dead Buffalo Bar back in Broken Arrow, just to find out she'd only been staring because she'd lost her glasses and thought he was her black-haired cousin.

"I'll take my chances," Carly finally said in a dry voice. "But..."

"I *hate* to pull rank, but I *am* the boss. If I want to go with you, I'll go with you. Now, what's first, the vet's office?"

Sage mulled over his options for a moment. Then, with an elaborate shrug to convey that it made no difference to *him* what she did, he put the truck into gear and glanced into the mirror. "Dr. Burton's office down this street?"

She nodded. "First turn to the right and halfway down the block. It's a red brick building with a white sign out front."

If he didn't know better, he would think she'd looked almost disappointed that he hadn't argued further. Maybe she was spoiling for a fight as badly as he was. Did that mean she was as bothered by him as he was by her? She *had* kissed him back.

When he went into the vet's she waited in the truck, but when he came back she was hanging out the open window, talking to a dark-haired woman who was holding a baby on one hip.

"I'd heard you were married," she was saying, "but I didn't know you'd had Billy. He's a little doll."

Both women looked up when Sage came back to the truck. He nodded and tipped his hat slightly to the other woman, then went around to the drivers' side.

"Debbie, this is our new trainer from Oklahoma, Sage Edwards," Carly said when he was behind the wheel. "Debbie Stewart and her son Billy."

Debbie eyed him curiously as she said hello. Sage returned her greeting and smiled at the toddler who was peering at him.

"Cute kid."

"Thank you," Debbie said. "Carly, it was nice to see you. Come into town and we'll have lunch sometime soon."

Carly said goodbye to her friend while Sage started the truck and looked at her expectantly. "Do you want to go to the grocery store next? Some of the things Rosa needs will wilt pretty quick in this heat."

She shook her head. "I need to stop at the drugstore. Anything you want there?"

He said no, determined not to be seen at her elbow if he could help it. He knew how small towns were and hated the idea of people discussing her later.

"I'll wait in the truck."

Her eyes narrowed and she nodded slightly, as if she'd just come to some kind of conclusion. "Fine," she said, glancing at her watch. "After the drugstore I'll buy you lunch at the Rocking R Grill, then we'll pick up Rosa's groceries and head back to the ranch."

Sage was just about to open his mouth when she raised a deterring hand. "I'm hungry," she said, "and I wouldn't enjoy my lunch, knowing you were sitting in the hot truck waiting for me."

She watched his face, calculating his reaction to her bossy attitude. When his mouth straightened into a mutinous line, she tried another tack.

"I hate to eat alone," she said, lowering her lashes. "I'd really appreciate it if you joined me." She didn't stop to think why it was so important to her, but waited while he appeared to think over her new approach.

"Okay," he said on a sigh. "Thanks."

Sage did go into the drugstore, heading for the toiletries section as Carly went toward the skin care products. The sun could burn her fair skin if she didn't apply sun block and lotion religiously. As she was waiting in the checkout line, Sage came up behind her, holding a tube of toothpaste and a bar of soap. When the clerk, a woman

Carly had gone to school with, rang up her purchase, she introduced Sage.

"Do you know everyone in town?" he grumbled as the two of them walked back to the truck.

"Probably," she replied. "After all, I did grow up here."

He opened her door, but she merely tossed her sack inside, took his and did the same. "The restaurant is right down the street. You don't mind walking, do you?"

He glanced in the direction she indicated. "Nope. Lead the way, boss."

His expression was bland, but she'd heard the slight emphasis he'd placed on the word boss. Some imp took over and she linked her arm through his, knowing the gesture of familiarity would annoy him. "Let's go," she said, smiling coolly. "I could eat a horse."

He frowned down at her but did nothing about their linked arms.

"Not a palomino, of course," she added, nodding to an older couple. She looked back up at Sage and could have sworn he'd almost smiled.

They sat across from each other in one of the grill's padded vinyl booths, and lunch started out awkwardly, but by the time the food came, Carly was relieved to see that he was beginning to relax.

"Anything else?" the waitress asked, smiling widely at him.

He shook his head and grinned back, while Carly found herself glaring at the young woman. Pouring a small pool of catsup next to her French fries, Carly assessed Sage unobtrusively.

He was stirring sugar into the iced tea he had ordered and didn't notice her staring. In the bright overhead light the single stud he always wore in one ear gleamed; his eyes were screened by short, thick lashes below the straight slash of his brows.

When Carly's attention wandered to his mouth, she had to swallow and glance away. He was probably the last man on earth she should be sitting there eating lunch with. Not only did they not have one single thing in common, their paths were going in totally different directions. Hastily she turned her attention to her chicken sandwich when he raised his head.

"Know the waitress, too?" he asked dryly.

"No. After my time, I'm afraid."

Mischief gleamed briefly in his eyes. "Too bad. I might have liked an introduction."

Carly ignored the sudden flash of jealousy and temper that flared and followed the direction of his gaze. The waitress was just disappearing into the kitchen, her short, tight uniform hiding nothing of her rounded derriere and curvaceous legs.

Carly shrugged indifferently. "I'm sure you could manage that on your own."

His smile faded. "Perhaps," he said quietly, studying her. "But I don't have the time."

Carly wasn't sure how to take his words. She avoided a reply by biting into her sandwich, conscious that Sage was watching her. He bared his white teeth and tucked into his own roast beef one.

"Food's still good here," she ventured when she'd washed the bite down with a swallow of cola.

He nodded, following her change of topic. "What's your favorite food?"

She thought a moment, toying with a French fry. "Anything I don't have to cook myself," she said finally.

Sage grinned. "Don't like to cook?" he asked. "Somehow I could have guessed that you're not very domestic."

His words seemed to carry some hidden meaning, implying more than just that she didn't care for household duties. His expression said that he considered her a little wild, untamed, something that Carly took as a compliment.

"Do you cook?" she parried.

He sat back, grinning. "Sure. We didn't have a housekeeper right away at Comanche Creek," he told her. "And the only thing Mac could do was soul food. I got tired right quick of black-eyed peas and ham hocks."

Carly was surprised that he brought up the ranch and Mac so casually. She nibbled on a pickle and asked more questions about Comanche Creek. But before she'd found out a fraction of what she would have liked to know, he turned the tables and began questioning her. Barely realizing what was happening, she was soon telling him stories about growing up on Rolling Gold, an only child.

"I don't mean to imply that I was always lonely," she said hastily. "After mother died, my father let me watch him work the horses sometimes, but he was pretty busy." She had spent a lot of time with her father, but somehow had never felt he approved of her. She reached for another fry and was surprised to find her plate empty.

"You want anything else?" Sage asked, swallowing the last of his iced tea.

Carly glanced at the clock on the wall. It was time they got back. Ben wanted that medicine, and they still had to stop and get groceries. She sighed, wondering where the time had gone. "I suppose we'd better go," she said reluctantly, reaching for the check.

Sage's hand closed over hers. "I'll take care of it."

Carly started to protest, but one look at his expression stilled her tongue. "Thank you," she said instead.

He released her hand and reached for his wallet, dropping several bills onto the table as she slid out of the booth. While he settled with the cashier, she glanced at the headlines on the front of the Fort Worth newspaper.

He came up and touched her elbow. "All set?"

She nodded and he held the door open. Suddenly very aware of his lean body, she brushed past him and headed back down the street.

While Carly paid for the groceries, Sage took them out to the truck. When they were done, he helped her into the cab. As she climbed past, the side of her breast brushed against his elbow. Reaction warmed her cheeks, and she glanced at him involuntarily. His gaze locked with hers, his eyes glittering. The lighthearted mood that Carly had cultivated all through lunch shattered, leaving aching awareness in its wake.

Swallowing, she fumbled with her seat belt. As soon as Sage started the engine she flipped on the radio, filling the cab with the rollicking country sounds of fiddle and guitar. Her thoughts were a jumble of unwanted feelings. Next to her, Sage was silent. Silent as a wooden Indian, she thought, swallowing a giggle of near hysteria. She wondered what he was thinking about. Probably wishing he could soon get back to his ranch.

They were headed down a flat stretch when he glanced into the rearview mirror and swore beneath his breath. Before Carly could ask what the problem was, he signaled and slowed the truck, pulled it onto the gravel shoulder and stopped so abruptly that she pitched forward.

"Probably your boyfriend," he grumbled; Carly turned to see a police cruiser pull in behind them, lights flashing.

"You weren't speeding!" she exclaimed.

"Technically I was, by about two miles an hour." Sage opened the door and stepped down. Grady Harper approached the truck, one hand resting casually on the butt of his gun, the other peeling off dark glasses. Sage pulled out his wallet before Grady could speak.

"Pushin' it a little, weren't you?" he asked as Sage slipped his license out of its plastic sheath and extended it.

Carly unclipped her seat belt and slid over, poking her head through the open window. "He wasn't..."

Sage turned, silencing her with a look. "I'll handle this."

"But you weren't..."

"Miss Golden," he said, his voice carrying a warning.

Carly glanced from him to Grady, whose expression was watchful. Then she sighed noisily and sat back. Men!

Grady went on to lecture Sage about his speed, driving habits, responsibility to his passenger and the inconvenience of having his license taken away. Carly was biting her tongue at the unfairness, waiting for Sage to jump in and defend himself. To her surprise he remained silent.

"You're a guest in our state," Grady concluded in a patronizing tone. "Don't be thinking that it's okay to come down here and terrorize our roads."

Carly was almost ready to interrupt, whether it made Sage angry or not, when an insistent voice came over the radio in Grady's patrol car. He cocked his head toward the sound for a moment, then shoved Sage's license back at him. "I'll catch up with you another time," he said threateningly. "Watch how you drive on back to the ranch, you hear?"

Carly slid over, and Sage hauled himself back into the truck. Seconds later, the patrol car whipped around them, spraying gravel as it raced past, lights and sirens going.

"How could you just stand there?" Carly demanded before Sage could turn the key. "I'm surprised you didn't shuffle your feet and tug on your forelock."

The look he turned on her would have silenced a more cautious woman, Carly reflected, but she was almost too incensed by Grady's unfair attack to care.

"He lectured you as if you were some reckless teenager out joyriding," she raged. "And you didn't utter one word in your own defense."

A muscle twitched in Sage's cheek, he started the truck and pulled back onto the road. He didn't look at her again, but suddenly Carly realized from the hard line of his jaw and the white around his nostrils that he was furious. She threw up her hands in exasperation.

"I don't get it."

"Of course you don't," he snarled. "You're white."

"And what are you?" she snapped back. "Zebra-striped?"

"No, lady, I'm a half-breed! We don't get out of line when *the man* is talking to us. It isn't worth the grief."

Carly opened her mouth to argue and closed it again. What did she know about what he was saying, after all? She'd grown up the daughter of a successful, respected rancher. Sage had told her his mother had abandoned him. He hadn't mentioned a father except to tell Mollie that the man was white, and Carly realized she had no idea what Sage might have been through.

"Didn't you—?" she finally began again.

He slammed the flat of his hand against the steering wheel. "Shut up."

She gaped at him. "Don't you dare!"

"Lady, I'm warning you. I don't much care right now that you're my boss. Just leave it alone, would you?"

Carly wasn't about to let him have the wrong impression of her concern. "All I wanted was to know why you didn't..."

Sage ground out another curse, glanced into the mirror and turned abruptly onto a dirt road.

"Where are you going?" Carly cried as they bounced over ruts and potholes. "This is a dead end!"

She thought she heard him say something that sounded like "How appropriate," but wasn't sure. A half mile farther on, he braked sharply in a stand of trees. Then he killed the engine and turned to look fully into her face.

The savage attraction of his features hit her like a blow. Angry, he was dangerously compelling. And the full force of his fury was directed at her.

She held up an unsteady hand. "Just a minute," she squeaked. "I think you misunderstood me."

In less than a blink, Sage changed from enraged male to aroused predator. She had never seen him this intent.

Sage must have read something of her alarm on her face. He froze, then dragged in a long breath and took off his hat, tossing it onto the dash. "You don't know me," he told her, his voice grating. "You don't understand me or have a clue about what I've had to do to survive." His gaze flicked over her with the sting of a whip. "What do you know of real pain, of hate or poverty?"

"I..." Words stuck in her throat.

"You think I don't know what you were trying to do today, introducing me to your friends, taking me to lunch, acting as if we had something going? What is this, Be Kind to a Redskin Week?"

His words seared Carly to the bone. Her own temper exploded. "How dare you!" She doubled her hands into fists, but before she could decide what to do with them, he had imprisoned her wrists and dragged her close. His eyes blazed into hers.

"Damn you!" He ground out the words. "Damn you for making me ache, for making me want—" His mouth slammed into hers, cutting off his own words. He released her wrists and wrapped his arms around her, pinning her against his hard chest as his hot mouth ravaged hers.

Carly tried to resist, but he refused to let her, his mouth demanding a response while his hands swept over her, rubbing, stroking, molding her even closer. She began to melt against him. This was nothing like the tenderness he'd shown her before. She was clinging to her last bit of control when he suddenly slowed.

His lips began to nibble softly, his touch gentling as he caressed her back and shoulders. A moan rose into her throat when he lifted his mouth from hers. Common sense fled. Her hands, trapped between their fused bodies, gripped the fabric of his shirt in an effort to bind him to her.

Uttering a groan, Sage pulled her across his lap and turned her toward him. Beneath her, his thighs were like iron. He eased his mouth over her cheek and down the side of her throat, teasing her sensitive skin with his teeth, then soothing it with a stroke of his tongue. Moving to her shoulder, he exposed it by freeing two of the snaps on her Western shirt.

When he buried his face in the sensitive hollow, a burning sensation raced through Carly with the heat of a fireball gone out of control. She whimpered. His fingers gripped her chin, holding her still while his mouth returned to tenderly ravage hers. Past her teeth his tongue slid, plunging to tangle with her own. The heat inside her grew. Breathing became almost impossible. When he released her jaw and slid one hand down to cup her lace-covered breast, scraping his thumb across the beaded nipple, she jerked and cried out.

Sage made a harsh sound in his throat and pressed his face into the deep cleft between her breasts. Carly raked her fingers through the coarse silk of his hair and arched into the drugging caress of his mouth. The passionate scraping of his tongue on the upper swells of her breasts drove her higher.

Carly shifted on his lap, her movements dragging another groan from Sage. Her hands were reaching for the buttons on his shirt when his long fingers bit into her waist. Suddenly she realized that he had gone still. Only his hands were moving restlessly. He raised his head, then pressed it against her hair. His breathing rasped, rapid and shallow; her own felt strangled.

She wanted to ask him what was wrong, why he'd stopped, but the words wouldn't come. Finally she licked her dry lips and slid off his lap onto the passenger side of the seat. Sage flung open the door and got out, turning away. His broad shoulders were rigid.

Carly sat as still as possible, her hands shaking. She tried without success to make sense of her confusion. There was so much about him that she didn't understand. The fires he'd started inside her still burned, driving back the reason she tried to regain.

Good Lord, what had she been thinking of, crawling all over him like a cat in heat, welcoming his touch and begging for more? Suddenly the cab was stifling hot, even with both windows open. She wrenched at the passenger door and jumped down, keeping her back to Sage.

"Where are you going?" His voice was a sudden intrusion in the roar of silence.

"No-nowhere," she stuttered. "I was too hot."

His laughter was mirthless. "God, I guess! Hotter than original sin."

She didn't know what to say, couldn't face him. Then she heard his boots crunch as he came around to her side of the truck. In the bright sunlight he looked curiously vulnerable without his dusty black hat.

Carly glanced at him hastily, then looked away, studying the toes of her boots as if she'd never seen them before. Now what did he want?

He stopped in front of her, but she didn't meet his gaze until his fingers trapped her chin and gently forced it up.

"I'm sorry," he said, surprising her. "That should have never happened."

"Why did you stop?" She wanted to retrieve the telling words as soon as she had spoken them.

His expression was a curious mixture, tender yet grim. "Because that's all I have to give you," he said roughly, gesturing toward the cab of the truck. "And you're a woman who needs more. Who deserves more."

Pride straightened her back and set her shoulders. Her wanton responses had given him a totally wrong impression. "What makes you think I want anything from you?" she shot back.

His grin was wry. "Let's not have any misconceptions between us," he said. "You come back for more of the same, you know what you're getting."

Her cheeks flooded with anger and embarrassment. The arrogant bastard!

"Don't get me wrong," he continued. "I'd like nothing better than to bed you. I'd give damn near anything to feel those long legs of yours wrapped around me." His voice grew hoarse. "But I won't give up my land, my dreams, for anyone. So I have nothing left for you."

Carly remembered her own willingness when he'd kissed her and grew even angrier. "And don't you forget *this!*" she cried. "I'm leaving, too. I have a life and it's not here." Her gaze raked him contemptuously. "You have *nothing* I want. Nothing!"

She glowered at his expression of surprise and disbelief, then slammed back into the truck. Sticking her head out the window, she shouted, "Let's go! I don't have all day to stand around talking about your adolescent male fantasies."

Sage was silent when he climbed in beside her and jammed his hat back onto his head, but the look he sent in her direction spoke volumes. It was all Carly could do to keep from protesting again that he had nothing she wanted.

But how could she expect him to believe her when she didn't believe it herself?

Chapter Six

"I'm sending a check for my share of this month's rent and expenses," Carly said into the receiver. She was sitting at her father's desk, talking to Donna Martin, her roommate back in Houston. Donna also worked at Dwyer Shipping, as the receptionist in the executive offices. She and Carly had been friends since Carly had been promoted to the general manager's executive assistant.

Donna was dark and petite, with a flirtatious personality that seemed at odds with the cool professionalism she presented at the entry to the suite of offices that held the upper echelon of Dwyer's management staff.

"You shouldn't have to pay when you aren't even staying here," Donna said. "It doesn't seem fair."

"Nonsense," Carly replied, doodling idly on the desk pad. "It certainly isn't costing me anything to live here, and I don't expect you to cover the bills by yourself. We have an agreement." She and Donna had been roommates for six months, an arrangement that suited them both very well.

"Well, if you're sure," Donna said slowly.

"I am. Now tell me about your vacation. When are you leaving?"

Donna was happy to talk about the week she and her boyfriend were spending in Bermuda. Carly listened half enviously, but her thoughts were of tropical evenings with Sage at her side. Abruptly she cut into Donna's recital.

"Is everything going okay at work?"

"Well," her roommate drawled, "Lisa would have you believe she's handling it very smoothly, but I heard Mr. Bass yelling at her yesterday. She'd misplaced an important file."

"Oh, dear," Carly moaned, feeling guilty. "He's been so nice about the time I'm taking, too." She was lucky that he had granted her an open-ended leave of absence instead of finding a permanent replacement. Maybe she should be relieved that Lisa wasn't doing a better job in her absence; otherwise Mr. Bass might reconsider and offer Lisa the position permanently. Carly was torn between her responsibilities in Houston and those at the ranch.

"I know he'll be very happy when you come back," Donna reassured her. "Any idea when that will be?"

"No." Carly thought a minute. "I suppose once the ranch is listed for sale, I could commute here on the weekends if I had to. Ben and Sage could run things." She glanced at the silver-framed photo of herself on the corner of the desk. Next to it was a baby picture of Mollie.

"Sage?" Donna asked. "Is that the new trainer you hired?"

"Yes." Carly was tempted to add more, but managed to still her tongue.

"He sounds dreamy from what you already told me. Anything *personal* going on?" Donna's voice was teasing. Carly's lack of serious interest in any of the men she'd dated in Houston was a source of constant worry to her roommate, who thought that a happy woman was a committed woman. She and her own boyfriend planned to marry when he finished graduate school. When Carly had tried to tell her that she hadn't yet met the right man, Donna had told her she wasn't looking hard enough.

"Personal?" Carly echoed now. "You know that I'm coming back to Houston as soon as I can. Sage has land in Oklahoma he's eager to return to. Besides that, we have nothing in common except horses. And you know that life no longer holds any attraction for me."

"Hmm." Donna was silent for a moment. "I know you want to believe that's true. But I really thought that once you went back... Well, I just don't think the ranch is as far removed from your heart as you want to believe. In fact, I thought that by now..."

"You're wrong," Carly said forcefully. "That's all behind me. I told you I could never run things the way my father wanted. I gave up trying to please him a long time ago."

"If you say so," Donna said doubtfully. "Well, I'd better get back to work. Talk to you soon."

Carly said goodbye and Donna thanked her again for the check. She hung up and swiveled her chair toward the wall of pictures behind the desk. Each photo showed her father with one of the champion palominos he had raised and trained. How could she match a legacy like that?

She turned again, this time to look out the window, directing her thoughts to her job at Dwyer Shipping. But her hands were tied until the ranch was in shape to sell.

* * *

While Carly was thinking about the sale, Sage was pitching hay into the stalls along one wall in the stallion barn. The air was close and humid, and he wore a bandanna tied around his forehead to keep the rivulets of sweat from dripping into his eyes. Until a few minutes ago Mollie had been with him, chattering like a compulsive magpie. Sage had made an occasional reply to indicate that he was listening, but his mind was preoccupied with what Carly had told him just days before. She wasn't staying on the ranch. Where was she planning to go? Back to Houston? Who would run the ranch then? Not Ben; he didn't want the responsibility. Surely she wouldn't trust Tony to handle it. Sage shrugged, wiping the sweat from his face with his arm. Maybe he would just have to ask her.

One of the horses nickered softly and he realized that he could no longer hear Mollie's chatter. He straightened and looked around, but she had disappeared. He wasn't worried; Mollie spent a lot of time around the stables and knew what not to get into.

Sage stabbed another forkful of hay, grinning to himself as he recalled some of her constant questions. Suddenly, from outside, came the trumpeting blast Sky Walker made whenever anything spooked him. For a moment Sage didn't react, and then, as he remembered something Mollie had said about having sugar cubes in her pocket, a chill flowed over his skin, cold as a dead man's touch.

She wouldn't!

He gripped the pitchfork with both hands and ran.

He cleared the doorway and heard Carly scream Mollie's name. Sage rounded the corner of the barn and skidded to a stop, watching helplessly as the child took one step after the other across one of the small paddocks, a cube of sugar in her outstretched hand. Sky Walker was standing in one corner, trembling all over at her intrusion into his space. Sage could hear Mollie's high-pitched voice as she coaxed him to take the treat.

Out of the corner of his eye Sage saw Carly running toward them from the direction of the house. Carefully he held up a detaining hand, hoping she would understand and stop the headlong rush that might spook the unpredictable horse even more.

"Mollie," Sage called quietly.

Her golden head spun around. Sky Walker snorted and pawed the ground. Sage gripped the pitchfork tighter.

"Oh, hi, Sage." Mollie was clearly unaware of the danger she was in.

"Listen to me and do what I say." Sage prayed she wouldn't argue. "I want you to stand very still," he continued in the same even voice. "Don't move your hand. When I tell you to, I want you to start backing toward me very slowly."

"But I want to give Sky his sugar." Mollie's tone had a stubborn edge to it that would have made Sage smile under other circumstances.

"Sage!" Carly pleaded. "Do something!"

All he could do was nod. If he raised his voice to answer, he risked Mollie's safety. "Do you often give him sugar?" he asked her conversationally.

"Sure. When he's in his stall I do. But he wouldn't come to the fence today, so I have to go to him." She took another step and Sky Walker rolled his eyes, showing the whites. He trumpeted again. The sudden blast made Mollie hesitate.

"Don't do that," she scolded the horse. "It scares me."

"Mollie," Sage said, thinking fast. "Sky isn't in the mood for company today. I want you to back up very slowly. Then, when you're outside the fence, we'll see if he'll come over for the sugar. Okay?''

Sky Walker's ears swiveled at the familiar voice, then he pawed the ground again.

Sage dragged in a deep breath as Mollie took one step back and then another, her hand still extended toward the horse. A bugling challenge from a stallion in a nearby paddock distracted Sky Walker, and Sage took the opportunity to slip through the fence rails. He stood only a dozen feet from the little girl.

"Please be careful," Carly said from somewhere behind him. For a moment Sage allowed himself to believe that she was worried about his safety then realized she knew he was Mollie's best chance to escape unharmed.

Carly was moving closer, each step in agonizing slow motion. Her heart had almost stopped when she saw Mollie in the paddock with the volatile young stallion. Carly had seen firsthand what damage Sky Walker's hooves could inflict. And Mollie was so little. So little and trusting. Carly's pulse rate doubled when Sage joined her little sister.

Barely daring to breathe, Carly watched while the four-year-old took one hesitant step after another, the hand holding the sugar cube wavering with her efforts. Carly could hear Sage's deep voice as he encouraged Mollie to keep moving toward him.

He had carefully set the pitchfork against the fence and Mollie was almost within his reach when a sudden gust of wind flipped up the full skirt of her blue-checkered dress.

Sky Walker exploded. Mollie screamed and so did Carly. Sage grabbed Mollie in one smooth motion and pushed her under the rails toward Carly, then grabbed the pitchfork and lunged at the frenzied stallion, forcing him back into the corner of the paddock.

Carly rushed forward and dragged Mollie, who had started crying noisily, into her arms. "Hush, baby," she soothed. "It's okay." She watched Sage anxiously; he made one last feint at the horse, then scrambled over the fence himself.

For a moment Sky Walker drummed his hooves in frustration then abruptly grew calm. He studied the now-empty paddock, then eyed the two adults who were brushing off Mollie and trying to stem her tears. What's the fuss all about? he seemed to be asking as he bent to delicately lip the sugar Mollie had dropped in the dust.

Carly didn't know if she should cry or scream in rage at the near tragedy. She would have liked to touch Sage, to reassure herself that he, too, was safe. If she hadn't already been holding Mollie, she would have flung her arms around his neck. Instead she hugged Mollie tighter.

"My dress got all dirty," the child said, squirming loose. "And I skinned my knee."

Carly kissed her cheek, trying not to think about what could have happened. "That's okay, punkin. We'll put a Band-Aid on your knee and Rosa can wash your dress."

"You're squeezing me," Mollie complained.

Carly's gaze met Sage's over the youngster's curly head. Although his expression was grave, there was an underlying glint of humor in his gaze. "Don't squash her," he cautioned.

His words were the last straw, and tears filled Carly's eyes. Her lower lip began to tremble. "I don't know how to thank you," she said and gulped.

His gaze cut to Mollie and he shook his head in warning. "No big deal." It was obvious that Mollie hadn't understood the extent of her danger, and he didn't want her frightened.

Carly made herself let go, and Sage immediately squatted beside Mollie. Despite Carly's fright, her gaze fastened on his hard thigh muscles as they flexed beneath the worn denim.

"I want you to promise me something," he said to Mollie in a solemn tone.

She had stopped crying, and there were dirty streaks on her face where she'd swiped at the tears with her fists.

"What's that?" Her voice was filled with curiosity.

Sage took both of her small hands into his. "This is very serious," he said. "I want you to promise me that you'll never go into a stall or paddock or a pasture with any horse, unless Carly or myself is with you and we say it's okay."

"Not even Polka Dot?"

Sage shook his head. "Not even Polka Dot." His gaze flicked to Carly and back to Mollie.

"Okay," she said after a moment. "I promise. Now can I go to the house and have Rosa put a Band-Aid on my knee? She might give me a cookie."

Sage straightened. "Yes," he said. "But I want you to remember your promise, okay? It's very important that you do."

"Okay." Mollie nodded emphatically and her curls bounced. "Bye." She ran toward the house.

"Walk slow, honey," Carly told her. "I'll catch up to you in a minute." She watched until Mollie was out of immediate hearing, then looked up at Sage. His face, too, was streaked with grime below the red bandanna that held back his hair. The sun overhead emphasized the chiseled planes of his face. His thick lashes shadowed his narrowed eyes.

"I don't know what to say," Carly began. "If you hadn't been there..."

Sage raised his hand. "I should have been watching her closer. She was with me just a couple of minutes before this happened."

"No." Carly didn't question the burning need to make him understand that he wasn't to blame. "Watching Mollie isn't one of your duties. She knows better...."

"A child forgets," he said easily. Then he glanced at Sky Walker. "I'll work with him more often. This kind of thing can't happen again."

"Damned right it won't!" Carly burst out. "I'm having him gelded as soon as the vet can get out here."

Sage's attention returned to her face, his expression unreadable. "Give me a little more time," he said. "A week."

"No!" Carly shook her head adamantly. "He's getting off easy as it is. He deserves to be shot for what almost happened."

Sage's hand closed over her shoulder. "A week," he repeated. "When I'm done with him, Sky Walker will be much more valuable as a stud then he ever would be gelded."

Carly searched his face, wondering why he was so determined. Did he somehow identify with the unpredictable horse? "Okay," she said finally. "But keep him in his stall when no one's with him, okay?"

Sage let out a long breath. "Okay," he said. "Thanks."

"Why does his fate mean so much to you?" Carly asked.

For a moment his expression closed and she thought he wasn't going to answer. "I want him," he said suddenly, his words catching her totally off guard. "Not now, of course, but someday, if he's still available."

"I should give him to you for saving Mollie," Carly said quickly.

She knew he would refuse, and he did. "Just keep it in mind," he told her. "And give me that week with him." For a moment he looked as if he wanted to say more.

She nodded slowly. "Okay."

He had never asked about her statement that she was leaving, either. It probably didn't matter to him *what* she did with her life, as long as Red Rocket covered his mares first.

As Carly watched him walk away, wondering if she would ever understand him, Ben pulled up in the ranch truck and got out.

"What's going on?" he asked, glancing from Sage's re-treating back to Carly's face.

"Carly, come on," Mollie called from where she'd been waiting in the middle of the driveway.

"I'll fill you in later," Carly said to Ben. "Right now I have a knee to bandage."

He shrugged. "Okay," he said. "You're the boss."

Ben was in the bunkhouse late that evening, sprawled across his bed as he stared at a paperback Western with-out seeing the words. Carly had filled him in earlier, and he had wasted no time in adding his thanks to hers the next time he saw Sage. Ben loved Mollie as if she were his own granddaughter. Now he broke into a sweat, thinking about how the incident could have turned out. But even so, when Carly told him what she'd wanted done with Sky Walker, Ben was relieved to hear that the animal had been given a reprieve.

The sound of the bunkhouse door opening made him glance up and he saw Rosa come in, carrying a covered plate.

"Did you bring me something?" he asked, rising from the bunk. The only other person there was Sage, who was mending a silver-studded bridle. Tony and Joey had driven into Hamlin to have a few beers.

Rosa slapped Ben's hand away as he reached for the plate. "These are for Sage," she scolded. "A dozen of my butterscotch oatmeal cookies. Fresh baked."

Sage glanced up in surprise. "Thanks," he said, standing politely and removing his hat. "But why me?"

While Ben watched, Rosa stepped forward and placed a kiss upon Sage's dark cheek. "For what you did today," she said softly. "I wanted you to know that I appreciate you risking your hide to get Mollie away from that devil horse."

Ben thought Sage looked distinctly uncomfortable. He ducked his head, toying with his hatband. "It wasn't really anything."

"Well, then," Rosa said, pulling back the plate, "maybe I'll just give these to Ben, after all."

"Oh, that's okay." Sage grinned, taking it from her. "I'll put these cookies to good use. Thank you." He uncovered the plate and offered it to Ben, who glanced at Rosa and declined, before biting into one of the cookies himself.

"Mmm," Sage groaned, mouth full. "Delicious."

Rosa smiled at him. "Glad you like them." She looked at Ben, who was studying the now-relaxed ranch hand with curiosity. "Walk me back to the house?" she asked.

Leaving Sage to his reward, Ben followed her out the door.

"What do you think about those two?" Rosa asked him as soon as they were out of hearing range.

Ben was wishing he'd taken a cookie. She was a wonderful cook. "What two?" he asked absently, folding one hand around hers.

"Carly and Sage," Rosa exclaimed impatiently. "Something's going on there, I can almost feel the heat."

Ben chuckled. "That heat's from us," he said, leaning close to drop a kiss onto her neatly waved gray hair.

She pulled away. "Oh, you big tease. You know what I mean. Don't pretend that you don't."

"Don't forget that we'll all be leaving here when the ranch is sold." Ben had his own ideas of how he and Rosa might spend their retirement, but wasn't ready to share them with her yet. A little of the concern he'd been feeling about Carly entered his voice. "I know what you mean, though. I've been tempted to say something to her myself. For a city girl, I don't think she knows all that much about men. Especially men like Edwards."

Rosa stopped and turned to peer into Ben's face. "You don't think he'd...take advantage of her, do you?"

Seeing that she was genuinely concerned, he hesitated. "I don't think he'd hurt her on purpose," he said slowly. "But he might not be able to keep from it."

"I was right." Rosa sighed, shaking her head. "Those two are headed for trouble. I just knew it."

"They're adults," Ben said, releasing her hand to slide his arm around her shoulders. "All we can do is pick up the pieces, if it turns out that way."

"Hmm," Rosa snorted. "So *you* say."

Finally the day came when Ben and Sage determined that Comanche Princess was ready to mate with Red Rocket. The mare had passed the vet's exam with flying colors and was exhibiting unmistakable signs of being in heat. Ben told Carly at breakfast that they'd be overseeing the pair of horses later that morning at the breeding shed.

After glancing at Sage, who was quietly watching her, Carly managed a response and returned her attention to the plate of waffles in front of her. *Relax,* she told herself silently. This is what happens on a breeding ranch. It's routine. This time will be no different than all the others.

Her silent lecture was having no effect on the tension that had shot through her when Ben spoke. Somehow the idea of her stallion being bred to Sage's mare was upsetting. Not exciting, not erotic, just upsetting. Perhaps it was because Carly knew that Red Rocket was rough on the mares he covered, and she had developed a special fondness for Sage's gentle ladies.

"Princess won't mind," Sage said quietly as soon as Ben and the others rose to leave. "She's a good mother, and I think she enjoys her pregnancies."

"How would you know that?" Carly looked at him archly.

Sage grinned. "Don't you know that I have a special affinity with horses?" It was the first time he'd teased her, and she didn't know how to respond.

"Besides, the mare's content when she's expecting," he continued. "When I run my hand over her distended belly, I get the feeling that things are the way they're meant to be."

For a moment Carly stared up at him, and he thought that he would drown in the intense blue of her eyes. The sudden image of her big with child, *his* child, hit Sage with the impact of a runaway train. The picture was even more intimate than all the times he'd dreamed of her in his bed, locked in his arms.

He swallowed dryly; heat poured through him. Yes! He wanted that. He wanted to plant his seed deep and watch her flower.

He turned away abruptly, wondering where the hell the forbidden image had come from. "I gotta go," he said roughly, "I forgot something at the bunkhouse."

Carly's smile faded. He jammed on his hat and pushed open the door. Could she tell what he'd been thinking? Hell, no, or she'd probably have slapped him silly. Women like Carly didn't long for mixed-blood brats. Or covet the men who could give them those brats. They had perfect blond babies with blue eyes. And white skin. And white *fathers* who could give them money and security. He needed to remember that most of all.

Carly, who had watched the parade of emotions cross Sage's face, was puzzled by his sudden departure. For a moment she'd allowed herself to think of his big, gentle hands on her instead of his pregnant mare. She'd grown hot and trembly with the idea of belonging to him, then good sense had rushed back. They had nothing in common but horses, and Carly wasn't going to make a life around *them* or anyone else dealing with them. Her father had been wrong to think she would.

Still, she had no idea what random thought had annoyed Sage so much. Maybe he was still having problems with his stiff-necked pride, even though she felt their deal was more than fair. Sage would only work here for a fraction of the six months they'd agreed on, but his expertise with the horses was well worth the stud fees.

Once again the image of his dark hands on her body rose to taunt her, but she pushed it aside and began to clear the breakfast dishes. In a matter of weeks, a couple of months at the most, he would be on his way back to Oklahoma and she would be happily ensconced at work, dealing with ships and schedules instead of horses, hay, manure and sweat. And unpredictable men who made her heart race and her imagination sing with desire.

* * *

Later that morning, Carly found herself wandering toward the breeding shed. The men were all there, overseeing Red Rocket's union with Comanche Princess. The stallion neighed piercingly when he caught the mare's scent, and Carly could hear Ben's voice. She slipped inside to watch. Sage was holding his mare's halter and talking to her quietly while he kept a careful eye on the big red stallion. Tension was thick.

For a few moments Carly watched the proceedings quietly, but when Red Rocket lunged at Princess, sinking his teeth into her golden hide and making her squeal with pain as he mounted her, Carly realized she couldn't take another minute.

She looked at Sage who, to her surprise, was watching her instead of the horses. His features could have been carved from stone, but his eyes were alive with hunger and burning need.

Beneath the intensity of his gaze she felt herself go red and begin to tremble. Then, sure that she must have misread him and mortified by her reaction, she turned and rushed out the door.

"Carly!" Sage had seen how upset she was by Rocket's roughness. He wondered if she had ever watched a mating before and, if not, why she had chosen to watch this one. For some reason, Sage himself had been deeply affected by the tension-filled atmosphere and the primitive sounds the horses made. And he had watched the same thing many times. It was all part of horse breeding.

The door slammed shut behind Carly and he cursed under his breath, wishing he could follow her and make sure she was okay. Instead he turned his attention back to his mare, while Ben and Tony dealt with Red Rocket.

Carly heard him shout her name but didn't stop. What if he had seen her response? What if he thought she was embarrassed by the scene, like some squeamish city girl who didn't know what life on a ranch was really about? She had no choice but to keep going. She would work inside the office for the rest of the day, until her mortification had cooled and Sage had forgotten all about how she had acted in the breeding shed.

Late that night Carly was still wishing that *she* could forget. It wasn't the memory of the horses' screams that kept her awake so much as the image of Sage's frozen features and the light in his silver eyes as his stare locked with hers across the room. No matter how many times she told herself that her vision had been distorted by her own fantasies, she knew she *had* seen desire stamped on his dark face. Primitive, naked, all-encompassing desire.

She *hadn't* been mistaken. For a few moments out of time he had wanted her as badly as she desired him. Impossible it might be, but hunger had swept across that room and branded them both. And now the echo of that hunger was keeping her awake.

She tossed restlessly, her sheets a hopeless tangle and her long, silky nightgown twisting uncomfortably around her thighs. To add to her discomfiture, the late-night air that filled her room was stifling, a preview of summer nights to come when all breezes died and the atmosphere around the house grew hot and sultry.

It was the kind of night that had sent Carly, when she lived here before, to the relative privacy of the swimming pool behind the house.

The thought of cool water lapping against her heated skin was a powerful lure. She scrambled from her bed and padded silently across the carpet to slide open the drawer where she'd tossed the pieces of a minuscule red bikini. She had thrown it into her luggage at the last minute. Now she was glad she had brought it, and even gladder it was dark out, so no one would see her in the scanty costume she hadn't really thought she'd be here long enough to use.

She pulled on the bikini, which was even skimpier than she had remembered, grabbed a thick white towel from the adjoining bathroom and cautiously opened her door. After she had listened for several moments, ears straining in the silence, she decided that the rest of the house was asleep and tiptoed down the stairs.

There was a bright moon in the night sky, but the area behind the house, bathed in silver, was deserted. Carly walked barefoot across the raised wooden deck, past the latticework screen that shielded the hot tub from view, went down the wooden steps and dropped her towel onto the ground. Glancing around at the silent landscape once again, she stood poised for a moment, then dived into the water.

The coolness felt wonderful. After she had floated briefly, Carly began to do laps back and forth the length of the pool, stroke, kick, breathe. Turn and go again, slicing through the water. Swimming was something she enjoyed. Although this was the first time she had taken the time to swim at the ranch, she'd always exercised regularly at the full-size pool at her apartment house in Houston.

Finally she had to rest. She paused at one end, resting her elbows on the edge of the pool while she caught her breath, and realized how much she had missed the regular workouts.

And the exercise hadn't helped in banishing the ghosts that had kept her awake, she realized. She still felt edgy…and restless…and unsettled. With a toss of her wet head, and uttering an exasperated groan, she pushed away from the wall and began to glide across the pool to where she had left her towel.

The moon was partially hidden by a cloud, but there was still enough light for her to see that the white towel was gone from where she had left it. Treading water, she glanced around.

And almost sank to the bottom.

At the side of the pool she spied her towel. A man whose bare chest and powerful shoulders were bathed in moon-glow was holding it out to her.

Sage.

Slowly she stroked her way closer. His face was in shadow, but the moonlight made his earring sparkle when he moved his head. He took in a breath and his smooth chest expanded. He shifted the towel and she watched, fascinated, seeing the muscles of his shoulders and arms ripple with subtle power. Even the diagonal scar on his abdomen added to his attraction.

''Where did you come from?'' she asked inanely.

''My mother, the moon, sent me to you.'' His voice was hypnotic in the night.

Carly stared, her senses awakening as he continued to gaze at her.

''Come here.'' The words caressed her, a part of the night and the fantasy that was unfolding around her.

Soundlessly she swam closer. Her gaze was fused with his. When she touched the edge and put her foot on the bottom step, he took her hand. She reached the deck and he stepped back, his gaze trailing down her body and up again with an agonizing slowness that left little fires blazing wherever it lingered.

Carly stared, too, at the wide chest above the jeans that rode low, zipped but unfastened, as if he had put them on in haste. He came closer, wrapping her in the thick folds of the towel as tenderly as someone putting a butterfly back into its cocoon.

"What are you really doing out here?" she asked as he began to dry her body with gentle strokes. He bent and scooped her into his arms.

"I couldn't sleep. I was walking when I heard you."

She glanced down and saw scuffed boots on his feet. Then he shifted her against his chest and her fingers dug into his shoulders, feeling his strength and the steady beat of his heart.

Freeing one hand, she spread it across his warm skin, which immediately tensed beneath her touch. "I can feel your heart beating," she mused aloud.

"It beats for you." His voice was low.

She slid her hand around his neck and into his long hair. "And mine beats for you." The words were like a pledge, binding them, but she knew this was only one night's fantasy. A fantasy she intended to live to its fullest degree.

"Let me feel it," Sage murmured; he bent his head. His lips touched the upper curve of her breast, exposed by the brief bikini top. Beneath his mouth her heart went wild. A moan was torn from her throat.

He looked into her eyes. "I burn for you."

"Yes!" she gasped, unable to tear her gaze from the searing glitter of his.

The moon sailed from behind the clouds and she saw him smile. He bent his head again.

Chapter Seven

Sage had been standing in the shadows, watching the house and wondering if Carly was asleep, when he saw her slip outside into the moonlight and go to the pool. For a moment he thought his imagination had conjured her up. Then she dropped her towel and he had to bite down hard to stifle a groan. This was no dream.

Carly hesitated for a moment before she dived into the pool, and his hungry gaze swept over her, burning that image forever into his memory.

Her breasts swelled lushly above the scrap of material that covered her nipples, and little else. Her waist dipped in before her hips flared, hips he ached to imprison between his hands. The swimsuit bottom was cut high, revealing long, sensual thighs that melted into delicately curving calves and ankles. At the apex of those gorgeous legs the suit widened slightly to conceal her most feminine secrets. Above that, the smooth line of her flat belly made him ache to rain kisses over her moonlit skin and to dip his tongue into the indentation there.

His blood was on fire, racing through him to settle heavily, arousing his body past the point of pain and into madness. He fought to hang on to at least a shred of control, but calling to mind all the reasons he should leave her alone was a futile exercise in the magic of this night. As Carly swam back and forth, the sounds of her strokes almost a lullaby to his fevered senses, Sage was finally able to recapture a small measure of restraint, but even that was not enough to turn him away from her altogether.

He forced himself to wait until she stopped swimming of her own accord. Silently he moved around the edge of the pool, stopping to pick up the towel she had dropped.

Then he waited, forcing the breath in and out of his tortured lungs, making his hands hold the towel easily, forcing himself to move slowly when she finally looked up and saw him.

When she rose from the pool he folded her into the towel and took her into his arms, close to the heart that threatened to burst from his chest. With ruthless control, he made himself hold her with tenderness and look upon her calmly. The gods had sent him to find her, and he hadn't the will to refuse their gift. When he was sure Carly wanted him, too, he finally allowed himself to kiss her tempting lips.

His mouth descended, and Carly had the sudden thought that her life was about to change forever. For a moment some deep instinct of self-preservation urged her to pull away, to break loose and run as if the very demons of hell were after her immortal soul.

And then Sage's warm, firm lips touched hers. She was lost. Lost in a spinning, swirling whirlpool of desire finally set free. There was an elemental rightness about being with him that she didn't question.

There was no sense of being carried anywhere, but then Sage set her down gently upon a double-width chaise lounge that was shielded by the latticework screen around the hot tub. Slowly he unfolded the towel, his gaze on the body he exposed. Carly heard a soft groan and then his eyes lifted to hers.

"You're the loveliest thing I've ever seen." His voice was husky with sincerity.

Carly reached up one hand and laid it against his hard cheek. "You have an untamed beauty of your own," she said.

He pulled away and she thought she had embarrassed him, but he was only bending to slip the bikini strap from her shoulder. The fabric slid down, exposing one nipple, already beaded and tingling.

Sage touched it with his finger, and a river of fire burned through Carly's body.

"So pale," he murmured as she gasped. "You're so pale against my dark hand."

"Does that bother you?" She forced the question through lips that longed for another kiss.

"Not tonight."

His words brought a dozen more questions to the tip of her tongue, but before she could voice them, he covered her breast with his warm hand and pressed his mouth to hers.

This time his kiss was rougher, the heat and moisture of his open mouth seducing her until her lips parted to admit his questing tongue. His thumb caressed the sensitized nub of her breast and she arched helplessly while his mouth absorbed her passionate cry.

Sage's hand slid behind her back and he released the catch on her top, dragging the fabric away with impatient fingers. Then his hands returned to stroke her, while his tongue explored the inside of her mouth.

Carly grabbed his upper arms, digging her fingers into the hard muscles. Then, with hungers of her own, she slid her hands across his bare shoulders and down the smooth expanse of his chest. Beneath her touch his muscles jumped. When he released her mouth and lowered his head to lave first one breast and then the other with his tongue, Carly's hands fell still.

His lips moved toward the nipple that waited, quivering. Wild sensations tore through her. When he finally pulled it into his mouth and sucked hard, Carly's fingers curled helplessly, her nails digging into his skin. Then she found the small nub of his nipple and plucked at it. Lightly she scraped the sensitive disk with a fingernail and heard a ragged groan.

Sage buried his face against her breasts. He'd been sitting on the wide chaise next to her but now he shifted, covering her body with his. The denim of his jeans was a rough caress against her bare legs. Bracing himself on his forearms, he slowly lowered his chest and dragged it against her sensitive skin.

Carly's hands stroked his back, wandering down his spine. Her fingers dipped into the loosened waistband of his jeans. They were all he wore. She ran her fingers along the firm curve of his buttocks, feeling them flex beneath her touch. He pressed closer, and she felt how passionately he wanted her.

Again Sage's mouth fastened upon hers. His hands were at her waist. Carly barely noticed when he stroked the bikini bottom downward until his marauding fingers burned a path from her navel to one shivering pelvic bone and then back across her stomach to her other hip.

His hand skimmed down, only to skate back up along her inner thighs, urging them apart. Then his fingers drifted to the most intimate part of her body. He caressed her and she moaned. His touch was turning her body to pure flame.

Finally he withdrew his hand, when she began to writhe helplessly, and shifted on the lounger. He kissed her again, deeply. When he lifted his head, she cried out with disappointment. Immediately he put a hand lightly over her mouth.

"Shh," he cautioned. "This night is for the two of us alone."

He replaced his fingers with his lips, giving her another quick kiss. Then he rolled away and sat up. Carly's hands reached out to him.

"No..." she moaned, senses swirling. "Don't leave me."

He glanced at her over his shoulder and she could see his smile in the moonlight. "Impatient little cat," he scolded. "I'm not leaving."

He pulled off his boots and dipped one hand into the pocket of his jeans. He then peeled them off and was fully revealed to her, a beautiful male, fully aroused and throbbing with power. Carly gasped softly and reached out her arms.

"Do you want me?" he asked, not moving.

"Yes," Carly breathed. "I want you *now*." She was burning up with need.

Uttering a satisfied sound, he came down onto the lounge, holding her close to the length of his body. "You feel so damned good," he muttered.

Carly tried to press even closer.

Briefly he turned away, then he was back. He rose over her and urged her legs apart with one knee. His questing fingers found and stroked her again. She cried out, arching toward him, and he moved his hand to cup her hip. When his mouth covered hers in another soul-shattering kiss, Carly thought she would go mad from the passion that raged through her.

"Are you ready for me?" he gasped.

Her arms struggled to pull him closer. "Yes," she sobbed. "Oh, God, yes!"

Positioning himself, he thrust into her with a controlled wildness that took her breath away. For a moment he lay still, buried deep. Then he moved again and sent her soaring. As her arms tightened around him and she began to convulse, his thrusts became faster, deeper, until suddenly he, too, was straining toward release. For a moment they were as one.

When Sage finally stilled, she had barely enough strength to hold him close. After a moment, one of his powerful arms curved around her and he shifted to his side, drawing her head to his shoulder while he fought to slow his breathing.

Carly felt as if her insides had been melted and then re-shaped. A great peace was descending over her, and she refused to think past the present moment while she savored his touch and the caress of his breath against her skin.

Finally Sage lifted his head and his eyes bored into hers. He opened his mouth to speak and a sudden fear raced through her. She covered his mouth with her fingers and shook her head, wanting nothing to break the moonspell between them.

Sage frowned, but she managed a smile as she pushed him gently away and reached for the pieces of her bikini.

Bunching them in one hand, she stood and looked down at him for a long moment. His eyes were alive with unspoken messages. She wrapped the big white towel around herself and began to walk back to the house. She heard Sage rise to his feet. Opening the back door, she looked at him one last time, drinking in the sight of the moonlight caressing his perfect male body as if he were a spirit of the night sky.

Carly made herself turn away and go through the door, shutting it quietly behind her. She floated up the stairs to her room, where she knew that eventually she would have to sort out all the feelings and sensations that still whispered through her in response to Sage's lovemaking. For tonight it was enough to pull her pillow close, to know that her desire for him had been fulfilled, and to sink into a dreamless sleep.

Behind her on the deck, Sage spent a long time looking at the stars. How much of himself was he going to leave behind when he went back to Oklahoma? He had no choice in the path his feet had to walk, but the next time he saw Carly, he was sure as hell going to ask what *her* plans were.

Sage got his chance the next afternoon. Ben and Tony were busy with the vet, and Joey had gone to the doctor to have his arm checked. Carly hadn't been at breakfast, but no one had said anything about her absence and he hadn't liked to ask. He'd wondered if she was deliberately avoiding him, if she was sorry for what they had shared.

Part of him regretted it, but another part could not. Holding her, making her his had gone beyond anything he had ever experienced. He couldn't make himself feel remorse for that.

Carly hadn't wanted to talk afterward, and maybe that was just as well. He didn't know what he could have said. He had already told her that he had nothing to give her. And he had no idea what she wanted. He didn't believe that Carly was the kind of woman who would make love with him for the novelty of it. Some women had; he'd found that out early. But not Carly. So then why had she?

The question ran through his mind as he walked past the pool and through the back door of the house. He didn't hear Rosa in the kitchen, so he went down the hallway to the office where Carly could often be found during the day. Before he could knock on the partially closed door, he heard her voice.

"I need to get together with you very soon. If I'm going to list the ranch for sale, I need some idea of an asking price."

Sage leaned against the wall, aghast at what he had just heard. She had everything he had lost and wanted back, and she was tossing it away. How could she bear to sell the *land?* How long had it been in her family? Land that her father had sweated over and died for, passing it on to her. Ben had told Sage that the man had been on his way to look at a new stud when he and Mollie's mother had been killed.

Sage should have realized that Carly had no intention of giving up her life in Houston. His earliest impressions of her had been correct. She didn't belong here. And she sure as hell didn't belong with him. Seen in that light, what they had shared last night made even less sense. If only he could put it from his mind.

While he waited impatiently for her to conclude her telephone conversation, there was a pause, as if she was listening to the person at the other end.

"Yes, everything goes," she said. "I'll want to set up retirement funds for two of the employees and severance pay for the others. Mollie and I will be taking some personal things with us, but everything else, including the stock and the furniture, will be sold."

Sage asked himself how she could sound so calm, her voice devoid of emotion. He listened while she made plans to meet with the other person a couple of mornings later.

As soon as she hung up, he knocked lightly.

"Come in," she called.

He got his emotions firmly under control and walked into the room. At least he thought he was under control until he saw her.

She had risen from behind the big desk. Her hair was loose and, while he watched, her cheeks went pink. The breasts he had touched and kissed rose as she took a deep breath. The tip of the tongue he had tasted slid across her lower lip.

Sage's hands curled into fists at his sides; he fought to keep from reaching out.

"I missed you at breakfast," he told her.

Carly's eyelids fluttered and she glanced away. "I was busy. I ate later."

"Busy cataloging the silver?" he asked dryly, then bit back a curse.

Carly's chin went up at the challenge. "You were eavesdropping!" Her voice had chilled.

"Not intentionally. But since I did hear, why don't you explain to me what's going on?" He dropped into a chair in front of the desk, crossing one ankle over the other knee. The hand that itched to reach out and shake her curved around the tooled leather of his boot.

For a moment Carly glared at him, then she, too, sat down. She stared out the window while he studied her profile. Did she mean to tell him anything?

"My father had plans for this ranch," she said eventually. "And he had plans for me. Unfortunately, the two of us didn't get along very well. It took me a long time to accept the fact that nothing I did could ever measure up to Joseph Golden's expectations." She hesitated, cleared her throat and glanced at Sage. "Finally I left. Went to business school in Houston. Then I came home for a little while, but it was even worse than before. Father had remarried by then."

"Surely you didn't expect him to remain alone?" Sage asked. Could Carly be that possessive, that unreasonable?

"No, of course not." She made a dismissive motion with her hand. "I got along fine with Susan. But Father and I couldn't agree on anything. Nothing I did was right, nothing I wanted to do went along with *his* vision, so finally I went back to Houston. The rest, as they say, is history. I never came back to stay, only for brief, occasional visits. The last couple of years I didn't come home at all."

Sage was surprised to see that her eyes had filled with tears. He rose, but she shook her head, as if annoyed at herself for letting her emotions show.

"I could never run Rolling Gold the way *he* wanted. Don't you see?" she pleaded, blinking rapidly. "He left me no choice."

Sage watched her closely. "But the ranch is yours now, yours and Mollie's. You could run it the way *you* want. Wouldn't it be better to do nothing final until you're sure?"

Carly stood, shoving back her chair. "I am sure. Besides, if I don't return to Houston soon I could lose a wonderful job and a great apartment with an amiable roommate.''

Sage got to his feet. "What about our deal?" he asked. "You knew when we made it that you weren't going to stay." He wanted to add, "What about us?" and "What did last night mean?" but didn't.

"And I knew you were leaving, too," she replied. "I need you here until the ranch is sold. After that our deal will be concluded."

He snapped his fingers. "Just like that?" What more did he want?

She raised her chin. "Just like that."

He studied her for a moment, pride urging him to reject her offer. She was all but giving him Red Rocket's services, and they both knew it. Then he stepped closer and took her hand.

"At least be honest about why you want me here," he said. "Even if you can't be honest with yourself about why you won't consider keeping the place."

Carly yanked her hand away. "Stop trying to analyze me. I know what I'm doing! What do you want from me, anyway?"

He reached out and gripped her shoulders, barely resisting the urge to shake her. How could she pretend that the night before had never happened? "I told you. Be honest!" he exclaimed. "You want me and I want you. Admit that, and you have my word that I'll be here as long as you need me."

Angrily, she shrugged out of his grasp. "I need a ranch hand I can count on," she said harshly. "If you think last night was the start of something big, think again."

Sage would have liked nothing better than to kiss her into submission, but knew that wouldn't solve a thing.

"We both have places we need to go," he said, "but there's no reason why we can't be together while we're here."

Carly's eyes glittered, and her voice was dangerously soft. "I'll keep in mind what you've told me."

There was nothing left to say. If Sage wanted anything more from her, he couldn't have it. And Carly didn't want anything else from him. Why wasn't he feeling elated that they understood each other?

"I have work to do," he said shortly. "I'll see you later."

Carly watched him leave the room. Why did she feel so alone when he was gone? What had last night meant to him? She had thought, foolishly, that it would satisfy the hunger building within her since he'd first come to Rolling Gold. Now, seeing him again, she knew she had been wrong. Staying out of his arms was going to be difficult, perhaps more so than she could stand. Maybe it would be better to take what he offered while she could.

She sat down again and tried to return her attention to the papers she had been going over before she'd called Sam Ferguson, the real estate salesman from Fort Worth who had been a good friend of her father's. After a few futile moments she closed the file and shoved her chair back, staring sightlessly at the painting of Red Rocket on the far wall of the room.

She had wanted to get along with her father. For years she had knocked herself out to live up to his expectations, but had never managed it. And now she never would. The best thing for her, and for Mollie, was to sell up and go back to the life she *could* succeed at.

It would be hard for a while. She would need to arrange day care for Mollie while she was at work, and they would have to find somewhere else to live. At least with the proceeds of the sale, as well as her generous salary, money wouldn't be a problem. Finding the right school for Mollie and bringing her up were challenges Carly looked forward to.

She loved Mollie, and the child had told Carly just yesterday that she and Sage were her two favorite people. Then the little girl had looked worried for a minute and asked if Carly thought her mom and dad would mind her saying that. Carly's smile had been wobbly, she recalled, as she bent down to sweep Mollie into a hug.

"You can be my two favorite *alive* people," Mollie had said in a practical tone, forcing Carly to turn away, barely in time to hide her tears.

As far as any kind of future with Sage went, there was nothing to be gained by thinking of it. Even if she had wanted it, he had made it painfully clear he didn't want or need *her,* except on the most temporary basis. That would have to be enough.

"I don't know what to make of it," Rosa said to Ben one evening as they sat on the deck. She was peeling apples for a pie, and Ben was whittling a small block of wood into the shape of Mollie's pony.

"What's that?" He didn't look up; Rosa would tell him in her own time.

"Carly and Sage," she replied, dropping a denuded, quartered apple into a bowl of water and lemon juice to keep it from turning brown. "Has he said anything to you?"

Ben's eyebrows went up. "Did you expect him to? Sage isn't exactly talkative," he said. The man hardly ever spoke unless it was to ask a question or give Ben some information pertaining to the horses. "Has Carly confided in you?"

Rosa snorted and laughed. "The only one who confides in me is Mollie. She's got a pretty active imagination when it comes to 'her two favorite people' and what she wants for all three of their futures.''

Ben peeled another shaving from the tiny animal he was carving. "I can see trouble coming," he said gravely. "Trouble for all of them. If only Carly would reconsider selling this place. I know she's going to regret it."

Rosa sighed, dropping more apple pieces into the bowl. "Carly has a life in Houston that's important to her."

Now it was Ben's turn to snort.

"Sometimes I wonder if romance is worth the hassle," Rosa mused.

He glanced at her and rose slowly. "Sometimes it is," he said, dropping a hand onto her shoulder. "When two people are mature enough to know what they want."

Rosa glanced up at him. "You'd better not say such things when we've both got knives in our hands. One of us is liable to get rattled and lose a finger."

Carly was walking around the side of the house, enjoying the evening's relative coolness, when she heard the indistinct drone of voices. She was about to join the two older people on the deck, but when she saw Ben lean over Rosa's chair, she decided they might prefer their privacy to her company. On more than one occasion Carly had noticed the way her foreman watched the housekeeper. Perhaps they would end up spending their retirement together, she mused. They could do worse.

Walking slowly down the driveway and listening to the sounds of the ranch bedding down for the night, Carly reminded herself that her own future was with Mollie, not with the man who never strayed far from her thoughts.

A masculine figure appeared in the open barn doorway, silhouetted against the light from inside. She recognized Sage instantly. For a moment she debated the wisdom of returning to the house, but the desire to see him was too strong.

He waited while she came closer.

"Hi," he said softly when she was only a few feet away. "I thought I recognized your white blouse."

"You aren't still working, are you?" she asked, feeling slightly self-conscious as he stared into her face.

"No, just checking on the gelding Mr. Hawkins brought over to board. He was a little spooky when we unloaded him, and I wanted to make sure he was settled in okay."

"And is he?" Carly stopped, folding her arms across her chest in a protective gesture. Her whole body was alert to Sage's nearness, desire urging her closer. In his tense expression she thought she saw the reflection of her own awareness.

"The horses are all fine. But how are you?" His voice was deep, filled with hidden messages.

Carly tried her best to act as if nothing was going on between them. "I'm glad the horses are okay," she said.

"I'm glad you're here." He shifted, and Carly wished she could see him more clearly. He glanced around and reached out to take her hand. She hadn't forgotten how warm his skin was, how enticing his touch. Part of her wanted to resist as he urged her to join him in the barn, but she looked into his shadowed face and was lost.

Their hands linked, he led her into an empty stall. Then he turned to face her, releasing her hand to cradle her jaw with his fingers. His thumb rubbed across her lower lip, and the slight friction made her gasp.

"I was a fool to think once was enough," he muttered, half to himself. "You've been crowding my thoughts all day."

"I know what you mean." Carly sighed, raising her hand to touch his earring and then to caress his cheek. His hair was damp; he must have showered.

He caught her fingers in his and gave each a tender kiss. Then he imprisoned one with his lips, drawing it into his mouth. The damp heat and the rasp of his tongue were a sensual adventure Carly had never experienced. She found his closeness overwhelming. Her nostrils flared, drinking in the clean male scent of soap and after-shave. Her knees quivered weakly, and her free hand splayed against the front of his shirt. She wasn't sure if she was trying to hold him off or hold herself up!

His eyes glittered down at her, molten silver, as his tongue teased the sensitive skin between her fingers and scraped boldly across her palm.

Carly's fingers curled protectively, and her head dropped back. She studied him through a haze of passion. "What do you want?" she asked softly, melting at the way he was watching her. As if she were a sweet confection he wanted to gobble up.

He smiled, showing his teeth. "You know what I want." He put his lips to her ear, whispering words that were explicit and heated. Carly's fingers tightened on the fabric of his shirt and she moaned softly; he bent his head and his arms enfolded her.

She leaned into him, tipping her head back. His mouth covered hers in a searing kiss. She clung to him, the only solid thing in a raging sea of emotion. His hands swept over her, staking an unmistakable claim, as did his mouth, branding hers with fire. Eagerly she returned his hunger with a burning desire of her own to know again his passionate possession.

As the last shreds of reason drifted away, the sound of whistling finally penetrated the sensual cloud that was enfolding Carly.

"Someone's coming," she whispered, tearing her mouth from his.

Sage's eyes were dark with arousal. He froze, listening, then uttered a succinct curse. Soundlessly he laid a finger across her lips, tucking her into the darkness of the deserted stall. Then he left her.

She heard first his voice, then Joey's. The younger man wanted Sage to look at a horse in the other barn. Frustration almost made Carly groan aloud as she heard Sage agree. The two men walked away.

She couldn't very well hang around the barn, hoping Sage would come back. What if someone else saw her and wondered what she was doing? And she refused to go down to the pool again and be humiliated if he didn't show up. As soon as she was sure the two men had gone, she came out of the stall and looked around. The barn was empty except for the horses and one frustrated human female.

"Damn," she muttered, kicking at some loose straw, then stalked toward the house. She couldn't very well wait for Sage in the bunkhouse, and even he probably wouldn't risk coming to her room at night. There was nothing to do but try to ignore her galloping hormones and the knowledge of how sweetly he could tame them. And try to sleep, if that were possible.

Apparently she had managed to fall asleep after a soothing bubble bath and a stern lecture to herself about affairs of the flesh with unsuitable men. Otherwise a sound at her window couldn't have wakened her later.

Carly sat up and listened, staring into the darkness. The sound came again, a scratching on the glass. Since her room was on the second floor, she couldn't imagine what it was. When the scraping began a third time, she got up and padded to the window. Parting the curtains and looking out, she almost screamed when she saw a dark, masculine shape lurking there.

Then she recognized Sage and pulled up the sash. Her heart was still pounding at a runaway pace. "What are you doing here?" she demanded in a hoarse whisper.

He grinned and slipped inside the bedroom, straightening to stand beside her. Again his body was bare except for the low-riding jeans. "Why do you think I'm here?" There was laughter in his soft voice.

"I meant, how did you get here? This is the second floor, and I didn't know that flying was one of your talents." She tried to hide her pleasure with a show of annoyance. Her earlier sensible resolution to resist him had vanished like a puff of smoke in a strong wind.

"Flying isn't one of my talents," he said, lightly tracing the neckline of her gown with his finger, "but the painters were nice enough to leave their scaffolding up on this side of the building."

Carly glanced out the window. Of course. "Very clever."

He slipped the gown off her shoulders and let it slide to the floor. "I'm a very clever fellow," he muttered in a rough whisper. "I'd climb a giant bean stalk to get to you."

He scooped Carly into his arms and carried her across the room, while she slid her hands over the satiny skin of his wide shoulders. Then he tumbled her onto the bed and, stripping off his jeans, followed her down. His hands and lips began to reawaken the fires he had kindled earlier, and she forgot everything except the joy of possession.

Chapter Eight

Listening to the night sounds that drifted through her window, Carly turned in Sage's arms. "So how was the mare Joey wanted you to check on?" she whispered, stroking his forearm with her fingers.

Sage took her wandering hand in his, pressing his lips to her knuckles. "She didn't look to me like she was going to deliver tonight," he murmured against her skin. "And in case I was wrong, I told Joey to wake Ben."

Carly turned to look up at his strong features. Once more his lovemaking had carried her to heights she had only dreamed possible. How much longer could she convince herself that her heart wasn't involved? "Good thinking. I wouldn't have wanted Joey knocking on my door an hour ago."

She felt him smile against her fingers. "No, two interruptions in one night would have made me wonder if we were cursed."

Carly sat up, pulling the sheet with her to cover her breasts. "You don't believe in things like that, do you?"

His eyes narrowed in the dimness. "Of course not. If I did, I'd have to think I'd been blessed, not cursed." While she wondered what his feelings toward her were, his teasing voice changed abruptly. "I'd better go. If Ben is awake, he might wonder where I've been half the night." He flipped the covers back and rose.

Carly would have liked to protest. Instead she took intense pleasure in watching him move. His muscular body rippled with power, subdued for the time being, but ready to explode at a moment's notice. She could have been almost content to just look at him for hours.

"I think Ben knows more than we give him credit for," she said softly, as Sage pulled on his jeans and slipped his feet into worn moccasins.

He bent over the bed, giving her a brief, possessive kiss. "No point in confirming his suspicions," he muttered. "I'll see you tomorrow, princess."

He slipped back out the window and was gone before she could reply, leaving her with a mouthful of questions and a head full of doubts and confusion. She was getting in deeper and deeper but, like quicksand, her attraction to him refused to let her go. When her heart was broken, as it surely would be if she kept seeing him like this, she would have no one to blame but herself.

For the next few days Carly managed to keep her distance. A couple of times she caught Sage watching her with speculation on his face, but he made no effort to get her alone. Then, early one evening, an older mare they were boarding began showing unmistakable signs of impending delivery. Since Ben had been up the two previous nights supervising foalings, Sage offered to keep Clover Patch company. The mare had a history of uncomplicated births, so Carly was surprised when he asked if she would mind helping. With Ben watching, she had no choice but to agree.

"Is anything happening?" she asked later that night as she sat on the floor of the stall with her back propped against the wall. She was watching Sage check out the bay mare, impressed as usual by his soothing voice and gentle touch. All the horses responded to him.

"Nothing yet. I think Clover Patch has decided to take her sweet time. She's been through this enough that it's no big deal to her, but once things start, they'll probably go fast." Sage straightened and came over to sit down again beside Carly, leaning forward to stretch the muscles in his shoulders.

She resisted the urge to rub the kinks out for him. His attitude had been strictly businesslike since she had joined him here two hours earlier. She was annoyed that he seemed to have no problem keeping his hands off *her*. Had he been having similar thoughts about not getting involved, or was he already tired of her?

"Tell me something," he said after a few moments, shifting so that he faced her.

As always, Carly found herself mesmerized by his dark coloring and predatory features. She didn't realize she was staring at his mouth until his lips quirked into a grin and he softly reprimanded her.

"Keep that up and you'll be on your back before you can blink," he growled.

Fierce color swept over Carly's cheeks. "Uh, what did you want to know?" she asked, attempting to ignore his provocative comment.

He took the time to pull a long straw from a corner and put it between his lips before he answered her. "Why are you really selling the ranch?"

His question caught her off guard. "I already told you," she said defensively. "My life is in Houston. Besides, I have no interest in running this ranch on a permanent basis."

Sage muttered an expletive. "You love this place. It's in your blood, just as Comanche Creek is in mine."

Carly turned away from his intense stare, selecting a straw of her own to twiddle between nervous fingers. "Nonsense. I'm here as a last favor to my father, and to see that Mollie's future is safeguarded by getting the best price possible."

"Odd the way your father neglected the ranch the way he did," Sage mused. "If, as you say, he was so determined that you take it over someday."

Carly sighed and leaned back against the wall. "I know. It wasn't like him."

"Perhaps he'd finally accepted the fact that you weren't coming back and he lost heart."

Her head snapped around. She stared hard at his unrevealing expression. "That's not true! He always knew I wasn't coming back to stay. I'm *not* the reason he let things slide."

It couldn't be. He had loved the ranch and the horses too much to let one disappointment affect him so strongly. There must have been another reason; perhaps he'd just gotten tired of the whole thing.

Sage shrugged and stood up to check the mare again. "If you say so."

"I wish we had made some kind of peace before he died," Carly found herself admitting. "I thought about coming back and trying to talk to him, but I always put it off." Tears threatened and she blinked them away. "If only I'd known."

Sage noticed that her eyes had filled. They reminded him of bluebells after a drenching rain. He reached out a hand and, when she took it, pulled her up with him.

"We all have regrets," he said gently, "but it seems to me that you could still win his ultimate approval. Stay here and raise Mollie where he meant for her to grow up." He stroked his hands up her arms, feeling her tremble, then gripped her shoulders. "It's not too late."

Even though Sage knew they had no future together, he would like being able to picture her here at Rolling Gold, not living a life in Houston that was totally foreign to him. If it was selfish of him to feel that way, so be it.

Carly was staring blankly past him, a brooding expression on her face. "Come," he said, settling them both on the straw and draping an arm around her. "I'll tell you about my childhood at the church of Saint Edward."

In the next few minutes, he found himself revealing a lot more than he had intended, but Carly's interest and the questions she asked whenever he stopped talking coaxed from him details he thought he had succeeded in forgetting.

"Joe Buchanan taught me a lot about horses," he said of the man who'd taken him from the church and given him a home when he was twelve. "He saw that I went to school and had what I needed. I worked hard on his ranch, but I learned a lot, too. Enough to make me want a spread of my own." He glanced at Carly to gauge her reaction to a poor boy's unrealistic dream, but she looked rapt with interest.

"What happened?" she asked. "Did you stay there until you went into the army?"

Sage wished he hadn't started talking about that part of his life. He didn't like to think about its abrupt end. "Yeah until I joined the army, but it wasn't exactly like you're thinking," he admitted reluctantly.

As if she sensed that he was about to reveal something painful, Carly turned toward him and laced her fingers through his. "Tell me."

For a moment he almost lost himself in her eyes. Then he set his jaw and went on. "Joe had been divorced years before. He had a daughter out in California, I think, that he didn't see too often. I'd met her briefly when she visited, but Joe finally persuaded her mother to let her spend the whole summer at the ranch."

As he spoke the memories returned, as vivid as if it had all happened just the day before. "Natalie was sixteen that year. She'd…ripened since the last time I'd seen her." He felt Carly stiffen beside him. Would she believe him, or would she think there was more to the story than he was telling? Some inner demon pushed him to find out.

"She followed me all over. I was eighteen and full of myself. It seemed that every time I turned around, she was there, tempting me. She went out with several of the local boys, but I guess that wasn't enough for Natalie."

He paused, raking his hair back, remembering the hell of what wanting that young tease had put him through. "I tried staying out of her way, but she was the prettiest girl I'd ever laid eyes on, and she let me know she was attracted to me." He glanced at Carly, who smiled encouragingly.

"It was a damn fool thing to do, I knew that as soon as I said yes." He shook his head, remembering his own stupidity. "She wanted me to meet her at the stable late one night, so we could talk. By then my hormones had pretty much blocked out any sense I had, but I would never have done anything to hurt her. I owed Joe too much for that."

"I know you wouldn't," Carly said with certainty. "So what happened?"

"Her father caught us kissing. I swear that's all we were doing, but I suppose it looked pretty bad." He let one bitter chuckle escape. "I might have been okay to take in, to give a job to, but I was still a half-breed, not good enough to put a dirty hand on Joe Buchanan's daughter." He took a deep breath, surprised at the hurt that still lingered. "He made sure he told me that when he kicked me out at dawn, with fifty dollars and what I could carry in a duffel bag."

Carly gasped. "That's awful! Didn't Natalie tell him what happened?"

"She tried to, but he wasn't in a listening frame of mind."

"Have you ever seen him since?"

Sage swallowed the humiliation that rose like bile. Might as well tell her the rest. "Once. I ran into him years later at a quarter horse show. He was with some other breeders and I went up to say hello. He looked me full in the face, and then turned away like he didn't know me from Adam."

Carly threw her arms around him. "I'm so sorry!" she cried. "You didn't deserve any of that."

Sage soaked up the unexpected comfort like a greedy sponge. "I never even told Mac that last part," he mumbled into her shoulder. Then he felt moisture against his neck and jerked away to stare into Carly's face.

The tears he'd seen swimming in her eyes earlier had spilled over. "It's too late to cry for that boy," he said. "He grew up a long time ago."

She shook her head, wiping at her wet cheeks. "I'm not feeling sorry for the boy," she whispered.

"Then why are you crying?" he asked suspiciously.

Carly realized there was no room for anything but the truth. She screwed up her courage and admitted what was in her heart. "I'm crying for the man you are now," she said, throat aching.

Sage's face darkened into a thunderous frown.

"For your dreams," she continued hesitantly, wanting to touch him, to comfort him in some small way, knowing he would never accept it. The man had been through so much. "For you and your stolen dreams."

More tears slid down Carly's cheeks, and the angry words Sage had been about to speak were frozen inside him. He couldn't remember anyone ever crying for him before. Some deep gut instinct told him it wasn't just pity that moved her. He could see the pain in her eyes. His pain. He had shared it with her and she had accepted it willingly.

Carly's tears ran down her cheeks unheeded. Finally she began to turn away, but Sage snagged her chin with his hand. He reached out cautiously and caught one of the silvery drops on the tip of his finger. He pondered it silently, too moved to speak. Then he opened his arms.

She went into them with a sigh and he gathered her close in a curiously passionless embrace. She gripped him around the waist. For a moment Sage allowed himself to absorb the comfort she was offering. His eyes burned. The heat of her soft body and the warmth of her caring began to melt the icy, self-protective wall he'd long ago allowed to form around his heart.

When he felt that wall of ice begin to thaw and his control to slip, instinct took over. He got up and moved away quickly. From the corner of one eye he thought he saw Carly shiver, even though the evening was still warm. She crossed her arms over her breasts, rubbing her hands up and down as if to ward off a sudden chill.

He wanted to say something, anything, but right at that moment, the third occupant of the stall, who had been standing quietly, uttered a deep, shuddering groan and flopped onto the straw.

"Damn!" Sage exclaimed as the mare's water broke. "It's show time!"

It was late morning when Mollie and Carly guided their mounts back into the stable yard after riding along the creek and back.

"I'm a good rider, aren't I?" Mollie asked as Carly pulled Dancer up and Polka Dot stopped beside him.

"Yes, you are, punkin. A good rider always takes care of her horse, you know." She helped Mollie dismount and then watched while the little girl led her pony inside, talking to him all the way. Her stepsister was a terrific kid. Carly was coming to realize how much the youngster loved the ranch, but there would be a lot of things in Houston, too, for Mollie to love, once she got used to it. Carly crushed down her doubts and led Dancer inside.

She had helped Mollie with Polka Dot and was seeing to her own mount when she heard footsteps. Ben and Tony had gone to a sale, and she hadn't seen Sage or Joey since breakfast. Clover Patch's delivery had gone smoothly, Carly and Sage working like a team until a captivating chestnut foal stood beside his proud dam, nursing greedily. Afterward Sage hadn't mentioned their emotional conversation and neither had she. Now her stomach tightened automatically, even though the steps didn't sound like his.

"Well if it isn't the big, hotshot boss lady." The hostile voice was slurred but still familiar.

Carly turned quickly. Behind her stood the groom she had fired when she'd caught him drinking in the barn one night.

"Artie, what are you doing here?"

His chin was scruffy with gray-brown whiskers and his pale eyes were bloodshot. He was taller than Carly, his expression threatening. When he came closer, she became aware that he must not have bathed in several days. His clothes were worn and dirty.

"You blackballed me, bitch. I can't get a job nowhere." Artie's breath was thick with whiskey fumes.

Carly glanced around to see if Mollie was watching, but the child had disappeared. Just as well.

"I did no such thing," she denied vehemently. "No one even asked me for a reference. But word gets around, you know, and your drinking is hardly a secret. It's your own fault that you can't find work. I offered to help you when I let you go." Carly could see that her words of reason were lost on him and wished one of the men would appear.

Artie's sneer was ugly, his tone venomous. "Some offer you made me! Wanting me to go somewhere and dry out." He pulled a flask from the pocket of his dark windbreaker and downed a gulp rebelliously. "Thass pretty extreme."

Artie had threatened her when she fired him. Even though he was making her nervous now, Carly told herself resolutely that she could handle one drunken sot on her own.

"I think you'd better leave." Her tone was forceful, confident.

Artie came closer. Carly wanted to hold her nose. "I'll leave when I'm ready," he said. "I told you I'd be back." He slipped the flask into his pocket and flexed the fingers of his dirty hands. "Not so high and mighty when you're all alone, are you?"

Carly glanced around for a weapon, anything to protect herself with. The pitchfork was out of reach. "All I have to do is yell," she bluffed. "You'd better get out of here."

His laugh was bitter. "Still think you can boss ever'-body around, huh? Maybe I'll just show you that some guys don't take orders from a woman!" His voice had risen so that he was yelling.

"You do and I promise you'll be very sorry."

At the sound of Sage's voice, Carly almost collapsed with relief. Mollie was behind him.

"This is Artie. He was just leaving," Carly said.

"The hell I was!" He glared at her, then turned to take a wild swing at Sage, who stepped out of the way. Mollie screamed.

Artie caught himself and jerked around, aiming another punch. It glanced off Sage's shoulder, and before Artie could recover his balance, Sage clipped his chin, dropping him to the floor like a sack of feed.

Mollie clapped her hands, and Carly sent Sage a smile of gratitude before looking down at her former employee, who struggled to a sitting position, holding his jaw.

"You'll be sorry," he snarled.

"What's this all about?" Sage asked Carly.

She explained briefly, glancing at Mollie, who was watching the whole thing with avid curiosity.

"Call the sheriff," Sage suggested. "Maybe some cell time will cool him off."

"I hate to do that." Carly didn't want more trouble.

"Better deal with it now, before it gets any worse." Sage urged her toward the phone in the tack room. "I'll keep an eye on him."

"You're gonna be real sorry for this," Artie said again. "Your father would never have treated me this way."

Carly didn't bother to say that she knew her father would never have condoned drinking around the horses. She went to make the call.

A few minutes later, a police cruiser pulled up and Grady got out. Just what she needed, more trouble.

"Your boy here giving you problems?" Grady asked, glancing at Sage as he came inside. Then he saw Artie, still seated on the floor, and he assumed a professional attitude. "What's going on?"

Before Carly could say anything, Sage told him in clipped sentences.

"Want to press charges?" Grady asked her.

She shook her head. "I don't think that will be necessary."

Grady hauled Artie to his feet.

"I'm not done with you!" Artie shouted at her. "You can't get rid of me that easy. You're gonna regret turning your back on Artie!" He yanked his arm away from Grady, who snagged it again.

"You sure about this?" he asked Carly.

She glanced at Sage, who was watching her.

"Yes, I'm sure," she said, decisively. "I don't want more trouble. Just get him out of here."

Sage bent and lifted Mollie onto his shoulders. "Let's go look at the foals," he suggested, ignoring Carly.

"Come on, man," Grady said to Artie, who lurched when he took a step. "I'll give you a ride back to town." His gaze met Carly's.

"Thank you," she said.

"I think you're making a mistake here. Call if you need anything." For a moment Grady looked as if he meant to add something, but then he turned away, herding Artie toward his cruiser. When they finally drove off, Carly heaved a sigh of relief and went looking for Mollie and Sage.

When she found them, she grabbed Sage's hand and inspected his knuckles, which were slightly swollen. "You need some ice for that," she told him.

He pulled away. "It's okay."

"I'm glad Sage was here to protect us," Mollie commented. "I went and got him when I saw Artie. He's a bad man."

"Well, he has a lot of problems," Carly said. "But I'm glad you brought Sage. He always seems to be rescuing me."

"I wish Sage could stay with us for always," Mollie remarked wistfully. "We could be a family. Sage could be the daddy and train the horses, and you could be the mommy and take care of me."

An awkward silence followed; Carly had no idea how best to deal with her sister's words. It surprised her, too, that Mollie's view of family roles was so traditional. Modern mommies did more than just raise their children. Mollie's own mother, Susan, had been involved in several charitable functions, as well as helping Carly's father show the horses.

It would have been easier to talk to Mollie if the two of them had been alone. Carly glanced at Sage for help.

"I can't stay here forever, little one," he said, lifting Mollie down from his shoulders. "I have my own ranch in Oklahoma."

"I thought his home was with us," Mollie told Carly.

"Only for a while, punkin."

"For how long?" Mollie demanded of Sage.

"I'm not sure." His glance at Carly was accusing. "We'll talk about it before I go, okay?"

Mollie's lower lip quivered. "Okay."

Sage looked at Carly again to see if she had anything to add, but she remained silent. Then it dawned on him that Mollie was talking as if she didn't know the ranch was going to be sold. He stared intently at Carly until she twisted her hands together and glanced away.

That was it! Mollie didn't know.

"I'll see you both later," Sage said abruptly. He needed to talk to Carly alone, but first he had to cool off.

Did she plan to take Mollie away without any warning? Or let her find out the truth when the For Sale sign was posted?

Late that evening he finally caught Carly alone. He had been waiting for her to come to the stables for her customary final check of the evening.

"What the hell do you think you're pulling?" he demanded, stepping out of the shadows when she walked down the aisle between the stalls.

Carly stifled a scream. "You scared me!"

"That's nothing compared to what you're doing to that innocent child. How's she going to feel when you turn her whole world upside down?" Something inside him rebelled against what Carly was doing. He could barely contain his anger.

"I'm doing what's best for Mollie," she insisted. "Besides, it's none of your concern."

"The hell it isn't! I care about her," he said roughly. "And I care about what happens to you. I hate to see you making such a terrible mistake."

Carly thrust out her chin. "It's *not* a mistake. I've just been waiting for the right time to tell her. She'll understand when she gets used to the idea."

Sage bit back an angry curse. "I wish you'd wait," he said, frustrated.

Carly seemed to sag. "There's nothing to wait for. Why should you care, anyway? You can't *wait* to leave here."

Her words made him aware that he hadn't been thinking about Oklahoma so often lately. Carly had filled his thoughts, clouded his senses. He grabbed her shoulders, and the warm feel of her beneath his hands ignited fresh flames of desire. "That doesn't mean I don't care if you louse up your whole future," he grunted. "You belong here." A tiny voice inside tried to tell him they belonged together, but he silenced it.

Carly searched his face, as if looking for something. "I know where I belong," she said softly. "Just like you do. We each have a destiny to follow, don't we?"

There seemed to be nothing more Sage could say. Instead of letting her go as common sense dictated, he yanked her close and covered her mouth with an angry kiss. Somehow her unguarded response both calmed and inflamed him. He deepened the kiss, drowning in her taste, savoring the desire she made no attempt to hide.

"I'll come to you later," he murmured, anger evaporating and control almost gone. Much more of this and he would lead her to the cot in the tack room, and to hell with the consequences.

"Is it safe?" she asked. "Someone might hear you."

"No one heard me last time."

"The scaffolding's not there anymore."

He grinned down at her, already savoring the idea of her wrapped in his arms with nothing between them but passion. "So I'll come in the door like regular people. Don't worry. No one hears me if I don't want them to."

"Yes," she murmured. "Later."

He kissed her again, gliding his fingertips over her breasts, feeling them tighten at his touch. Both hands slipped to her hips and he pressed his rigid arousal close to her for a tortured moment before letting her go.

"Later," he echoed, then slipped away. How was he ever going to leave her when the time came? The thought was almost enough to keep him from going to her that night, but when he pictured her in her bed, the covers kicked away and moonlight on her slim form, nothing could stop him.

Dawn was struggling with the night when he woke up. Carly was curled against him, breathing softly. Her scent filled his nostrils, and he responded instantly to the feel of her bare body tangled so intimately with his own. Then he looked at her clock and swore under his breath. He'd be lucky to get out of the house undetected.

In one fluid movement he slipped from the bed and pulled on his jeans. Grabbing his moccasins in one hand, he stopped to gaze down at her enchanting face, full lips slightly parted, thick lashes lying against her creamy cheeks. For a moment he wished he had time to wake her the way he wanted to. Then he cocked his head, listening for sounds. He heard nothing, so he eased open her door and padded down the stairs.

Rosa stood at the entrance to the dining room, with a towel in her hands. Her face was set in disapproving lines, but she didn't speak.

"Morning," Sage said, feeling as if he'd been caught with his hand in the silver drawer. "See you at breakfast."

Rosa turned away without responding. Not wanting to run into anyone else, Sage went to the entry and slipped out of the front door. He hurried back to the bunkhouse and was stripping off his jeans when Ben began to stir.

"You're up early," the older man observed.

"Yeah, couldn't sleep." Sage reached for his shaving kit and headed to the washroom.

He should have known he wasn't going to get off that easily. Ben cornered him later in the day, while he was watching Comanche Princess and her foal frolic in one of the paddocks and daydreaming about the future. He turned when Ben climbed onto the fence beside him, and they sat in companionable silence for a few moments, following the pair with their eyes.

"Good-looking filly," Ben commented. "So's your other one." Comanche Lady's filly was a lighter gold than Promise.

Sage nodded. "I was lucky."

"Speaking of getting lucky…" Ben began on a dry note.

Sage felt his face grow tight and braced himself for a lecture.

"It's none of my business. Carly's a grown woman." Ben was still watching the horses; it was as if the whole subject made him uncomfortable. He cleared his throat and began scratching his chin. "But Carly's father isn't here to speak for her, so I will. I've known her since she was born, and I know she's vulnerable." He looked at Sage expectantly.

"You're right about it being none of your business."

Ben shifted his perch on the fence rail. "She and her father had their differences," he continued determinedly. "I know she's a sensitive girl, and I think you could hurt her bad if you aren't careful."

"Carly's been to the big city," Sage said stubbornly. "She knows the score."

"Maybe not as much as you think. She hasn't worked through losing her dad yet." Ben climbed down. "Just don't hurt her," he insisted. "She's been hurt enough already." Without waiting for Sage's reaction, he walked toward the broodmare barn, calling out to Joey when he saw him.

Back at the paddock, Sage pondered what the older man had said. He'd told himself that Carly understood the situation. Hell, he'd been nothing but honest with her, right from the start. So why did Ben's words make him feel so guilty now?

Carly expected to feel more relieved when Sam Ferguson came over and she completed the paperwork necessary to list the ranch for sale. Instead, as she took Sam on a detailed tour, she was conscious of a faint wistfulness that she instantly dismissed.

After he left, promising to return when he had worked out the list price, she went to Joey and Tony and told them about her plans. At first they were surprised, but when she assured them that she planned to give them severance pay and glowing letters of recommendation, they accepted her news with resignation. She also cautioned them not to say anything in front of Mollie.

"The Browns' annual barbecue is next Saturday," Carly announced at the dinner table that evening. "We're all invited, and it will be fun. We'll double up on the chores to make sure they're done early and cover the rest when we get back."

"What's the big deal?" Sage asked Joey, who was sitting next to him. "They invite the ranch hands, too?"

"Yeah," Joey said around a mouthful of baked beans. "You don't want to miss it. There'll be a ton of food, lots of cold beer in tubs of ice, good music and pretty women to dance with.''

"The Browns invite everyone from the neighboring ranches," Ben added. "It'll give you a chance to meet some people."

Sage was thinking that he didn't much care about meeting people he wouldn't be around for long. He'd rather have the evening alone with Carly.

"Sounds interesting," he said politely. Not that he had any intention of going. Brown might invite the hired help, but it didn't mean he would expect someone like Sage to show up. He'd run into it before and did not intend to expose himself deliberately. Even when he had been showing his own horses, there'd been those who hadn't been willing to accept him. The thing he hated the most was knowing that Carly would be there, dancing in other men's arms, while he drove himself crazy thinking about it.

"I'm really looking forward to the Browns' barbecue," Carly confided later when she was watching Sage work one of the yearlings. What she was looking forward to most was showing him off. She glanced up shyly. Did he dance? All the women there would be trying to get his attention, he was so attractive. Even his long hair and single earring only added to his slightly pagan aura of pure male intrigue.

"I'd rather be with you."

His blunt words made her heart race with excitement. "We can be together at the party," she said, relieved. "That is, if you want to."

His usually enigmatic expression bore traces of surprise. "You'd like that?" he asked.

His question confused her. Didn't he know how she felt? "Of course I would. I'd be proud to go with you."

He looked away, shaking his head. "You really are color-blind, aren't you? Well, I hate to be the one to tell you, but the rest of the world isn't. You go with me and there'll be trouble."

Carly grabbed his arm, determined. "I don't care!" she exclaimed. "I'd rather go with you than with anyone else." She realized what she had just admitted and blushed, but kept going. "I think you're dead wrong about people and their reactions. These are friends and neighbors I've known all my life. They'll judge you on what kind of man you are, not the shade of your skin." His expression of disbelief egged her on. "And if someone says something, so what? You'll survive, and so will I."

Sage knew he could take it; he had before. But he did not plan to put Carly in a vulnerable position. The depth of his determination came as a surprise, even to him, and when he had the time he would examine it more carefully. Meanwhile he was having trouble believing what she was trying to tell him. He made a derisive sound in his throat, thinking that she was either incredibly naive or too stubborn for her own good.

"I mean it," she insisted. "Come to the barbecue with me, and I'll prove I'm right."

His silver eyes studied her warily. "All right," he said when she was about to give up. "You've got yourself a deal."

Chapter Nine

Sage wasn't sure why he had agreed to attend the Browns' party with Carly; he only knew he was looking forward to being with her. The idea of showing her off and seeing the envious looks of the other men there was not nearly as tempting as the thought of holding her in his arms while they danced and being the one to take her home when the party was over.

Turning restlessly on his bunk, Sage tried not to wake the other ranch hands who slumbered and snored around him. He knew he was venturing onto dangerous ground, testing his feelings toward Carly beyond all good sense. Not that he had shown any good sense when it came to her so far. In fact he had ignored his survival instincts altogether.

He could tell himself he wanted another chance to try to persuade her not to sell the ranch, but that was only a small part of the truth. The big question was whether he would be able to let her go at all, when the time came.

He rolled onto his back, hands behind his head, and stared out the window into the dark night. These feelings of possessiveness were new, and a part of him sensed that they went far deeper than the physical attraction that just burst into flame whenever he was with Carly. But there was one lesson that life had taught him well; those he came to care for always left him.

The only thing he could truly count on was his land. Reclaiming it, living on it and making it productive again was his only purpose, and he would allow nothing to stand in his way. Nothing, not even his growing feelings for a woman he had known from the beginning he could never keep.

He raised himself and turned again, thumping his pillow and releasing a gusty sigh.

"Get a drink of water or take a piss," Ben growled out of the darkness. "But quit thrashing around like a dogie stuck in barbed wire. I want to get some sleep."

"Sorry." Sage lay still for a long time, but sleep didn't come.

It took a bit of planning on Carly's part to arrange transportation back and forth to the Browns', but it was finally settled that Ben, Rosa, Tony and Mollie would take the sedan Carly's father had always favored. Carly, Sage and Joey were riding over in the ranch pickup later, when the others returned. That way the horses wouldn't be left untended, and Rosa could put Mollie to bed before she got overtired. Carly remembered Artie's threats but wasn't worried. It had been the booze talking; he didn't have it in him to really do anything.

At the Browns' party, the food and music would last for hours, in order to accommodate similar schedules at other ranches. People would be coming and going all afternoon and well into the evening.

Carly had thought for a long time about what to wear to the party. She hadn't brought anything that was really suitable, so one day she drove into Fort Worth. While she was there, she stopped at Sam Ferguson's office to okay the ranch listing. He wanted to put a For Sale sign at the main road, but because of Mollie, Carly had to refuse.

"You'd better tell her," Sam cautioned, "before she finds out from someone else."

"I will," Carly insisted, "when the time is right."

At a specialty shop at one of the malls she found a sundress that was perfect. At other stores she bought new shoes, lingerie and stockings to wear with it.

When she got home she took her purchases into the house and put them into her closet. It had been fun to take the day off, and she had brought back gifts for Ben, Rosa, Mollie and Sage. After she had left Sam's office, she had not allowed herself to think about the ranch again, keeping her mind on what she was shopping for instead.

Carly changed for dinner and went to Mollie's room, where the little girl was playing with her dolls.

"I brought you back something from Fort Worth," Carly said, handing her sister a bag. "I hope you like it."

"Ooh, thank you." Mollie pulled out a red-and-white-striped party dress with a white lace collar and red buttons down the front. With it was a full petticoat trimmed with red ruffles. "It's the prettiest dress I've ever seen!" She laid the items carefully upon her bed and reached back into the bag to take out white tights and red patent leather shoes. "Can I try it all on?" she asked.

"Sure, punkin. I thought you'd like a new dress for the Browns' barbecue. Need some help?" Carly sat down on the bed.

"Yes, please." In minutes, Mollie whirled in front of her mirror. The dress and shoes fitted perfectly, the fancy petticoat flaring out as she twirled.

"You look like a princess," Carly told her.

Mollie raced over to her, arms outstretched. "Thank you, Carly," she mumbled as they hugged. "I love it all."

"You're very welcome. We'll have a good time at the barbecue."

"Are you going to dance with Sage?" Mollie asked while she was changing back into her play clothes. "Rosa told me there would be dancing."

Carly smiled as she hung up Mollie's new dress and put the other things into drawers. "Probably. If he knows how to dance."

"He knows," Mollie said. "I already asked him."

Carly wondered what else Mollie had asked, but decided it might be better not to know. "If you can keep a secret, I'll show you my dress," she said.

It was late afternoon the next Saturday when Carly went upstairs to shower and change for the party. Rosa, Ben, Tony and Mollie had left hours ago and would be back soon. The weather had been perfect all day, sunny and warm with a hint of a breeze. The evening ahead promised to be a pleasant one.

Rosa had liked the silver earrings Carly had brought her from Fort Worth, putting them on right away, and Ben was wearing his new suspenders. Carly was having second thoughts about Sage's gift and hadn't decided when to give it to him. The masculine bracelet, which was made from one flat, curved band of silver, would suit him and look good against his dark skin, but she worried about how he would react to the gift. While it hadn't been expensive, she knew that Sage was sensitive to their respective financial situations, and she didn't want to embarrass him.

After she had showered and dried her hair, Carly slipped into the new sundress. It was a deep forest green, the full skirt lined with its own underslip trimmed in eyelet lace. The lace peeked below the skirt's hem and also edged the dress's strapless bodice. Its simple style gently hugged her curves. Beneath the dress she wore only white panties and sheer, thigh-high nylons topped by bands of stretch lace. Her white sandals had high heels and skinny straps.

Carly thought about wearing something around her neck, but nothing she had with her was quite right, so she settled on tiny gold hoop earrings as her only decoration. The white eyelet lace made her skin look a honey tan, and the dark green of the dress turned the hair she wore loose around her shoulders to spun gold. After spraying a cloud of her favorite floral scent into the air and walking through it, Carly was ready to go.

She took one last spin in front of the mirror, then descended the stairs to wait for the men. When she was two-thirds of the way down, the front door opened and Sage stopped in the doorway. In a black leather vest over a white, Western-cut shirt and new black jeans, he was breathtaking. His hair was brushed back from his face and he was carrying his hat, cleaned up for the occasion, in one hand.

"Damn!" he exclaimed in a rough voice as the door shut behind him. "If you aren't the most beautiful woman I've ever seen." He walked to the base of the stairs and waited.

Carly, who had stopped when the door opened, floated down into his arms. "Thank you. You look very nice."

He seemed pleased by her compliment. For a moment he just looked at her, then lowered his head, taking her mouth in a brief but possessive kiss. When he let her go, Carly moved away, so affected by his appearance and the touch of his lips that she needed some space to get her reaction to him under control.

"I brought you something," Sage said, digging into his pocket and extracting a small box. "I hope it's okay."

He handed her the present and for a moment he looked anxious. Carly was speechless with surprise.

"When did you get this?"

"One day when I went into town. Open it." He gestured impatiently.

She lifted the lid and looked down at the exquisitely fragile gold chain and glittering pendant. "Oh, you shouldn't have," she murmured as she lifted the necklace from its box. The pendant was a small gold horseshoe, each nail head a tiny, winking diamond.

His expression hardened. "I wanted to."

"It's wonderful." She held it up. "Would you put it on me?"

"You don't have to wear it."

"But I want to. Please." She urged him to take it.

Some of the pleasure she was feeling must have shown in her eyes. She saw the taut line of Sage's mouth soften as he set his black Stetson on a side table. She spun around and lifted the back of her hair. For a moment nothing happened, then she felt the warmth of his lips against her bare shoulder. "You smell like heaven," he whispered.

Carly shivered with excitement while he drew the chain around her neck and fastened the tiny clasp. When he was done, she crossed to a mirror and admired his gift.

"It's really exquisite. Thank you."

Sage came closer, his intent easy to read. Suddenly Carly remembered the present she had gotten him. "Wait right here!" Ignoring his astonished expression, she quickly raced back up the stairs to her room. When she came down and handed him the gaily wrapped box containing his bracelet, he studied it intently.

"It's for you. Open it," she urged.

He looked into her eyes. His were puzzled. "I didn't expect anything."

"Neither did I. Great minds think alike, I guess," she said, touching one finger to the tiny horseshoe he had given her.

Sage made quick work of the wrapping and gift box, but instead of taking out the silver band he merely looked at it.

"Don't you like it?" Carly asked. "If not, I could..."

"It's great." His voice was husky.

"Try it on," she said impatiently. "Does it fit?"

He slipped the bracelet on. It curved around his wrist, fitting perfectly.

"Is it okay?" she asked. "I didn't know..."

He turned his arm, flexing his hand back and forth. "It's great," he repeated. She had been right. The simple band of silver glowed against his skin. Then he looked up and she saw something in his eyes she couldn't immediately understand. Instead of their usual glinting silver, they were smoky and soft.

"Thanks," he said in a low voice. "I really like it."

Carly sighed with relief. "I'm glad. I love my present, too." She lifted her face toward his. To her pleased surprise, his hands gripped her upper arms, and he turned what she had meant to be a simple kiss into one filled with heat and promise. There was a new tenderness in his touch that almost undid her, and when he finally released her, she was shaking.

"We'd better go," he muttered, his voice deep and rough. "Joey will be wondering where we are, and the others are due back."

"Oh, yes." For a few moments Carly had forgotten all about the party, about everything except for the wildly attractive man who stood before her. He broke the spell by grabbing his hat and putting it on. She picked up her small white purse and followed him outside. Shutting the front door, he took her hand into his. His glance was questioning, and she didn't try to curb her happy grin. His expression relaxed as he opened the drivers' door of the pickup. Joey was already there, sitting by the window.

The sedan was coming down the driveway. It stopped alongside the truck. "Good party," Ben said, getting out and scooping Mollie into his arms.

"I had fun," she said.

Carly went over and took her from Ben. "I'm glad, honey. I bet you were the prettiest girl there in your new outfit." She gave Mollie a big hug and a smacking kiss on her cheek, making the little girl giggle. "See you in the morning," Carly said, handing her back to Ben.

"He liked the food best," Rosa teased him; she came around the car to pat his belly.

"And you liked the dancing," he countered. "You were so durned busy it was all I could do to partner you. A mature woman oughta act more settled." The last comment came out as a grumble.

Rosa laughed self-consciously. "Everyone was having a great time," she said to the other three. "You all will, too."

"Thanks for taking Mollie. See you later," Carly said. She turned and Sage helped her into the truck.

"You look great," she said to Joey, admiring his plaid shirt and bolero tie as she slid in next to him. "I bet you'll be danced off your feet."

Joey's fair complexion beneath his tan Stetson turned a bright shade of red. "Th-thanks," he replied. "You look real pretty, too."

She fastened her seat belt and Sage started the engine. When he shifted gears, the bracelet she had given him caught the late-afternoon sun.

The three of them drove down the highway, while Carly asked Joey about other parties at the Browns'. Pretty soon he was telling them about every amusing and embarrassing incident he could remember. Even Sage chuckled at some of the stories. Finally Carly directed him to turn down the next dirt road.

The Browns' house, an impressive two-storied sprawl of adobe, tile and intricate wrought iron surrounded by tall shade trees and flowering shrubs, was barely visible from the main road. There were cars and pickup trucks parked everywhere, and Carly could hear the music before Sage opened his door.

"Sounds like it's in full swing," Joey commented. "I'll see you both later." He headed toward a group of young men playing horsehoes.

"Come on," Carly told Sage. "I'll introduce you to Bud and Maxine, and then we can get something to eat."

Sage looked at her, his expression unreadable. "I still don't know how you talked me into this," he muttered, but she linked her arm through his and pulled him toward the massive double doors of the house. They were standing open and there was a crowd inside.

For a moment Carly wondered if Sage could be nervous about the party, then she dismissed the thought. He'd been to shows and sales. He'd also undoubtedly been to plenty of social gatherings with other horse people.

When she introduced him to their host and his wife, Bud Brown shook Sage's hand and invited him to help himself to food and drink. Carly paused to exchange a few words with Maxine and another woman she knew. When she finally turned to look for Sage, he was filling his plate from the groaning buffet table. An attractive brunette who looked vaguely familiar to Carly was at his side, pointing to the various dishes as she talked to him.

Withstanding the urge to rush over, Carly helped herself instead to a glass of wine and joined another group that was discussing an upcoming quarter horse show in San Antonio.

"Carly!" exclaimed one of the men. "It's good to see you. How are things going at the ranch?"

She smiled. "Nice to see you, too, Rick. We've been busy, but everything's going well. The ranch is for sale, in case you hadn't heard, but we've got some promising yearlings, if you're in the market."

"I'm not surprised to hear you're selling, since you live in Houston," said one of the women, Angela McKenna. "What I want to know is who's that hunk you came in with."

One of the men groaned.

"You mean Sage Edwards." Carly forced a smile to her lips. "He's a trainer from Oklahoma."

"Mmm. I hope they play a ladies' choice later."

Carly was shocked by the possessiveness that raged through her at Angela's remark. She had known that Sage would command some interest and thought herself prepared for it. Obviously she had been wrong.

"He's an excellent horse trainer, but I don't know about his dancing skills," she said lightly. "You'll have to find that out for yourself."

"A pleasure." Angela was almost purring, studying Sage as he went to sit on a bench outside, the brunette still with him, and began to eat.

One of the men in the group observed that Angela already appeared to have competition, but Carly had heard enough. Mumbling something about being hungry, she drifted away.

By the time she had worked her way out back, stopping to talk with several people she hadn't seen since her father's funeral, Sage had finished eating and joined a group shooting arrows at a target placed against a stack of hay bales. The brunette was nowhere around.

Carly was headed in his direction when she overheard one of the men make a loud remark about an Indian having an unfair edge over the competition. She hurried closer.

Another man she didn't recognize looked at Sage, then announced, "Perhaps we should give him a handicap, make him shoot while he's hanging off the side of a running horse." He was holding a drink and his words were slurred.

"Yeah, good idea," chimed in the man who had spoken first. "Can you do that, Indian?"

At the sound of the loud voices, several more people had stopped to stare. Carly could tell by Sage's expression that he was holding on to his temper with difficulty.

"I'll shoot from a horse if you will," he said quietly to the two drunks. "But I'm half-white, so I should also get a shot from here, like you did, too."

A couple of the others chuckled, then Bud Brown stepped forward. "Charlie, Hank," he said, addressing the two cowhands who were giving Sage a bad time, "I've got a new roping horse I just brought back from Arizona. How'd you two like to have a look at 'im?"

The men glanced at each other and quickly agreed, obviously pleased to have their host's attention. He led them away and another man stepped forward, hand extended to Sage.

"Don't mind them," he said. "They never did have any sense. I'm Harry Widdows. Didn't I used to see you around at some of the palomino shows?"

Sage looked at Harry's hand and Carly wondered if he was going to ignore the overture. Then he stepped forward and shook it. "Sage Edwards," he said, glancing at Carly.

She moved closer, content to listen to the conversations that resumed around her while people waited for their turns at the target.

After a few moments, Harry excused himself to look for his wife. Tipping his hat to Carly, he left them. Sage held out his hand and enfolded hers, drawing her closer.

"Is it permissible to go down to the barns?" he asked, his narrowed eyes gleaming. "I'd like to see some of Browns' horses, and I'd love to get you alone for a few minutes."

Carly felt her cheeks coloring at the intensity in his gaze. "I need to get something to eat first." The last thing she wanted was to run into the two drunks who had insulted him. "Would you come with me? I'm sure you could manage a little more, couldn't you?"

If he was disappointed, he hid it well. "I guess. Have to keep my strength up for the dancing later."

"Going to dance with that brunette who was talking your ear off?" Carly asked, then could have bitten back the words.

His brows rose and he grinned. "Jealous?" he murmured, bending closer.

Carly shook her head. "Of course not."

"Liar." His after-shave drifted around her, enveloping her senses.

"I wouldn't admit it if I was," she teased back. "Your ego's big enough as it is."

His grin widened. "Oh, is that right, boss?"

"Why, I'm surprised your hat still fits," she said, trying to look stern. "Is it getting tight?"

He lifted it, then set it back upon his head. "No," he murmured directly into her ear, "but my jeans will be, if you keep looking like you want to take a bite out of me."

"Ooh!" Carly exclaimed. "You are impossible!" She took a plate from the end of the buffet table and began to fill it, hardly paying attention to what she was taking.

Behind her she heard Sage chuckle. "Nothing's impossible when I'm with you," he said softly. "I thought I proved that the other night."

She whirled, almost spilling the contents of her plate. "Shh!" she scolded, glancing around. "Behave yourself."

He rocked back on his heels, watching her appreciatively. "Guess I'll have to if you won't go to the barn with me."

Carly laughed out loud at his disappointed expression. He murmured that he would see her in a little while and went over to greet a breeder she knew by sight. After watching the man grab Sage's hand and clap him on the back like a long-lost buddy, Carly became aware that she was holding up the food line and hastily resumed filling her plate. Then she got another glass of wine and joined some women she knew at one of the tables scattered across the neatly trimmed lawn.

By the time she had finished eating and visiting, the sunlight was rapidly disappearing. Some of Bud's men had begun to light the hanging lanterns when Sage reappeared at her side.

"I didn't mean to stay away for so long. We got to talking about training techniques and the time got away from me."

"No problem," she said, smiling. "I've been renewing high school acquaintances." She didn't add that most of her friends had families of their own now. "Did you run into someone you know?"

"Yeah. And I met a few more." He glanced toward the huge deck, where the band had just resumed playing and several couples were already dancing.

"Would you care to give it a try?"

Carly couldn't resist a teasing remark. "Mollie assures me that you know how to dance, so I assume my toes are safe with you."

He took her hand and walked up the steps. "Sweetheart you're always safe with me," he murmured as she stepped into his arms. "Just as safe as you want to be."

Carly wasn't sure what to say and was relieved when the band abruptly swung into a faster tune. She matched her steps to Sage's as if they'd danced together for years, reveling in the envious glances they were getting from some of the others.

"I need a breather!" she gasped when the music finally slowed to a sentimental waltz.

Sage's hand tightened on hers. "Not just yet." His eyes had grown dark, and he gently pulled her closer. His gaze burned her, then he tucked her close as if she were the most precious thing in his life. Tears stung Carly's closed lids, and she allowed herself to wish for a moment that it was true. Then she let the music flow over her, determined to put aside unhappy thoughts and enjoy every minute in his arms.

It was getting late and the crowd was finally thinning when Joey came up to them. They were enjoying one last dance.

"I got a ride home," he said. Carly glanced at the girl nestled in the crook of his arm. She had long, honey-brown hair and eyelashes that were almost too thick to be real. "See you later."

Carly resisted the urge to make a teasing remark, knowing it would embarrass him too much. "Okay," she said instead. "See you later."

As Joey and his friend moved away, Sage looked into Carly's eyes. "Let's get out of here."

She nodded, suddenly too full of unfulfilled desire to speak. In minutes they'd said goodbye to their hosts and were traveling back down the highway in the pickup, Carly tucked against Sage's side, while one of his hands curled possessively around her knee.

He could still smell her perfume in the confines of the cab, and had to struggle to keep his passionate need of her under control until they got back to the ranch. Dancing had been both a thrill and a trial. He had absorbed every laughing glance she'd bestowed upon him, almost bursting with pride that she was so obviously pleased to be with him, while still trying not to embarrass himself by revealing his overwhelming physical response. Now his body felt as if he had been waiting for her forever.

"Did you have fun?" she asked in a low voice, resting her hand upon his thigh.

His muscles tensed instantly at her touch, but her fingers continued to idly stroke the soft denim covering his quivering skin until he thought he would explode.

"Yes," he managed in a strangled voice. "It was a good party."

"It was fun catching up on everyone's news." She slid her hand the length of his thigh, stopping at his knee, then traced the outside seam of his jeans back toward his hip.

He gritted his teeth. Did she realize what she was doing to him? "One more thing you'll leave behind if you sell the ranch," he commented.

Her hand froze. "Not still trying to talk me out of it, are you?"

"If I can't, you're going to have to tell Mollie about your plans pretty soon. How else can you explain to her the potential buyers who'll be poking into everything?" He couldn't keep a trace of bitterness from his voice. She had everything he had worked so hard to achieve and then lost, and was throwing it away. How he wished he knew more about his heritage, even his father's name—things she took for granted.

Carly removed her hand from his leg. "I'll take care of Mollie," she said, her tone warning him off as clearly as a No Trespassing sign would. "I know that I'm doing the right thing."

He wondered whom she was trying to convince, him or herself. Why did he keep on when he knew he was destroying the mood that had been building between them all evening?

"You'll break Mollie's heart," he said stubbornly.

"She's a little girl. She'll get over it."

"And what about you?" he persisted. "How will you get over it when you realize what you've done?" He turned down the road to the ranch, aware she had shifted her body slightly away from his. He felt the sudden chill of being without her.

"Don't worry about me," Carly said, sliding still farther away from him. "You just don't understand."

Frustration washed over Sage like an icy wave. He was losing Carly as surely as if she had already sold up and returned to Houston. He could feel it.

"Tell Mollie soon—" he ground out the words "—or, by God, I'll tell her your plans myself. She deserves to be prepared before she sees her belongings thrown into a moving van."

He slowed the truck at the front of the large white ranch house, and Carly turned toward him. "Stay out of it," she hissed. "It's *my* ranch and *my* sister. I'll handle *my* business in my own way."

He stared at her in the darkness, wishing there was some way to call back the earlier sense of oneness he had felt with her. "I wish we could work this out," he began.

"No, you don't," Carly retorted. "You only wish I'd do what you want. God knows why you care. I suppose it's just the old male instinct to be in charge and have everyone doing what you say."

"That's unfair!" No one could make him as angry, as quickly, as Carly could.

"Unfair?" she shot back. "Think about it. You don't want me in your life, but you don't want me to have the life of my own that I've chosen, either." She opened the passenger door. "Thanks for the ride home." She slid out and shut the door softly behind her.

Sage shifted gears; the gravel spat beneath his tires, and he uttered a stream of curses under his breath. Damn, but she was right. And, much as the truth hurt, there wasn't one damn thing he could do to change it. Even if he wanted to, he had nothing to offer her but a broken-down ranch that might or might not become successful again. She didn't even want the prosperous ranch she had.

He was beginning to sense that life without her would be no life at all, but knew he would rather be condemned to a hell of loneliness for all eternity than go to her with nothing at all to offer but himself and his broken-down dreams.

Chapter Ten

Carly hadn't told Sage anything about the real estate agent coming out the next morning. It would have only given him one more thing to object to.

"Good morning, Sam," she said, greeting the older man at the front door. "Come on into the office and I'll have Rosa bring us some coffee."

Later, when Sam had gotten the additional information he needed, they discussed a couple of other spreads that had sold recently. Carly had been surprised and pleased at the amount Sam thought he could get for Rolling Gold. After the bills were paid, there would be more than enough left to buy a house in Houston and set up a college fund for Mollie.

"Of course, the stock will have been sold at auction," he added. "And the equipment."

"Do you think the sale of the ranch will take long?"

He scratched his chin. "Ordinarily it might. This is a pretty big property. But I just heard of a man who's looking for something like this. I'll give him a call."

Carly sat back in her chair. "That would be great. The sooner we sell the ranch, the sooner Mollie and I can move back to Houston and get settled."

"You can't sell the ranch! I don't want to move to Houston! I want to stay here!"

Carly hadn't noticed that Rosa had left the door ajar when she'd brought the coffee tray. Now Mollie stood in the doorway with tears rolling down her flushed, round cheeks.

"I want to stay here!" she cried. "With Polka Dot and Sage and Rosa!"

Carly rose from her chair, sick with dismay. She had not wanted Mollie to find out this way! Sam's expression showed discomfort and a grim disapproval.

"Mollie, honey," Carly began earnestly, "listen to me." She had to make her sister understand that what she was doing was the best thing for both of them.

Mollie stamped her foot in a rare display of temper. "I won't listen! You can't sell the ranch! I won't let you!"

"Baby, let me explain." Carly felt smothered with regret and guilt; Mollie was very upset.

Mollie clapped her hands over her ears. "I can't hear you!" she cried. Before Carly could reach her, she turned and fled, her sobs echoing down the hallway behind her.

Carly turned to Sam, spreading her hands helplessly. "I'm sorry about this. If we're all done for now, I'd better find my half sister and calm her down."

Sam was still frowning. Carly's spine stiffened. She had handled things the best way she could.

"I'll call you in a few days," Sam said. "After I've talked to the gentleman I mentioned. Meanwhile, I hope you can sort things out around here."

He shook Carly's hand and she showed him to the door, thanking him again, then shutting it behind him. Then she leaned against it, pushed her hair off her forehead and took a deep breath. Her hands were shaking.

She hadn't meant Mollie to find out this way. She had pictured the two of them settled on the couch together while she told Mollie of the wonders they would see in Houston and the fun the child would have going to the local school and making lots of new friends. Instead, Carly now had to find the unhappy four-year-old and try to explain the best she could.

Mollie was nowhere to be found in the house. Carly walked toward the barns, her full skirt swishing around her legs and her flat sandals slapping against the hard-packed earth. Deep in thought, she glanced up and saw Sage coming down the driveway. His expression was thunderous, and Mollie was clinging to his hand. Carly could see that she was still crying.

"We need to talk," Sage said as soon as he was close enough for Carly to hear him. "But first there's something you have to discuss with your sister. You've got some explaining to do."

Carly gazed at Mollie, her heart aching for the pain she had inadvertently caused the little girl. "Of course I intend to talk to Mollie," she said defensively. "But I don't see what you and I have to discuss."

For a moment Sage's eyes burned with an angry light, then his face went blank as it always did when he wanted to hide what he was feeling. Carly felt a twinge of regret for hurting him, too, then quickly reassured herself. He just wanted yet another opportunity to try to force his will on her. Because he had lost his own ranch under such tragic circumstances, he refused to understand that she was doing the right thing in selling hers. She had to remind herself that his lack of understanding was a problem he would have to deal with.

Mollie sniffed loudly, and Carly's attention was drawn back to her. "Come on, punkin. You and I need to talk."

"I don't want to talk to you!" Mollie burst out. "I hate you!" She wrenched loose from Sage's hand and began to run toward the house.

Carly was stunned by the child's vehemence. She had had no idea that Mollie would be so deeply affected by the news.

"You look surprised," Sage said dryly. "What did you expect she'd do when she found out? What would you have done at her age, looked forward to being uprooted from everything you knew?"

Carly opened her mouth to protest, then it dawned on her that Sage was right. She *would* probably have reacted the same way Mollie had.

"I suppose you're glad she's been upset by all this," she said to Sage without thinking.

His eyes narrowed, their expression so cold Carly almost shivered from the chill. "I never wanted to see her hurt," he replied in a soft voice. "If you thought that, you don't know me at all. And I wonder if I really know you, seeing what you're willing to put Mollie through for your own selfish reasons."

Before Carly could protest, he turned on his heel and stalked off, back and shoulders stiff with anger. She glanced in the direction of the house, feeling as if she had been attacked from all sides. But before she could deal with Sage and his accusations, she had to find Mollie and comfort her.

Mollie was huddled on the floor of her closet, a place Rosa said she had often retreated to during the first days after the plane crash. Finding her there, Carly flushed guiltily, abruptly aware that Mollie hadn't fled to her private spot for weeks—until today.

Carly squatted so as to be on a level with the child, who was still crying softly. "Come out, honey, so I can explain things to you."

"No!" Mollie slid farther back, beneath the row of hanging clothes. "Go away. I want my mommy."

Sighing with resignation, Carly sank onto the rose-colored carpet, crossing her legs and rearranging her skirt. "I know you miss her, baby. I miss them, too. Sometimes our lives change in big ways, and we have to learn to accept them. It's one of the hardest parts of growing up."

Mollie watched her in silence.

Carly wondered what else to say, then began her argument by painting a tempting picture of Houston and all its attractions. For a few moments she thought she was making progress.

"Would we have horses?" Mollie asked when Carly stopped for breath.

"Well, not at our house or apartment, but we could board a couple somewhere, I suppose. Then we could ride on weekends."

Mollie looked less than impressed. "Would Rosa live with us?"

"I think Rosa wants to retire. We'd do our own cooking."

Mollie thought a moment, her brow furrowed. "Would Sage come to visit us in Houston?"

There was no way around that one. "I don't think so, punkin. He'd have gone back to his own ranch in Oklahoma by then. Broken Arrow is pretty far away from Houston."

Fresh tears poured down Mollie's face. "What would I do all day if I couldn't see Sage or Rosa and we didn't have horses?"

Carly pasted what she hoped was an encouraging smile onto her face. "Why you'd be in preschool during the day, with lots of other children, while I was at work. And in the evening . . ."

"I don't want to go to school," Mollie said stubbornly. "And I don't want to move to Houston. *I'm* going to stay here, with Sage and Ben and Rosa."

Carly eyed the determined expression on her sister's face and decided she was getting nowhere. Perhaps the best thing to do would be to drop the subject for a while.

"Well," she said, rising to her feet, then bending to peer into the closet, "I think I smelled cookies baking on the way up here. I bet that Rosa would give you a couple with a glass of milk, if we asked her real nice." She held out her hand. "Want to see?"

For a moment she thought Mollie was going to refuse, but then the little girl scrambled out of the closet, wiping her cheeks with her fingers. She didn't take Carly's hand, but she did follow her down the stairs.

After Carly had settled her at the kitchen table, explaining briefly to Rosa what had happened, she set out once again for the barns. If Sage wanted to talk, she would oblige him. And if he expected her to shut up and listen without talking back, he had a surprise coming. Carly was in no mood to listen.

She'd had enough of listening to him insist that she would have regrets later on. The way she felt right now, her only regret would be that she had met him and been foolish enough to fall in love. Why couldn't she have given her heart to someone in Houston, a city boy with a business degree and a promising career, one who wanted nothing more than a house in the suburbs, a wife and 2.3 children?

Instead she had fallen for a renegade with more foolish, touchy pride than sense, an absolutely unwavering idea of his destiny, and the ability to turn her heart to mush and her body to an inferno of desire without even touching her.

Carly stomped into the barn with fire in her heart, spoiling for a confrontation that would release some of the pent-up guilt, anger and doubt that had been building since she had first heard Mollie's heartbroken wail. She looked around slowly. Except for several horses, the barn was empty. She was about to stalk off to the other barn when she heard a thump and a muttered curse in a little-used corner storeroom.

She walked over and flung open the door.

"What are you doing in here?"

At the sound of her voice, Sage turned slowly from the file cabinet he had been bent over. "What does it look like I'm doing? I'm trying to find some old training records. Ben thought they might be in here." He had straightened and now he was looking down his arrogant nose at Carly.

"You wanted to talk," she said.

For a moment his glittering gaze raked down her body. Then he moved forward and kicked the door shut behind her.

"No," he said. "I'm through talking." He backed her up to the wall, splaying his hands against the wood on either side of her as he leaned close.

Carly was well and truly cornered. His anger fueled her own, and any sense of caution she might have had went up in smoke. Raising her chin, she poked her finger into his chest.

"You wanted to talk, big man, so I'm here to talk. It's about time someone gave you a piece—"

"I would never want to see Mollie hurt," he interrupted. "And you ought to know better."

Arrogant male. Didn't he understand anything?

"Of course I know that!" Carly was fuming by now. "If you would have let me, I was going to apologize for saying what I did. I lost my temper and I'm sorry." Suddenly she knew without question that he would never hurt either of them, not intentionally, no matter how angry he was. Before she could say as much, Sage wrapped his fingers around her chin, forcing her to look deep into his eyes.

"You make me crazy," he growled. "Ever since I first came here and saw you fighting that fool horse, you've driven away any shred of sanity I ever had."

"I did?" she asked foolishly.

He snaked his other arm around her waist and yanked her close, hand splayed possessively against her hip. His arousal pressed into her stomach, and his narrowed gaze searched her face. The air in the closed room was suddenly stifling, almost too heavy for Carly to breathe.

"I can't get enough of you." His tone was fierce, accusing. "Half the time I walk around so hard I think I'll die from it." His fingers tightened on her jaw. "You've spoiled me for any other woman. What the hell am I supposed to do now?"

"I, uh, don't know," Carly muttered, dazed by the emotion that was pouring out of him.

"Well, I sure as hell do." He reached over and dropped the latch on the door, locking them in. Then he tipped her head back, still holding her jaw, and covered her mouth with a kiss so hot she thought she would burst into flames right there in his arms.

Her hands grabbed at him in an effort to keep from falling, and her lips parted for the thrust of his tongue. His hips pinned her to the wall, while his marauding mouth took everything she had to offer and gave back even more.

Carly's head began to spin, and her lungs were threatening to burst. She felt feverish, shaky, disoriented, and any rational thought she had come into the storage room with was completely gone, as if it had never existed. Looming over her, Sage groaned deep in his throat, held her hips with his hands and moved against her. Then he grew still and dipped his head, looking into her eyes. His own had gone dark, accentuating the raw passion she could see in his face. The room was silent except for the sound of their tortured breathing.

"I want you," his voice rasped in her ear. "Now."

All Carly could do was nod. She arched against him, crushing her breasts to his chest, wild for the feel of his hard body against hers. This was the man she loved, the man she needed above all else.

Uttering another groan, Sage bent and slid his hands up her bare legs beneath her full skirt. She thrust her head back as his fingers dipped beneath her panties, caressing her intimately. Love and passion and the urge to become one with him were all swirling within her.

Sage released her, and she clung to his shoulders, legs trembling. She heard the clink of his heavy buckle, then the sound of his zipper. Before she could suck in a breath, his hands had pushed aside her skirt and pulled off her panties. Then he cupped her bare buttocks, lifting her. She clutched his shoulders and wrapped her legs around his hips. When he thrust into her, shoving her hard against the wall, Carly almost cried out her welcome. Her legs held him tighter, her arms locked around his neck, and she buried her head into his shoulder.

He surged again, straining, and she shuddered. Once more; now her sensitive flesh was quivering around him, her pleasure so intense she was biting her lip to keep from sobbing. Another thrust, deeper yet, and she felt the explosion of his release. His hoarse cry sent her over the edge, and she followed him into oblivion.

For long moments there was nothing in the room but the sound of their ragged breathing and the scent of heat and sex. Then Sage moved back and lowered her slowly to her feet.

"Can you stand?"

She nodded, even though her legs felt like rubber. One by one she forced her fingers to uncurl from his shoulders.

He smoothed down her skirt and turned away to rearrange his jeans. "Did I hurt you?" His voice was gruff.

Carly moistened her swollen lips. "Hurt me?" she echoed. "You could never do that."

Slowly he turned to face her, his expression unreadable in the light from the bare bulb overhead. "I..." He stopped and raked a hand over his face, muttering something. It sounded like, "I don't have the right," but Carly couldn't be sure.

Words of love rose to her own lips and died there. They were better left unsaid.

"I care about you," he said finally. "Believe it. I'm sorry for all the hurts you suffered here, and I hope that whatever you decide, it's right for both of you." Their gazes met and held for a timeless moment. There was so much she wanted to say, wanted to ask him. Then he pushed past her and unlatched the door. Before she could speak, he was gone.

Sage and Ben left the next morning with the pickup and the big horse trailer for a palomino show in Austin. Carly might have gone with them, but Sam Ferguson had called with the news that his client was definitely interested in seeing Rolling Gold. They came while Ben and Sage were gone, and the client, Rod Silverthorne from Denver, seemed to like everything he saw.

"I've got Arabians," he told Carly as they walked from one barn to the other. "My place is getting too small, and we've always wanted to live in Texas." He glanced around, grinning. "Can't wait to see my Arabs filling those stalls and paddocks. They'll give the place some real class."

He pointed while Carly choked on an imprudent response. "I'll put another barn right over there. Paint all the buildings blue, with white trim, just like my place now." Then he chuckled and gave Sam a playful push. "First you have to get the little lady here to accept my offer."

Carly and Sam exchanged glances, and Carly knew her smile was forced. The house and barns had been white as long as she could remember, were even now newly painted. It would be strange to think of the ranch without her father's palominos. Of course, it would no longer be Rolling Gold, either. Silverthorne had already told Carly that if he bought it, the first thing he was going to do was erect a big sign at the main road, Silverthorne Arabians.

After the men left, Sam promising to return with a written offer, Carly went inside and wandered into her father's office. During his inspection of the house, the potential buyer had commented that his wife would want the interior gutted so she could start over. She liked chrome and glass and modern art. Carly looked at the paneled walls and reminded herself briskly that the new owners would naturally make changes.

It had not occurred to her before that she would never be able to come back once she had sold the ranch, but she understood now that it would be too painful to see the changes a new owner would make. She would have to say her goodbyes when she left. The ranch, her father and her childhood would be well and truly behind her, with no going back.

There were still a couple of personal files in the office that she hadn't gone through. Pulling out the folders, she found a fat, unmarked one full of newspaper clippings and other papers. Opening it, she saw that the clippings were all articles about the horse shows and junior rodeos she had entered as a girl. Surprised that her father had cared enough to save them, she glanced at several of the write-ups. She had done better than she remembered, though it had never seemed good enough for her father's expectations at the time.

Under the clippings were copies of her report cards and progress reports, along with school pictures from kindergarten all the way through her high school graduation. There was a postcard she had sent from camp one year, along with birthday cards she'd made for him when she was little. Carly's finger traced over the drawing of a strange-looking animal she remembered was supposed to have been a horse. She had made it for him when she was five or six. And he had saved it. Now her gaze roamed the far wall of the office without really focusing.

He had cared. He had even been proud of her. Though he'd never found the words to tell her while he lived, he was telling her now. Tears filled Carly's eyes and a great weight shifted.

She sifted through the papers in the folder again. At the very back of the pile was a letter, unsigned and apparently unfinished. Recognizing her father's handwriting, she started to read.

Dear Carly, I'm writing this down because I can never seem to put my feelings into words.

She stopped for a moment. He had never written her since she'd moved to Houston. Susan had written or he had telephoned. She looked at the letter again, smoothing it out with a hand that was not quite steady.

He went on to say that he wished he could have told her more often how much he loved her. He mentioned his own parents, who had died before Carly was born. They'd been hardworking and undemonstrative, even though he'd known they cared for him in their own way. That was no excuse, he wrote, but he wanted her to understand and not to make the mistakes he had. He still hoped that someday she would return home to work the ranch with him.

The writing stopped at that point. Carly tucked the letter carefully into the folder before dropping the whole thing back into the file drawer. She went outside, walking quickly past the outbuildings and down to the spot by the stream where she had met Sage that evening. There she sat down on the bench and stared at the slow-moving water, thinking about the ranch that had meant so much to her father.

She didn't realize she was crying until she felt a tear drip from her chin onto her bare throat. Had he somehow had a premonition of his death? Or had some deep frustration moved him to commit to paper what he could not say aloud? She would never know why he had written that letter. Or why it had never been sent.

But now she did have a good idea why he had neglected the ranch during the last two years of his life. It had been about that long ago when she had finally made him believe over lunch in Houston that she loved her life there and was never coming home to stay. That day she had seen herself as independent and strong-willed, but now she felt only a sharp ache at the memory of her father's expression when he'd left her.

Fresh pain assaulted her senses. How she wished she'd had just one more chance to see him, to talk to him! To tell him that she understood. If only he could have known how much she did love the ranch, the horses, the land. If only there'd been some way to tell him that she loved *him,* too. Maybe he had needed the words as badly as she had.

She looked around again; the sun warmed her face and a breeze touched her hair. An idea was forming. She began walking slowly back to the house. Joey shouted a greeting, but she only waved absently, deep in thought. When she went back inside, she was drawn again to the office, where her father had spent most of his time when he wasn't with his beloved horses.

Carly crossed to the massive executive chair and sank into it, the scents of after-shave and pipe tobacco rising faintly around her as the worn leather creaked beneath her. Her hand reached out to trace the embossed border of the desk pad she had given him for Christmas one year. Of course there was still a way to show him how she felt, perhaps the best way of all.

Taking a deep breath, Carly became painfully aware of the magnitude of what she was considering and its far-reaching effects. She could show him how much she loved him and the legacy he had left her by keeping it, by working the ranch and breeding the horses, by raising Mollie here and showering her with all the love their father would have wanted her to have.

Carly expected to feel overwhelmed by the idea of such a drastic change of plans, but instead a sense of peace stole over her; maybe she was headed in the right direction now.

Now she could admit, if only to herself, that she had not really been anticipating her return to Houston, to the noise and the crowds, to the deadlines and pressures of her job. To the apartment she shared with Donna, one small cell in a gigantic beehive. She would miss her roommate, but maybe Donna would come to the ranch for a visit. Carly's other friendships in the city had been shallow ones; perhaps she had always subconsciously held back part of herself, she reflected wryly.

If she had been of a fanciful turn of mind, she might have imagined her father standing at her shoulder, his expression finally approving as he drew on his pipe. Since she wasn't, she merely smiled to herself, knowing in her heart that wherever he was, he was pleased.

"I'm sorry to be giving you the news over the phone, Mr. Bass, but things have changed here." Carly listened to her former boss's deep voice; he was complaining about making do with a temporary assistant when he could have been looking for a permanent replacement.

"I know you've been more than reasonable and I'm very grateful for your understanding. If I had realized it at the time, I would certainly have told you right away."

While his voice droned, she looked outside, watching several of the broodmares and their offspring graze in the nearby pasture.

"Oh, I won't change my mind again. I'm sure this time."

He made a sound of disbelief, then raised another point.

"Yes, I suppose that's the least I can do," she agreed reluctantly. "If you want me to come in for a day or two, I will. I need to pick up my things, anyway."

She drummed her fingers on the table while Mr. Bass complained again about the inconvenience she had caused.

"I can't tell you enough how considerate you've been," she said when he began to run down. "I'll be glad to come in the first of the week and take care of any loose ends I can. I'm sure Lisa will be pleased to accept the position permanently."

From the dining room she could hear the others gathering for lunch. "I'll see you on Monday, then. Thank you again. Goodbye."

She replaced the receiver, and the realization that she had taken an irreversible step washed over her. Burned her bridges for sure, her father would have said.

She had already told Donna of her decision to stay at the ranch before speaking to Mr. Bass, offering to pay her share of the apartment expenses until her friend could find a new roommate. Carly was cutting the ties to her old life as surely as if she had severed them with a knife. The next person she had to call was Sam Ferguson. He'd have every reason to be angry with her over the fat commission he would lose.

She decided not to mention her decision to anyone at the ranch until Sage and Ben were back from Austin. It was hard not to tell Mollie, who was still very upset over the idea of moving, but the little girl would never be able to keep the news to herself.

Carly wanted to see Sage's reaction with her own eyes. Hugging herself, she wondered if her decision might affect his own plans, but knew she would have to wait two more days to find out.

* * *

Before she tried to call Sam that afternoon, Sam surprised her with a visit. Carly was dismayed to see that he'd brought Rod Silverthorne with him.

"I hope we aren't intruding," Sam said when she let them in. "Rod's flying back to Denver and he remembered a couple of things he wanted to check on first."

"Okay if I leave you two to thrash out the paperwork while I take another look around?" the prospective buyer asked, pumping Carly's hand enthusiastically.

She glanced at Sam. This was going to be terribly awkward.

"Actually I was going to call you this afternoon," she told him. Then she cleared her throat, trying to dislodge some of the embarrassment that felt as if it had settled there like a wad of cotton. "I've decided not to sell."

Her announcement was met with stunned silence. She sneaked another, guilty look at Sam, her father's old friend. He didn't look that displeased. Silverthorne, on the other hand, had flushed a dusky red and was beginning to sputter.

"What kind of nonsense is this? I've wasted valuable time here when I could have been looking at other places. You *have* to sell to me!"

Carly looked at Sam for guidance.

"No, actually she doesn't," he said blandly. "I'm sorry for the inconvenience, but if Miss Golden is sure about changing her mind, I suggest there's nothing much for us to do but leave." He looked at Carly and his wrinkled face softened. "I take it you've decided to stay?"

She nodded. "I can't allow my father's legacy to be dismantled and sold piece by piece. Not when I love it here so much myself."

Rod Silverthorne uttered a snort of displeasure.

Sam clapped a hand upon her shoulder. "We'll talk later," he said, smiling.

"I'm going to sue that young lady," Silverthorne boomed as he followed Sam down the front steps.

"Believe me, you have no grounds," Carly heard Sam say while they walked to his car. "Besides, I just heard of a lovely spread south of Dallas that I'd like to show you before your flight back to Denver. I'll call the owner on my car phone and see if I can set it up."

Carly watched Sam's Lincoln pull away. She hoped the angry horse breeder would find a new property and forget his anger.

The day that Ben and Sage were due back, Carly found herself going to the front porch repeatedly to stare down the highway, searching for a glimpse of the truck and trailer. When she was inside the house, her ears were straining for any sounds of their arrival. By the middle of the afternoon she was as jumpy as a cat in a roomfull of balloons, and she hadn't gotten one thing accomplished.

After she'd managed to get into a minor argument with Rosa over what they were having for dinner, and to scold Mollie with unjustified impatience for watching too much television, Carly decided that a ride on Dancer might soothe her jangled nerves. She invited Mollie to go with her on Polka Dot, but after a moment her sister frowned and shook her head wistfully.

"No, thank you." Mollie's very politeness was a reminder that Carly was not yet forgiven.

Carly changed her clothes and walked to the barn. Saddling up Dancer, she told Joey where she was going.

"When they gonna get here?" he asked, peering down the driveway.

"That's what I'd like to know!" She mounted and urged Dancer into a trot, heading toward her favorite path along the river.

Sometime later, when she had finally slowed her mount and turned his head back toward home, she saw a tall, dark rider approaching at a fast pace. No one else sat a horse like Sage. Carly's pulse rate quickened and she urged Dancer forward, eager to tell him her news and to share an idea that could affect both their lives.

What would his reaction be when she offered him a permanent position at Rolling Gold?

Chapter Eleven

Sage watched Carly kick her mount into a gallop, and his body tightened at the sight of her as they raced toward each other. Her hat had come off her head, tethered only by the strap; her hair flowed behind her like a golden banner. He had missed her; the excitement of being back at a horse show hadn't come close to the way he felt when he was with Carly. Of course, that would all change when it was *his* horses he was showing.

They both came to a halt, and Sage pulled up his mount alongside hers. His arms went around her and she kicked her stirrups loose, dropping the reins to ground-tie Dancer. Sage's horse sidestepped when he felt Carly's extra weight, but Sage controlled him with his knees.

She was barely settled in front of him when he covered her mouth with his own, starving for the taste of her. Carly's response was everything he remembered. His arms tightened and his heart slammed against his chest. She moaned a greeting and then her lips parted, welcoming him. Her hands were in his hair. One of his anchored her against him, the other cupped her breast. Beneath his fingers her nipple beaded.

Sage lifted his mouth and gazed deep into her eyes. "I missed you." His voice was raw with unspoken feelings. Things he didn't dare say.

Carly traced her finger down his cheek. "I missed you, too."

He wasn't ready to let her go and talk about the horse show. Instead he lowered her to the ground and dismounted quickly. She seemed content to stand in the circle of his arms, while his gaze roamed her face from her glowing eyes to her soft lips. He bent his head again, gathering her close to his body that was throbbing with need. He was about to draw her down to the soft grass when her hands tightened on his shoulders.

"We have to talk!" She was smiling.

What could be so important? Then it hit him. She had sold the ranch while he was gone and couldn't wait to tell him. Sage felt as if he'd taken a hard punch to the gut. Releasing her, he turned away. He would have to let her go now; there was no other way. Gathering his control around him like a protective cloak, he faced her again.

"About what?" His voice was rough.

To his surprise, Carly didn't answer immediately. She was still smiling, but now lines of worry marred her forehead. As she turned to study their horses, grazing close by, one hand went to the horseshoe pendant he had given her. Then she looked full into Sage's face and he braced himself for the bad news.

"I'm keeping the ranch, not selling it. I want you to stay on as my trainer."

It took Sage a moment to take in what she had said. To absorb the meaning of her words. It was probably the last thing he had expected to hear. "You haven't sold the ranch?" he repeated, just to be sure.

She tossed her head, eyes sparkling. "Never."

"You're staying? You aren't going back to Houston, after all?"

"I'm staying forever." She threw out her hands expansively. When he kept staring, her grin wavered. "How about you? Will you stay, too? Will you help me with the horses?"

The meaning of what she was asking hit him with the resounding sting of a hard slap. He had never thought it through when he'd pictured her living at the ranch instead of in Houston. He'd only wanted to have her nearer, to know that she and Mollie were safe and happy on land of their own. Now she had made the choice he wanted her to, but she expected him to remain here with her.

"Why?" he asked, still dazed by her unexpected announcement. "What changed your mind? You really aren't going back to your fancy life?" Had she lost her job?

Carly looked impatient; it was as if she didn't want to answer his questions, but wanted *his* answer instead.

"I saw the light," she quipped, then shook her head, folding her arms across her chest and gazing out over the land. "No, it wasn't that simple. I guess I finally realized that in fighting my father's plans for me I was fighting myself." She swung around in a half circle. "And I couldn't bear to let this all go, to see his life's work erased as if it had never existed." There were tears in her voice, and Sage reached to comfort her.

"No," she said, holding up a detaining hand and stepping back. "I'm okay with this. I feel good about it. What I want to know now is, what are *you* going to do?"

She was waiting, and there was no more dodging the question. Sage looked at her with all the love and longing he had come to feel for her. And gave the only answer he could.

"I'm going home," he said. "Now that you've decided to stay for good, you'll want to start looking for someone permanent. I can give you a little more time here, but I've got a life of my own that needs getting back to."

For one stunned moment Carly stared at him, her eyes wide with pain; he saw the color drain from her face. When she spun around, he thought he saw tears, but couldn't be sure. Quick as his own reflexes were, she was mounted and whirling Dancer away before he could put a hand on her.

In a heartbeat Sage had mounted as well and was after her, riding hard and urging even more speed from the horse flying beneath him. By the time he'd caught up with Dancer and snagged the horse's reins, Carly had gone from shock to fury.

"Let me go!" she cried, almost spitting the words at him when he pulled her up. "I heard your answer loud and clear."

He knew she was furious because she had allowed him to see her pain. He had pain of his own and no way to relieve it. Frustrated, he lashed out in his turn.

"It wouldn't work!" he shouted. "Don't you know that I couldn't stay here, content to work for you, to crawl into your bed at night and sneak away before the dawn? It would kill me to live like that. It would kill everything we feel for each other."

Renewed hope lighted up her entire face, and her hand clutched at his. "It wouldn't have to be that way," she said quickly, her words tumbling over each other in her visible haste to get them out. "I could make you a partner. We could run the ranch together. If you wanted, we could even—'' She stopped abruptly, hesitating.

He regarded her silently, the impossibility of each of her words striking him like flaming arrows.

"If you want, maybe we could get married," she said softly. "Then the ranch would be yours, as well as mine and Mollie's."

It took every bit of Sage's willpower not to grab with both hands the offer she dangled in front of him. Instead he forced indifference into his voice, though his heart felt as if it had turned to ice.

"And what do I bring to this partnership?" he asked. "My prowess in bed?"

She looked as if he had slapped her, but he forced himself to continue coldly. "You can't buy me with a partnership and a marriage proposal. I couldn't be a man, knowing I was being kept like a pet."

"That's crazy!" Carly's eyes were blazing. "You would be bringing your horses and your skills as a trainer. You wouldn't be coming empty-handed. You have a talent with animals that any breeder would want. Together we can raise wonderful palominos."

He remained silent. He had to stop her before he succumbed to temptation, but the necessity of hurting her was shredding his gut like the talons of a hawk.

Her voice dropped to barely a whisper. "If you love me . . ." she began.

Sage cut her off, hating himself. "That's the problem. If I did, perhaps I could accept all that you want to heap on me like a generous reward to a stud you found pleasing."

Her sharply indrawn breath almost made him stop. He forced himself to go on, to finish it. "As it is, I can't be expected to give up my own life for yours. We had a deal, and if you insist, I'll stick to it. But sooner or later, I'm going back to Broken Arrow, to Comanche Creek. That's where I belong, just as you belong here.'' He had a sudden fear. ''I hope you won't change your mind about staying....''

She raised her chin in the way that almost always made him smile, but he had never felt less like smiling.

''I'm staying,'' she said. ''I'm sorry if I embarrassed you with my offer. I'm sorry if I assumed too much—'' she raked him with her brittle gaze ''—about your feelings. Of course you're free to go whenever you want.'' She stopped and an expression of frustration crossed her face. ''I'll need to find a replacement, if you can give me a little more time, but I promise not to hold you up any longer than necessary.''

Sage could see how much she hated to ask. Undoubtedly she would have taken great pleasure in ordering him off her land at gunpoint. Despite the anguish that was churning inside him, he was glad to see her put the good of the ranch before her own pride.

''Of course,'' he said, wishing he could touch her. ''I'll stay as long as you need me.''

Her nod was brisk. ''Good.'' Before he could speak again, she was riding away.

Carly couldn't have stayed with him another moment. Her composure was cracking like an earthen dike under the pressure of a thousand tons of floodwater. Tears blurred her vision, so she trusted Dancer to find his own way home. If only Sage would just leave her alone until she'd found some way to cover the raw wound his cruel words had ripped open.

She shook her head, hardly able to believe she had assumed he loved her, had gone so far as to offer him marriage. As if she needed to throw herself in to sweeten the deal!

She glanced behind her and slowed Dancer. Sage was no longer in sight, and she needed some time to compose herself. She knew now that she had lost before she started. He couldn't stay with the awkwardness of an affair between them, and he didn't love her, so anything else was out of the question. She couldn't even go with him. He hadn't asked.

Perhaps she should be thankful he'd had the good sense to reject her rash offer. Now all she had to do was to convince herself it was for the best.

Far behind her, Sage allowed his horse to pick its way along the river. He tried to tell himself that he had done the right thing. The only thing. No way could he accept her generosity, taking a partnership in the ranch like a handout, acquiring a wife like a lottery prize, when he hadn't even the price of a ticket.

He'd done what he had to. All that was left was to go back to Oklahoma and try to forget her. Now it was painfully clear that he had been wrong to think he had nothing to give Carly. When he left Texas—and her—behind, he would be leaving his heart.

For the next couple of days Carly managed to talk, to listen to the others making plans to stay on at the ranch, even to smile. If they guessed that all was not quite right with her, they were too polite to comment.

The only bright spot in the darkness was Mollie's renewed happiness. When Carly told her they weren't moving to Houston, after all, the little girl asked a stream of questions before she allowed herself to believe they were really staying.

Her caution showed Carly, as nothing else could have, how deep the hurt would have gone if Mollie had been uprooted from the only life she knew. At least some good had come of the decision to stay. Carly hoped her own life would right itself in time and that she, too, would find, if not real happiness, then perhaps contentment.

Despite her performance in front of the others, she was desperately relieved when it was time to fly to Houston. On the plane she could finally let down her guard and allow the smile she had been wearing like armor to fade. Her tears she refused to release, but thoughts of Sage and his cold words buzzed in her head like angry bees.

How could she have been so wrong about his feelings?

She'd seen little of him since their confrontation at the river. He had become an elusive shadow, as good at avoiding her as she was him. If Rosa wondered why, all of a sudden, neither had time to join the rest of them for meals, she kept her thoughts to herself. Or perhaps she shared them with Ben. Carly didn't much care, as long as she didn't have to answer painful questions.

Mollie finally gave up asking her why Sage was never around anymore, and Carly hadn't the strength to jeopardize her sister's newfound happiness by telling her of her hero's imminent departure.

It was enough for Carly that Rosa, Ben and the others had all agreed to stay on. She had already begun the search for another trainer, but at this time of year, with several important shows coming up, she hadn't much hope of finding one who wasn't committed. If she had to she would just hire another groom and release Sage from their agreement, now that she knew how badly he wanted to go.

The pilot broke into her thoughts when he announced the plane's descent into Houston. Carly was eager to get there and finish what she had to so she could go home again.

While she was in Houston, she wasn't entirely successful in keeping images of Sage at bay, but by the time she got back to Rolling Gold two days later, she had begun the painful adjustment. For now that was all she could hope for.

Late one night after her return to the ranch, something dragged Carly from a deep sleep. She had tossed and turned for hours before finally taking one of the pills she had been given after her father's funeral. Now she forced her eyes open, feeling as if she had been brought up from the depths of a dark hole.

Her first thought upon waking was that Sage had come to her. Then she sat up in bed, fighting her way to full consciousness, and became aware that the sound that had penetrated her slumber came from outside. From one of the barns.

Carly's blood chilled. It was the smoke alarm. Above the harsh blast she could hear the screams of frightened horses.

She was pulling on her jeans even as she dashed to the window. What she saw was terrifying in its intensity. The sleeping pill had kept her under far too long. The barn was lit by a hellish orange glow, flames visible through some of the lower windows. Dark figures were running back and forth, silhouetted in the light from the fire; horses were milling about in two adjacent paddocks. Pausing only to ram her feet into boots, Carly ran for the staircase, stuffing the tail of her nightshirt into her jeans before she fastened them.

At the foot of the stairs she saw Rosa holding a frightened Mollie.

"I was coming to get you," Rosa said. "Fire department's been called. The boys are getting the horses out. Ben said the fire came from several places, hard to fight. I'll stay with Mollie. You tell those boys to be careful."

Carly stopped long enough to give Mollie a quick hug and thank Rosa, then rushed out, absorbing what the housekeeper told her. The fire had started in several places.

Arson!

She sprinted down the driveway to the scene that looked as if it had come straight from the bowels of hell. The fire cast an evil glow upon everything around it. Smoke burned Carly's eyes and filled her nostrils. Even the roaring sound the flames made was frightening.

Tony was leading two horses from the barn. Before Carly could get his attention, he'd turned them into a paddock where several more terrified animals already waited, milling about nervously.

"How many left?" she shouted, grabbing Tony's arm. A wet towel hung around his neck, and his face was streaked with soot.

"Only Sky Walker. Sage went back for him. Thank God it wasn't the broodmare barn. Fire blazed up so fast, we didn't think we'd get them all out."

Carly's heart rose into her throat and stuck there. No animal was worth a man's life. And she would gladly give all that she owned before she would put Sage in danger. She looked through the open double doors to the inferno beyond. Then she took a step forward, but Tony's hand closed around her arm.

"Sorry boss. Harper's in there, too. Sage told me to keep you back when you got down here, or he'd show me some Indian torture tricks when this was all over."

Carly glanced at the police cruiser parked on the other side of the driveway. She hadn't noticed it before.

"Harper was on his way by on the highway when he heard the call," Tony explained. "He pitched right in and brought out several horses himself."

Before Tony could say any more, Ben came over from where he'd been playing a hose upon the leaping flames. He, too, was black with soot, and his shirt was riddled with burn holes from falling debris.

Carly heard a siren in the distance. From the looks of the barn, the fire truck would get here in time for the cleanup.

"Any sign of Harper or Edwards?" Ben asked Tony.

He shook his head. Just then a blindfolded horse burst through the doorway, someone holding tight to his bridle. Though the eerie light played tricks on her perception, Carly knew instantly that it was Sage. She ran toward him.

He turned the terrified horse over to Tony, who hurried him away.

"I just woke up," Carly said. "Are you okay?" She wanted to throw her arms around him, but forced herself not to. It was enough for her that he was still alive.

"I'm okay. You stay away from that barn." For a moment his hand gripped her arm, hard. His eyes were red, his face black. His hair was wet from the towel he'd undoubtedly been holding up against the smoke. The fabric of one sleeve was seared away, the exposed skin an angry red.

"That arm needs attention!" she exclaimed.

"Later. Where's Harper?"

"I didn't see him come out." She glanced around. Headlights were coming down the driveway and red lights flashing; the siren abruptly fell silent. Sage pulled her onto the grass.

"The horses are all safe. Everyone but Harper's out. I'm going back for him." He pulled the wet towel from around his neck and put it over his head, holding the ends across his face.

"No!" Carly clutched at him, terrified. "The firemen are here now. Let them go."

"There's no time!"

For a moment their eyes locked. The message he gave her was wordless, but it went straight to her heart. He was *not* unfeeling about her, despite what he had said. As she absorbed the truth from his glittering eyes, her fingers relaxed their grip and he broke away. Despite her scream of protest, he raced back into the heart of the inferno.

"Stop him!" she cried to the first of the fire fighters who were rushing toward the barn. Others were dragging hose that had been connected to a huge tanker truck.

"How many inside?" demanded one of them.

"One other, I think, besides him!" she shouted above the sounds of the fire. "Please hurry!"

Just as they were about to go in, two blackened figures appeared in the doorway, one half carrying the other. Carly ran toward them.

Sage pulled the semiconscious Grady Harper from the burning ruin and lowered him carefully to the ground.

"This man needs first aid!" he shouted. Immediately several men came over. Sage had barely straightened when Carly flew into his arms.

"You're safe!" she cried. "I was so frightened."

His arms locked tight around her and her feet left the ground; he hugged her close. "So was I, babe, so was I. I was lucky to find him in all the smoke."

Behind them Grady was coughing and trying to sit up, shoving away the oxygen mask that the fireman had put over his face.

"Edwards," he croaked, another fit of coughing racking him.

Sage turned and went to him, still hanging on to Carly. "Yeah?"

Grady stuck out a grimy hand. "You saved my life. Thanks, man."

Sage grasped Grady's hand with his free one. "Thanks for helping out."

Grady's gaze went from Sage to Carly, his smile growing slightly crooked when he glimpsed their clasped hands. "Sorry about your barn."

"There's insurance," she said. "At least the animals got out and no one was seriously hurt. I want to thank you for your help, too."

She glanced again at the angry burn on Sage's arm. It must hurt like the very devil. "Get that taken care of," she told him in a brusque voice. "Or I'll smear ointment on it myself and I won't be gentle."

Sage didn't smile. "Yes, ma'am," he said instead, using the tone they both knew always infuriated her. This time she was too relieved that he was alive. Before she could say anything else, the chief came up and started asking questions.

It was hours before the fire crew was ready to pack up, and the horses from the burned barn were relocated and settled down. Carly had already called the insurance agent, who'd promised to be there first thing that afternoon.

Ben and Sage both insisted that the fire had apparently started in several places and spread rapidly. Although the fire chief was reluctant to confirm anything yet, Carly was sure the blaze had to be arson.

"It's hard to believe that anyone could do such an awful thing," she said to Sage. She was still churning with helpless frustration as the two of them sat behind the house, drinking coffee. Rosa had made several gallons and served it with sandwiches to everyone there. "Deliberately endangering the horses."

Sage stroked the back of her hand, then drained his coffee cup. "I can think of one man with a grudge against this place," he said, expression bleak. He'd cleaned up some, but there were raw places on his dark skin and circles under his bloodshot eyes.

Carly realized that his thoughts must parallel her own. Acknowledging the idea of such blind hatred was difficult for her. "Artie?" she asked.

"Don't you remember how he threatened to get even with you?" For a moment Sage's gaze turned cold.

Carly shook her head sadly. "I'd hoped that was just the booze talking," she said. "But I'm afraid you're probably right." She swallowed, remembering the agony of those moments before Sage and Grady had appeared in the doorway of the barn. She wanted to reach up and touch Sage's face to reassure herself that he was okay, but didn't.

He raked one hand through his hair. "Artie strikes me as a man who's capable of just about anything if he's liquored up enough. He was wild for revenge when I caught him with you."

"I hope somehow that we're wrong," Carly murmured.

"I reminded the sheriff about Artie's visit and his threats. He said he can't do anything without proof, but Grady promised to give the matter his special attention."

Carly yawned widely, covering her mouth with her hand. She had seen Sage and Grady talking before the deputy left. Suddenly she found herself sighing wearily; the excitement and horror of the night had sapped her energy completely.

"Go to bed," Sage told her, rising. "Everything's pretty much under control."

Carly nodded, then walked out to thank the fire fighters, who were loading the last of their hoses back into the remaining truck. Finally, after what seemed like another eternity, everyone scattered, Joey to the broodmare barn, in case the arsonist decided to come back, Ben and Tony heading to the bunkhouse. Carly looked around, but Sage had disappeared, so she went back to the house. After checking on Mollie and thanking Rosa for the coffee and sandwiches, she trudged her way back up the stairs. First a shower and then a nap before the insurance man came.

She was washing the smoke smell from her hair when the shower door was yanked open. Wiping the shampoo from her eyes, she peered at Sage, her gaze drawn to the diagonal scar across his naked torso.

"May I join you?" His voice was husky, his eyes blazing with the need his body could not disguise.

She opened her arms to him, and fresh gratitude for his safety surged through her. Gratitude, love and the passion he always ignited. He joined her beneath the shower's spray, and she pushed aside her doubts as to the wisdom of what she was doing, vowing instead to make the most of what could be their last time together.

Later, as Carly curled against him in her bed, Sage stroked her hair. "I'll stay until the arsonist is caught, or until I'm convinced you're no longer in danger," he said softly.

"I know you care for me," she whispered in reply. "It won't do you any good to deny it."

"Then I won't bother. But it doesn't change a thing. I still can't stay when I have nothing to offer you."

Damn his stubborn male pride! Before she could argue further, he had wrapped his arms around her and fallen asleep. His silver bracelet glowed softly in the moonlight.

Exhausted by the events of the night before and their violent, then tender lovemaking, Carly refused to think about his leaving. Instead she slid one hand across his chest and followed him into the land of dreams.

After the insurance agent's visit that afternoon and his assurance that the loss was completely covered, Carly made arrangements for a new barn to be started as soon as possible. She thanked God that one thing her father had firmly believed in was good insurance protection.

When she had woken earlier, Sage was gone. She had seen him outside from her window, but hadn't had a chance to talk to him.

"Will there be another fire?" Mollie asked from the office doorway. "What if our house burns up?"

Carly pushed her chair back and held out her arms. When Mollie came into them, she hugged the child, then kissed her cheek. "The house isn't going to burn, honey. We have excellent alarms to warn us."

"We had an alarm in the barn, too," Mollie said. "But somebody still burned it down." Apparently she had overheard some of the talk about arson.

"No one was hurt, though, and the horses are all safe," Carly said, giving Mollie another hug. "People and animals are much more important than buildings. But I still don't think you have to worry about the house. All the sheriff's men are looking for anyone who might have started the fire in the barn, and they'll catch him soon."

And then Sage would leave. Her feelings about finding the arsonist were decidedly mixed.

"Okay," Mollie agreed solemnly. "I won't worry."

"Thanks, punkin." Carly wished that she could stop her own worrying as easily.

* * *

While Mollie was in the office with Carly, Ben was talking to Rosa in the kitchen. "He's leaving," he said in a disapproving tone, "as soon as the police catch the guy who torched the barn. He told me himself. How can he leave Carly just like that?"

Rosa set aside the zucchini she was slicing for dinner. "I don't know," she said. "But we have to trust them to do what's right for both of them. Anyone with eyes can see they love each other. It will work out somehow."

Ben uttered a sound of disbelief. "Anyway," he said, moving closer, "now that neither you nor I is retiring anytime soon, I've got a proposition for you."

"A proposition?" Rosa's eyes danced.

"Well," he said, feeling the heat of a blush steal over his cheeks, "let's say a proposal."

"That sounds like something I might be interested in hearing," Rosa said, wiping her hands on her apron.

Ben glanced around to see if anyone could overhear. "I was going to ask you before we left here for our retirement," he resumed nervously. "But that all changed. Now I guess what I'm wondering is if you'd marry me. You've probably known for a long time how I feel about you."

Rosa arched one eyebrow. "And how's that?" she demanded.

Ben shifted his weight from one foot to the other, wishing she wouldn't ask so many questions. "I love you," he burst out at last. "And I want you to marry me and share what life we've got left on this earth. I've got money put by—"

"Never mind that," Rosa cut in. "I've got money put by, too, but it's the feelings that have to be dealt with first." She took his hand and gave it a squeeze, smiling into his face. "I love you, too, Ben. And I'd be proud to be your wife. Just as soon as we can arrange it." To his surprise she giggled and blushed like a young girl. "No point in wasting any of that time we have left, is there?"

Ben knew a good thing when he heard one. Relief made his knees wobble before he got the presence of mind to pull Rosa into his arms and give her a smacking kiss. "No, honey," he said. "No point in wasting time." And then he kissed her again.

Chapter Twelve

Carly wanted the days to slow so that she could savor every minute she spent with Sage, but they seemed to rush by. Apparently he, too, had decided to make the most of the time they had left, for he said nothing about his departure. Neither did he try to maintain the pretense that he had no feelings for her. When they were together Carly could see the love shining in his face, feel it in his touch, taste it when they kissed. The words were all he still denied her.

"I love you," she murmured yet again, awakening in his arms the morning of Ben and Rosa's wedding.

It was barely dawn. Sage kissed her nose and climbed out of bed to pull on his clothes.

"I overslept," he muttered, glancing out the window.

Had it not been for Mollie, Carly knew she would not have bothered to sneak around. She doubted there was a person on the ranch over the age of four who didn't at least suspect that something was going on between the boss and the horse trainer.

Sage snapped his jeans and sank onto the edge of the bed next to Carly. She had been sitting up, watching him, the sheet pulled over her breasts. Now he bared them and bent to bestow a kiss upon each rosy nipple before he pressed his mouth to hers.

"I wish we could stay here all day," he said when he finally broke the kiss.

"We'd be missed at the wedding." Carly tried not to let her feelings show, but couldn't help wishing it was *her* wedding day rather than Rosa's. How she longed for Sage to stay at Rolling Gold forever, to share with her the feelings she saw in his eyes when he looked at her, to choose her over the land that meant everything to him!

But no, his damnable pride would not permit him to do so.

Because of that pride, if Sage did stay, he would eventually be destroyed. And she loved him too much to let that happen. Instead she would smile at Ben and Rosa's wedding today, keeping her own pain hidden. When the time came, she would wish Sage good luck and let him go. With a smile if she could manage it, but at the very least without tears and without begging him to stay. She had promised herself that much.

If Sage could see in her expression any hint of the direction her thoughts had taken, he made no comment, but stood and slipped on his shirt.

"I wonder what shape Ben's in this morning," he said. "Poor man's been a wreck ever since Rosa accepted his proposal."

Carly managed a dry chuckle. "He's been a bachelor for a long time, so I guess we can't blame him for being ner-

vous. I'm told this is a big step for any man." Her gaze
locked on Sage, searching for signs of regret.

"Yeah, it's a big step," he agreed softly, bending to kiss
her again. "One some men can't afford to take. Ben'll
settle down once the ceremony's over. He's a good man.
They going on a honeymoon?"

"Just to Dallas for a couple of days," Carly replied,
pushing back his hair before he straightened. "It's too
busy around here for anything else right now, but I'd like
to send them off for a week this winter. Someplace warm
and sunny, where they can lie on the beach and bake their
bones." It was difficult for her to talk about someone else's
honeymoon. For once she wished Sage would leave her to
her private thoughts.

Buttoning his shirt and saying that he'd see her later, he
finally did. Carly wondered if this would be one of the
mornings he met Rosa on his way out. The older woman
had never mentioned seeing Sage before the rest of the
ranch was up, but she had asked Carly once if everything
was okay.

Today belonged to Ben and Rosa, she reminded herself
as she slipped from the rumpled bed and padded to the
shower. It was no time for sad thoughts, only happy wishes
for a couple who had waited a long time to find each other.

Later that day, Carly helped Rosa dress in a lavender
sheath with a matching lace overdress. With it she wore the
silver earrings Carly had given her and a bit of lavender
veiling on her gray hair, which she had pinned into a neat
chignon. A blue garter and a borrowed prayer book lay on
a small side table next to the bridal bouquet of Sterling
Silver roses that Ben himself had brought earlier.

Rosa peeked at her reflection in the mirror with a satisfied murmur, then surprised Carly by taking her hand. "I
pray every night that things will work out for the two of

you, too," she said gravely. "I'm sure that love will find a way in the end."

Carly blinked back sudden tears. It was sweet of Rosa to think about someone else on her own special day. "Some things aren't meant to be." Carly managed a shaky smile. "But today's a day for happiness, no sad thoughts allowed." Stepping back, she studied Rosa for a moment. "Ben couldn't ask for a prettier bride."

The housekeeper looked slightly flustered. "Thank you, sweetheart. It's been a long time since I was someone's wife, since Louis's father died when he was such a little boy."

Louis was a lawyer at the prosecutor's office in Corpus Christi. Carly was glad Rosa's son was coming home for the ceremony.

"I hope Ben gets through today without fainting," Rosa added, slipping the garter into place before she smoothed down her skirt and stepped into her high heels. "I've never seen such a nervous groom."

"He'll be fine," Carly reassured her. "He'll probably calm down as soon as the deed is done. You know, my father was the same way when he married Susan."

Rosa looked thoughtful. "Lord, I remember that. The man was even more nervous when Mollie was born. And him having delivered hundreds of foals, too." Rosa's smile faded and she studied Carly. "How are you doing, girl? I knew you cared for your father heaps more than you let on."

Carly thought for a moment and then nodded slowly. "Now that I've decided to keep the ranch, I'm more able to remember the good times I had growing up here, instead of just the times I disappointed him."

Her finger caressed one of the lavender roses in Rosa's bouquet. "He taught me so much—about the horses, about life. It must have been hard for him to raise me without a mother. I'd never thought about that before."

For a moment Carly's thoughts wandered, and then she remembered Rosa was still standing there. "His standards were high, but he was hard on himself, too. Now I've come to realize how much he cared for me, and that helps a lot." She had told no one about the letter she'd found in her father's desk. That was hers alone.

"Yes," Rosa said. "He was a hard man in some ways, but a good man. He mellowed a little after he married again, but I always used to wish he'd be gentler with you, more open about his feelings. He wanted so much for you, and I think he was afraid if he was too easy you wouldn't have the strength to run this ranch." She hesitated. "It sounds like you've made your peace."

Carly nodded. "I think I have." She glanced at her watch. "Almost time to make an appearance," she added as music drifted up the stairway. "I'm sure Father would be delighted that you and Ben are finally getting married. Are you ready?"

Rosa leaned toward the mirror, fussing with the neckline of her dress. "Ready as I'll ever be," she muttered. "I just hope that Ben doesn't disgrace us both and faint."

After the ceremony in the living room, unmarred by embarrassing incidents of any kind, there was a small reception, with a wedding cake Rosa had decorated herself and punch and finger sandwiches Carly had made. Mollie had helped by garnishing each silver tray with a lavender satin rose.

Ben's sister, Emma, came forward to give the new couple each a hug. Then she turned to Carly, who was standing with Sage. Unlike Ben, who looked uncomfortable in a new gray suit, Sage was dressed like the other ranch hands, in the same shirt and jeans he had worn to the Browns' party. The silver stud winked in his ear, and the hand that held his Stetson also sported the bracelet Carly had given him on the day of the other party.

"It was about time the big lug popped the question," Emma commented with a grin as she glanced back at her brother, who was talking to Louis, his arm around his new bride's waist. "Ben's been alone too long, and he was lucky to find a woman so well suited to him."

"We think the world of both Ben and Rosa," Carly said. "I'm glad they've agreed to stay on here."

Beside her, Sage made no comment.

"I'm glad you're keeping the ranch," Emma said, eyeing him with feminine interest. "Ben isn't old enough to retire."

"You're right," Sage said. "They'll be happy here."

"I wanted to thank you, too, for putting me up tonight," Emma told Carly. "I'll be on my way in the morning."

"I'm happy you could come for the wedding," Carly said. "It was a nice ceremony."

"I wouldn't have missed it." Emma moved on to speak to the minister, and Sage took the opportunity for a private word with Carly.

"I saw Harper in town last night," he said. "Told me he'd talked to Artie and put a little fear into him. Artie didn't have a very good alibi for the night of the fire, and Harper made it clear he'd be watching and waiting for him to make a mistake."

Carly shivered. "Grady would make a mean enemy. Do they have any clues yet?"

Sage shook his head, watching the small crowd of guests mill about, sipping punch and eating the sandwiches. Ben and Rosa had disappeared.

"They didn't find anything at the fire. We may never be able to prove who did it, but Harper hinted to Artie that they had something, just to see what he'd do."

Carly remained silent, and Sage wondered if she was thinking, as he was, that he would have no more reason to stay if the arsonist was caught. There was some money from the sale of his last champion stallion waiting for him in an Oklahoma bank, money he had put aside to start over, and his mares and their fillies were fit and able to travel. He was fast running out of excuses to stay.

Music from the stereo flooded the living room and drifted outside into the heat of later afternoon, and he grabbed Carly's hand, lacing his fingers with hers.

"Come and dance with me on the deck," he said, needing to feel her close to him.

Today she looked cool and serene in a fancy, peach-colored dress and high heels, her hair swept up into a classy style atop her head and a corsage of white roses over her heart. He was pleased to see she still wore the little gold horseshoe he had given her around her neck, but her unapproachable air made him ache to take down her hair and strip off her clothes, just to prove to himself that he was the one man who could melt her cool facade and make her warm and willing. His woman.

"I should stick around," she said. "In case the guests need anything." She glanced at the silver trays on the dining-room table, still half-covered with food. The crystal punch bowl was almost full.

"You've done your duty here." He needed her in his arms and he needed her now.

"Okay." Wondering at his sudden tension, Carly followed him silently, weaving through the small clusters of people and finally escaping out the kitchen door. She couldn't look at the pool without remembering the first night they had made love. She had known then that she was playing a dangerous game, and now she was paying the price. But if she succeeded in persuading Sage to stay with her, she would have to watch the erosion of his self-respect. And that she couldn't do. To save him, she had to put aside her own needs and let him go.

She was blinking back tears when they rounded a corner of the house and almost collided with Ben and Rosa. The two older people sprang apart as if they had been caught at something illicit. Carly and Sage stopped, embarrassed at having interrupted the tender scene.

"We were just talking about moving my stuff into Rosa's quarters," Ben said quickly, cheeks growing pink. Beside him, Rosa nodded.

"That's right."

To Carly, Sage's grin seemed bittersweet. "You've got permission from God and the state of Texas to hold each other whenever you want, without making excuses," he teased. "Pardon us for interrupting." With a wink at Rosa, he tugged at Carly's hand. "Let's go check out the new barn."

She followed him to the skeletal structure that smelled of newly cut wood, walking carefully through the dirt and sawdust in the pale peach shoes that matched her dress. She had been proud to stand beside Rosa earlier. Tony had been best man and Mollie, in frilly pink with a garland of daisies in her hair, the flower girl.

Now Carly stopped in the doorway of the new barn and gazed up at the partially finished structure. It was bigger than the old barn, with a covered practice ring in the middle and rows of stalls down both wings. Until the building was complete, some of her horses had been moved to the empty stalls in the broodmare barn, and the others were over at the Browns' ranch.

"This is going to be nice when it's done," Sage said. He dropped her hand and walked inside to run his fingers down a thick beam. "I'd like a barn like this one day."

His words sent a bolt of pain through Carly. "Tell me about Comanche Creek," she asked, following him inside. "What's it like?"

"Not much to tell." He jammed his hands into his back pockets and looked around. "I've got an old farmhouse that needs renovating, a big, old-fashioned barn with stalls for the stallions, and a stable that's not big enough for what I need."

"Tell me about the land," she murmured, stepping closer.

He closed his eyes and tipped his head back. "Ah, yes. Prettiest piece of land in all of Oklahoma. Two creeks I can count on all year long and all the acreage I need." He stopped for a moment, as if picturing the place in his mind. "Mac wanted his ashes scattered from this one rise...." He opened his eyes and looked at Carly. "He's still there," he said quietly. "Maybe you think that's kinda dumb, but sometimes I could feel his presence. I know he wants me there, raising the horses we used to talk about back in Vietnam."

Carly couldn't think of a thing to say. "I know you miss him," she finally ventured after a long moment of silence. "He'll be glad when you're back."

His gaze was questioning. "Then you understand?"

Carly couldn't prevent the bitterness in her tone. "I've always understood. That's why I can't let myself fight your decision."

They stared at each other, both frustrated and hurting. Then Sage opened his arms and Carly hurtled into them. For just a moment she let herself wish that he cared as much for her as he did for his precious land, then gave herself up to his kiss. Rational thought fled in the face of his all-consuming passion.

Carly, Ben and Sage pulled into the driveway late one evening a week later after several long days at a quarter horse show in Amarillo. Ben was taking a turn driving the pickup, which was towing the large horse trailer.

"It's good to be back," Sage muttered, stretching as best he could in the confines of the cab. His words broke the silence that had reigned for most of the last hour. They were all beat.

"Yeah, sure is," Ben said, pulling up outside the new barn, whose walls were now finished. "I've missed my wife."

Carly couldn't help but grin at his possessive tone. He'd called Rosa twice a day while they were gone and talked about her the rest of the time. She felt Sage nudge her ribs with his elbow; they'd shared their amusement at Ben's expense. Now she glanced up to catch Sage's wink.

"Think she's waiting up?" he asked Ben innocently. "I've heard that once they've got that gold ring on their finger they'll leave you a dry sandwich on the kitchen counter and go to bed early. Rosa's probably exhausted from runnin' around partyin' while you were away."

Ben's head whipped around and he glared at Sage before he noticed the teasing grin. Carly was trying with little success to stifle her giggles. Sage's teasing had gone from the subtle to the ridiculous since they'd left Rolling Gold.

"Aw, shucks," Ben said. "You know Rosa wouldn't do anything like that. She's probably waiting by the window with hot coffee on and a fresh pie to go with it."

Carly's mouth began to water. She hoped Ben was right. The meals they'd eaten on the run had been mediocre, at best.

As they dragged themselves from the truck, Rosa came bustling from the house to give Ben a big hug. "Pie and coffee ready in the kitchen when you have the horses bedded down," she said when he finally let her go. The three of them began to laugh, and she glanced around suspiciously.

"Sounds good," Sage said, walking to the back of the horse trailer. "We'll be in a little later."

To give Ben and Rosa a moment of privacy, Carly followed Sage. By the time they had the trailer open, Joey and Tony had come out to help.

"How's Sun Catcher's leg?" Tony asked. Ben had kept everyone back at the ranch posted by phone on each day's events. The filly had begun to limp after her class had been judged.

"Fine," Sage told him. "She must have just bruised it. What's new around here?"

"Not much," Tony replied, helping to unload the first horse, Golden Fire Dancer, half brother to Sky Walker. "Grady Harper's called a couple of times."

"Any news?," Carly asked.

"Naw. Personally I think it was set by some firebug who's long gone."

Carly looked up and noticed headlights coming down the long driveway. She stepped from the trailer and waited until a car pulled up and the lights abruptly went out.

"It's Grady," Sage said. "Maybe he's found out something new."

They waited expectantly while the deputy climbed out of his car and came toward him.

"Carly," he said, nodding. "Looks like you just got in. How'd you do at the horse show?"

"Pretty good." She was impatient to know why he was there. "We're going to put the horses up and go in for pie and coffee. Do you have time to join us?" She'd burst if she had to wait that long to hear whatever he'd come out to tell them.

Grady shook his head. "Thanks, but I gotta get movin'. Just wanted you all to know right off that we just caught Artie Maddock settin' fire to one of the stables over at Roy Henshaw's. The sheriff's taking him into jail."

"You don't say!" Carly exclaimed, feeling Sage grow tense beside her. She saw his hands curl into fists.

"I knew it was him," he growled.

"But what does he have against Roy?" Carly asked. "Artie never worked for him."

Grady removed his hat and slapped it against his knee. Carly thought that he probably enjoyed drawing out the news, then dismissed the thought as ungrateful.

"Seems the little talk I had with him before spooked old Artie. He got hold of a bottle this evening and somewhere between the first sip and the last decided to take the spotlight off himself."

"I don't get it," Tony said.

Carly grabbed Sage's arm. "Wait a minute!" she exclaimed. "Don't tell me he meant to start another fire and make us think there was some serial arsonist loose?"

Grady's grin widened. "A prize to the little lady," he said, pointing his finger like a pistol. "That's exactly what Artie had in mind. Too bad for him it didn't work out quite that way. All he accomplished was to get himself caught red-handed when Henshaw went out to see why his dog was fussin'."

"Any damage done?" Sage asked.

"Naw. Artie only had time to start one small fire, and they got it out with the extinguisher before it could do any real harm. I was the first one there, and Artie couldn't confess to both fires fast enough. I think Henshaw'd threatened to turn his dog loose if Artie didn't start talkin'. 'Course, I don't know that for sure. Confession wouldn't hold up if he gave it under duress. And I did read him his rights, but he kept on talkin'." Grady shrugged.

"Well," Ben observed, "if he'd gotten away with a second fire, he might never have been caught. We'd probably think exactly what he wanted us to, that some pyro was starting them."

Grady frowned, obviously unhappy with Ben's suggestion that the crime might never have been solved.

"Well, thanks for letting us know," Carly said, breaking the silence. "It was good of you to come out and tell us." She shook Grady's hand. "I'm sorry it had to be Artie, but I'm glad he was caught before anyone got hurt." She remembered again her terror when Sage had gone back into the burning barn to get Grady out and shuddered.

"Yeah," Ben added. "Glad you caught him." He, too, moved forward to shake hands. The others followed, and Ben said something about getting the horses unloaded.

Grady put his hat back onto his head. "Well," he said finally, "I'd best be gettin' along. We'll keep you posted about Artie."

"Thanks again," Carly said before climbing back into the horse trailer. She was glad her ex-employee was going to get what he deserved, but didn't dare look in Sage's direction. She knew if she did, she'd disgrace herself by bursting into tears.

Later they all gathered in the dining room for coffee and pie. Sage listened to the talk around him and watched

Carly unobtrusively. In the light from the overhead fixture she looked pale and tired. As he pushed the last bite of pie around on his plate, he tortured himself by toying with the idea of asking her to go back to Oklahoma with him.

He tried to picture her in the primitive kitchen of his house, an apron around her waist and her hair caught up in a bandanna, waving a wooden spoon and hollering that supper was ready.

"Yeah, sure," he muttered under his breath. The chance of that happening was as likely as his going back to find that his ranch had been transformed into a modern facility while he'd been gone. Compared to Rolling Gold, his place looked like a dirt farm out of the old West. On top of that, he had nothing to offer Carly but hard work and uncertainty.

The ranches they loved stood between them like two beds of burning coals that were impossible to cross.

Despite Sage's determination, he knew there was no guarantee that he could restore Comanche Creek to its former success. This time he could truly lose everything he had, so even if Carly had been willing, he'd have refused to let her take that kind of risk, especially when she had Mollie to consider.

Better to let Carly keep thinking he didn't want her, even though he knew he would never get over the golden-haired angel who came apart in his arms. Taking her with him was as impossible a dream as was staying here with her. He was going home, and he was going alone.

When he finally lifted his fork to his mouth, the last bite of pie tasted like sawdust. Scraping his chair back abruptly, he glanced at the others.

"I'm beat," he said. "See you all tomorrow."

A general exodus followed, and Rosa began to gather up the dirty dishes. Sage didn't let his gaze linger on Carly, but did see Ben slip an arm around Rosa's waist before he helped her to clean up.

Envy slammed through Sage. He knew the other man would be spending the night with the woman he loved, while Sage tossed and turned on his narrow bunk. Sleeping alone was something he would have to start getting used to all over again. He should be doing it right now, and he always stayed away from Carly as long as he could. But eventually a need he couldn't overcome would drive him back to her bed.

"But why does he have to leave?" Mollie's voice was an anguished wail. Carly gathered her closer in the living-room rocking chair and searched for words to help her understand.

"He stayed with us as long as he could, but now it's time for him to take his horses back to his own ranch." She was having a hard time not giving into the tears that hovered behind her own eyelids.

Mollie had started to cry when Carly first told her that Sage would be leaving them in a few days. Now Carly felt like barricading herself in her own room until he was far away. The pain of watching him leave would surely break her heart.

"I thought we were going to be a family," Mollie sobbed. "Like Ben and Rosa. Why can't Sage marry us and stay here?"

Carly shifted in the chair, cuddling Mollie and resting her chin on the little girl's head. Why, indeed?

"It's complicated," she began. "You know that Sage is part Comanche."

"I know." Mollie hiccupped.

"Well, he had a pretty rough time when he was a little boy. His father had gone away, and then his mother left him, too. I think the first real home he could count on was his ranch, and his land means everything in the world to him. We can't expect him to give it up."

"That's sad," Mollie said, straightening. "But the land isn't like people who can love you. He'd be happier living with us, and so would I."

Carly added her silent agreement. "Everyone has to decide for himself what will make him happy," she said finally. "We can't say what's best for Sage, any more than he could for us."

"But I love him," Mollie argued, "and I want him to stay here."

It was all Carly could do to keep from crying right along with Mollie. Her voice was unsteady as she replied. "Me, too, punkin. And that's why we have to let him leave, because we love him."

"That doesn't make any sense," Mollie grumbled, snuggling closer to Carly and wiping her eyes. "Grown-ups are very hard to understand sometimes."

"Sometimes it sure seems that way," Carly agreed on a shaky sigh.

Sage didn't dare let Carly see his anguish at leaving her, but he could let out some of the sadness he felt when he said goodbye to Mollie. As the others waited, he swept her into a giant bear hug and gave her cheek a smacking kiss. Her skinny arms clung to him.

"Goodbye, Sage. I'll miss you."

"Goodbye, princess. Take care of your sister for me." He looked around, but Carly still wasn't there. He hadn't expected her to be. They had said a private farewell early that morning, and he was almost relieved not to have to go through it again in front of witnesses.

She had been distant with him and very tense. Perhaps she was angry that he was leaving her in the middle of the season. Maybe she didn't understand, after all, but at least anger might make the separation easier for her to bear. He had no idea how *he* was going to survive it, except to wear himself out with work at Comanche Creek until he was so exhausted that he could fall into bed each night without dreaming of her.

One of Sage's horses kicked impatiently at the side of the big trailer he had borrowed from the ranch to transport them home. The one he had brought with him was too small.

"I'll bring this trailer back and pick mine up as soon as I have someone to keep an eye on my place," he told Ben.

The older man nodded and clasped Sage's shoulder. "Take care," he said gruffly, looking for a moment as if he meant to add more.

"I fixed you a lunch," Rosa said, handing Sage a package before she gave him a hug. "Make sure you eat properly."

"I will. Thank you." He set the bag upon the worn bench seat of his beat-up truck. "Take care of Carly," he said, "and Mollie."

"We will." Rosa's smile wavered.

There was nothing left to say. Sage glanced up, looking for one last sign of Carly, and saw a lone figure on horseback silhouetted against the morning sun. He stared until his eyes began to burn, then touched two fingers to the brim of his hat, bade her a silent goodbye and climbed into the cab. He felt as if his heart had been torn still beating from his chest. The engine of his old truck caught, and with a final wave he started down the driveway.

On a rise behind the buildings, the solitary figure watched the red pickup drive away. After a moment her vision blurred, the colors before her running together like the scene through a rain-washed window. Finally she buried her face in Dancer's neck and sobbed. Her mount stood patiently until her private storm had passed.

When she looked up again, almost doubled over by the pain clawing at her, the red truck was a tiny dot on the distant highway. She watched until long after it was out of sight and then, her tears drying on her cheeks, she turned Dancer's head toward home.

Time slowed to a hot, dry crawl. Even the horses failed to hold Carly's interest as they usually did, and consoling Mollie without breaking down herself took every bit of control she possessed. More than once she intercepted the worried looks Ben and Rosa exchanged over her head, or walked into a barn as the conversation between Joey and Tony turned abruptly into guilty grins.

Routine chores drove Carly crazy, and the things she used to enjoy, like riding Dancer or showing the horses, only made her want to go home and pull the covers over her head. Food had lost all appeal and, despite Rosa's tempting offerings, Carly's clothes were getting baggy.

Oh, Dad, she thought one evening as she watched the stars from a chair by the pool, *how I wish you were here so I could talk to you. Maybe you could tell me how you survived the loss of my mother, how you found the courage to keep on!*

Carly was wearing the red bikini. It was late, and no one was around. The day had been hot and the night was still uncomfortably warm. Perhaps swimming in the pool was a first step back. Blotting all thought from her mind, she went to the edge and dived in.

Back and forth she swam, establishing an easy rhythm, concentrating. Stroke, stroke, breathe. Over and over. Push off, glide and stroke again.

When she finally let herself stop, she came up looking for Sage. As soon as she realized it, she froze, cursing him soundly.

His footprints were all over her life.

He had made his choice and so had she. She was sick of being miserable, of hurting. Sorrow had not healed her, so perhaps anger would.

The more Carly thought about what had happened, the madder she got. He had left her, damn it. Left her for a patch of land he had admitted wasn't as good as the one she'd offered.

For a few days she chewed on that, fuming and snapping at anyone who ventured too close. Only for little Mollie did she drag up a ragged bit of patience.

Anger only gave her a headache and a guilty conscience. She was scolding Joey for failing to secure one of the paddock gates properly, when Ben came into the barn and touched her arm.

"We need to talk," he said in a serious tone.

She glanced back at Joey. "I'm right in the middle of something."

"Now," Ben said. "It won't wait."

Carly sighed, letting her impatience show. "Okay. Joey, we'll finish this later."

The young man's ears were red and his eyes failed to meet hers. "Okay." He turned and walked away quickly.

"Now, what's so damned important?" Carly demanded of Ben. Her hands were braced on her hips and she was fuming with impatience.

He glanced around, then led her to a bench along one wall. "Sit down."

Her eyes widened. He hadn't used this tone with her since she had been a little girl. Certainly not since she had come back to run the operation.

Carly sat.

"You were a mite rough on Joey, weren't you?" Ben watched her closely, as if looking for something.

"He had it coming. What he did was careless and could have caused problems."

"Mebbe so, but it's not like you not to give someone a chance to tell his side of it."

"I never—" Carly began hotly, then stopped. Had she given Joey a chance to defend himself? She wasn't sure, she'd seen that gate and just lit into him.

Carly looked up at Ben. "You're right," she said, shrugging. "I'll talk to him."

Ben nodded. "Now," he said, "how much longer are you going to put us all through this?"

"Through what?" Carly could feel herself getting defensive. Maybe she hadn't been her usual easygoing self lately, but she had a reason. Didn't anyone understand what she was going through?

Ben slapped his hat against his thigh. "Go after him."

"That's impossible." Carly picked at a spot on her jeans. She had already been over all the reasons why she could never try to change Sage's decision.

"Then let him go."

Her gaze flew to Ben's face. "I already have."

"No." He shook his head. "You're hanging on with everything you've got. And punishing everyone around you for not being him." Ben rose from the bench, reaching a hand to squeeze her shoulder. "I know it's not easy," he said. "But if you can't have him, you have to let him go." He continued to look at her for a long minute. "I'm sorry," he said softly, then walked away.

Carly stayed where she was, thinking about what Ben had said. She knew she couldn't have Sage. She was getting damned tired of grieving for something that had been doomed from the outset. Tears filled her eyes and she dashed them impatiently away.

Ben was right. From now on she *would* get over him. Filled with renewed determination, Carly rose and headed off to look for Joey. She had some fences to mend, and then perhaps Mollie would like to take Polka Dot and go for a ride.

Chapter Thirteen

Carly was working a yearling, her mind focused tightly on the horse, when she saw Grady's patrol car pull up outside the fence. She stopped what she was doing and called to him as he got out and glanced around, his eyes hidden by sunglasses. He waved and came toward her, so she left the training paddock, shutting the gate behind her.

"Any news?" she asked.

Grady shook his head. "Not since Artie pleaded guilty. The judge isn't going to pronounce sentence until next week, and then I'm sure Artie will be transferred down to the prison for a long visit."

"I hope he'll get some help with his drinking problem," Carly said, remembering how good Artie had been with the horses when he was sober.

Grady took off the sunglasses and studied them. "I didn't come here to talk about Artie."

Carly tensed. "Oh?" She hoped he wasn't going to ask her out again. Willing herself to get over Sage was one thing; accomplishing it took time.

Grady flushed; was he, too, remembering the time he had lost his temper and Sage had ejected him from her house? "You knew my brother Sloan, didn't you?"

Carly thought a moment. Sloan had been several years ahead of Grady and herself in school. She recalled him vaguely because he'd played football. "Yes, I remember. How is he?"

"He's fine, living up in Wichita Falls with his wife and four kids."

Carly pretended shock. "Four!"

Grady grinned, visibly relaxing. "They're expecting another before Christmas, but that's not why I mentioned him."

"Then why?" she asked. The sound of a truck pulling up on the other side of the new stable distracted her momentarily. Ben was over there; he would see who it was.

Grady kept speaking. "He's looking for a new mount for his oldest daughter. She's been riding since she could toddle, and now she needs a horse she can show. I told him to call you."

Carly smiled, relieved. "Thanks," she said. "I appreciate the recommendation, and I'll be sure to give Sloan my personal attention." She was glad Grady hadn't asked her out.

"Carly, someone to see you!" Ben shouted. A skinny youth with black hair and copper skin was with him.

She glanced at Grady.

"Well, I'd better get going," he said. "I'll let you know when I hear something about Artie."

"Thanks again." She followed him to where Ben was waiting, then watched Grady leave in his cruiser.

"This is Pete Swift Eagle," Ben said. "He brought our other trailer back from Comanche Creek."

Carly had already stuck her hand out; she understood what the boy's appearance meant. She was unprepared for the disappointment that curled bitterly inside her, making her heart ache. It hadn't been clear until this moment how much she had still been looking forward to seeing Sage one last time. Seeing the boy look at her strangely, she steadied the smile that had begun to slip and shook his hand.

"How is he?" she asked when they had exchanged greetings.

"He's doing okay, working hard. I help him most days after summer school." The boy's glance took in the new barn and the surrounding paddocks with their neatly painted white fences. "Nice place."

"Thank you," Carly said. "Did you have any problems with the trailer when you brought it back?"

He shook his head. "No, ma'am. Sage told me to be careful, and I was. Where do you want me to leave it?"

Carly glanced over at the unfamiliar green pickup. "Ben will show you. Then he can take you in to get something to eat before you head back."

"Thank you, ma'am." the boy said. "Sage told me to thank you again for the loan of the trailer and to wish you luck with your horses."

Carly wanted to ask if Sage had said anything else, if he ever talked about her, if he seemed happy, but glanced at Ben instead. "You don't mind showing him, do you? I want to finish working Daisy Chain."

"Sure." Ben grinned at the lanky teenager. "Come with me."

For long minutes after Pete Swift Eagle had walked away with Ben, Carly stood unmoving. Memories threatened the barrier she had erected against them, so before they could topple it completely, she turned her attention back to the horse in the training paddock and what she needed to accomplish with her before the next show.

The air was heavy and still, the heat in Oklahoma relentless. It was a month since Pete had got back from returning Carly's trailer, two and a half since Sage had come home to Comanche Creek. He was mucking out a stall in the rundown but spotless stable, his movements automatic. Sweat rolled down his forehead, stinging his eyes, and he wondered what had happened to the satisfaction he used to feel when performing even the most humble chore.

He had been driving himself harder and harder in his search for some measure of personal satisfaction, some sense of accomplishment. Now he stopped to rest his folded arms on the pitchfork handle and studied the mare he had released into a small paddock surrounded by a fence of weathered boards.

"Well, Lady, I hope you're happy here," he muttered, pulling a bandanna handkerchief from his pocket and mopping his face with it. "Maybe I just miss Mac. I can't seem to settle into anything." He stuffed the handkerchief back into his pocket; Lady wheeled and crossed the paddock to call to Comanche Princess in the next enclosure.

No matter how hard he worked, starting when dawn was beginning to light the eastern sky and finishing long after sunset, Sage had not been able to find any peace in the weeks since he had left Texas. He couldn't sleep, so every night he walked outside to search the heavens, but the darkened sky held only stars, not answers. Sometimes he wondered if Carly was looking at those same stars, too, then ruthlessly drove all thoughts of her from his mind.

He picked up the pitchfork and resumed his task. Why did he go on torturing himself? When Pete had gotten back from Rolling Gold, he'd told Sage how chummy Carly had been with a deputy who sounded like Grady Harper from the boy's description. Sage couldn't blame her if she had turned to the other man, but the images that formed inside his head of her in someone else's arms gave him such pain that he did his best not to think of her at all. Carly had been his, and he had let her go.

Had let her go for this.

He laid the pitchfork aside and went through the doorway, narrowing his eyes against the bright sky; he walked down the path and through a gate to a small rise. He'd had enough practice getting over people he had lost, so why wasn't he getting better at it?

Since he had come back to Comanche Creek, he was even getting used to Mac's absence. He no longer looked up expectantly when he heard Pete's footsteps, forgetting for an instant that Mac was gone for good. This hillock he stood on was where he had scattered his friend's ashes on the wind, and where he sometimes went to give voice to his own loneliness. It helped some, and he felt sure that Mac would understand.

A little while later, Sage was leading Lady back into her stall, his mood still black, when Pete came rushing in.

"Come quick."

"What's the hurry?" Sage asked, shutting the stall door behind his mare.

Pete was a good boy; the new priest at the church where Sage himself had grown up had recommended him.

Pete's black eyes sought the toes of his boots before he glanced back up at Sage. Pete's father had left for the big city two years before, leaving a wife and five children. No one had heard from him since. Sage had hired Pete on the condition that he also attend summer school to keep up with the other students his age. When Father Dominick had found a truck for Pete to drive to school and work, Sage had helped tune it.

Even now Pete was still sometimes wary. Sage remembered and understood that lack of trust. It was a buffer against pain. An edge against disappointment.

Pete pushed back his shaggy hair. "There's a fellow in a fancy pickup here to see you."

Sage wiped his hands on his faded bandanna and adjusted his Stetson. "Do you know who he is?"

"Naw, but his truck has some words painted on the door, curly letters I couldn't read."

Curious, Sage emerged from the barn, Pete following at his heels like a curious, overgrown puppy. In the rutted driveway stood a short man, his back to Sage, wearing a cream-colored Stetson. He had a horseman's build and was studying the open land past the rundown farmhouse.

When Sage got closer, the stranger turned. His face was dark and weathered beneath his hat and he had a paunch that flowed over his wide belt, all but obscuring the elaborate silver buckle. The pickup truck looked shiny and expensive, the driver's door sporting an elaborate logo. Sage's gaze lingered as he tried to make it out.

"I'm your new neighbor," the man said, holding out his hand. "My name is Bernard Sim."

Sage gripped the proffered hand and looked into his visitor's intense brown eyes, set between beetling black brows and a large, hooked nose. His English was faintly accented.

"Glad to meet you," Sage told him, introducing himself and Pete. "Can I offer you something cold to drink?" He wondered if there was anything in the house but tap water and doubted it. He never did get to the store until Pete badgered him.

Sim held out a detaining hand. There were heavy gold rings on two fingers. "Don't trouble yourself. I'm sure you have much work to do." He glanced around, then back at Sage. "Anyway, I don't want to keep you. I just stopped by to introduce myself and invite you, and your young friend, of course, to dine with me tomorrow evening at my home, Windy Hill."

Sage was surprised. The surrounding landowners were polite enough, but not one had gone so far as to invite him over, not when he and Mac had run Comanche Creek, and certainly not since he'd come back.

He glanced at Pete, who shrugged. There was no polite way to refuse. Besides, Sage was curious. He had heard rumors in town about the rich foreigner who had bought up the old Wicken place and most of the land around it, had the existing buildings razed to make way for new ones, and then brought in the finest horses and blooded cattle that money could buy.

"Sure," Sage said. "You can count on both of us. What time?"

The other man smiled, revealing a gold tooth. "Seven," he said. "Casual attire, please. There will only be the three of us."

Moments later the tan pickup eased carefully over the potholes in Sage's driveway. What did this Mr. Sim have in mind? No point in speculating; he would find out soon enough.

The next evening, Sage and Pete arrived at the sprawling stone ranch house right on time, got out of Sage's beat-up red truck and looked around.

"Holy cow," Pete muttered. The sprawling house was of white stone and dark wood, surrounded by lush greenery that had to have been professionally planted and maintained. Before them a wrought iron gate stood partly open, indicating the way past a lyrical fountain in a tiled courtyard to a massive set of carved double doors.

Bernard Sim himself answered Sage's ring. "Come in, please," he said, bowing. He was wearing tan slacks and a white shirt piped in blue. A bolero tie set with a large sapphire was around his neck.

After they had exchanged pleasantries and a manservant had served drinks for the two men and a cola for Pete, Sim led the two of them on a tour of the house and then showed them the rest of his impressive facility. Sage could see that no expense had been spared.

"It looks like you've thought of everything," he said, gesturing with his glass of bourbon to the massive stainless steel tub used for hydrotherapy on the horses.

"I like to think so," his host said, stroking his chin. "But enough for now. Dinner must be about ready."

At the massive dining-room table, each time Sage tried to find out why they had been invited for dinner he was politely but firmly sidetracked. The only thing Sim would say about the matter was that he never talked business on an empty stomach.

From the man's girth Sage could readily believe him, but he grew more curious as the elaborate meal progressed. Beside him Pete ate steadily, undoubtedly grateful for the variety and abundance of food he would never find at home or in Sage's haphazardly stocked refrigerator.

Finally, when the dessert dishes were cleared away, Sim led the two of them into a wood-paneled room carpeted in plush burgundy, offering brandy and cigars. Sage declined and, after a moment's hesitation, so did Pete.

"Now, then," Sim began as soon as they were seated across from each other on matching gray suede sofas, "I imagine it is time I satisfied your curiosity before you become truly annoyed at me."

"That would be nice," Sage replied dryly. He crossed one booted foot over the other knee and waited.

Sim rose to his feet and went to one wall, where a large map held a position of honor.

"This is Windy Hill," he said, pointing. "As you can see, it is large. But in order to run the cattle I intend, as well as the horses I showed you earlier, I need more acreage and, what is of even greater importance, more water."

He glanced at Sage, who waited silently for him to continue. After a moment Sim turned again to the map. "This—" he traced one border with his finger "—is where your property meets mine."

Sage sat up straighter; his suspicions of why he had been invited to dinner were being confirmed. Beside him Pete sucked in a sharp breath.

Sim returned to the opposite couch and sat down again. "As I am sure you have guessed by now, I want to buy your land."

"Impossible," Sage said automatically. "It's not for sale."

"Not even for a generous price?" asked Sim, naming a surprising figure. "A price that would allow you to buy again elsewhere and build the kind of place you must long in your heart to have?"

Sage thought of Rolling Gold, then yanked his attention back to what Sim was saying. "You haven't even looked over my land," Sage said. "You don't know..."

Sim's smile broadened. "I can assure you that I have researched your holding with great care. I know how many acres you have, down to the last square foot. I am aware of the water available and I know which repairs your buildings need the most."

Sage allowed his eyes to narrow. "You know my boot size and what brand of shampoo I use, too?"

Sim spread his hands, palms up. "I can find out."

"It's not necessary." Sage wondered what else the man knew about him. He felt as if he had been stripped in public, and the sensation was not a pleasant one.

"Comanche Creek is not for sale," he repeated.

Sim shrugged, pausing to light a cigar. "I know of the difficulties you and your late partner had," he said, sobering. "And I even heard about the poker game in which you wagered several years of your freedom against two broodmares in foal to your best stud that you had sold."

Pete had swiveled his head to stare at Sage. "You did?"

"It was a long time ago, and I won the game." He forced himself to remain cool as he looked back at his host. "You must have a nose for gossip," he remarked in a bland tone that belied his inner agitation. "But it's all very old news."

"And of no interest to me," Sim agreed. "I only mention it in wondering if you might not be persuaded to relocate. To somewhere in Texas, near Hamlin, say? Surely this ranch must hold unhappy memories for you."

"And some happy ones," Sage said, rising. He would not permit Bernard Sim to bring his past relationship with Carly into the conversation as an argument for him to sell out. He stretched out his hand, keeping his expression bland.

"I appreciate your hospitality," he said, "but morning comes early, so we have to be going."

"Will you at least consider my offer?" Sim asked, walking them out.

Sage shook his head. "I told you, my land isn't for sale." Without his land he was nothing, a man without roots, a man with no ties.

"I hope that we can become friends," Sim said bidding Sage and Pete a final good-night.

Sage let his faint smile be his only answer.

Later that evening, after Pete had left, Sage popped open a can of beer he found in the back of the fridge and walked out to the knoll where he had scattered Mac's ashes.

"Am I doing the right thing, old buddy?" he asked softly, staring into the darkness, picturing the way it looked in daylight, remembering how he and Mac had ridden out for the pure joy of being on land that actually belonged to them.

"Am I crazy to say no? I never thought about selling, you know that. And I never dreamed of getting this kind of an offer."

For a moment he allowed himself to picture Carly and the way her eyes had looked when they'd said goodbye. Like bluebells in the rain, drowned in tears she refused to shed. Did she still think of him? Or had she already found comfort in someone else's arms?

Sage's hands curled into fists. He could not bear the thought of her with another man. The pain was beyond anything he had ever imagined.

Yet what right did he have to object? He had left her. Left her for a large rectangle of dirt covered in scrub and bisected by two streams. Left her to return to the dreams he'd shared with a dead man.

He shifted restlessly and drained the can of beer. Although he had never smoked, he sometimes wished he did. This was one of those times. Instead he crushed the beer can, resisting the urge to hurl it into the darkness.

As usual, when he tipped back his head and searched the night sky, it gave him no answers. How long, he wondered, how long until this burning pain subsided? How long before he could put the love he felt for Carly behind him and begin the rest of his life?

He was no closer to an answer when he walked back into the house and tossed the flattened can into the garbage. Tired, for once, of his own company, he went into the small master bedroom, shedding his clothes and leaving them where they fell.

That night he dreamed of Carly. At first she was with him the way they had been back at her ranch, then the dream changed. She was with Grady Harper and their children, all wearing miniature khaki uniforms.

Sage fought his way up from sleep, waking with a roaring headache and a mouth as dry as the worst part of Oklahoma during a drought. His bedding was tangled and soaked with sweat, but his body was shaking and chilled. He wondered how much longer he could endure the memories without going mad.

Over the next few weeks, Bernard Sim returned twice to visit Sage. Each time he presented a higher offer. Each time Sage turned it down, conscious of Mac's presence beside him. The third time Sim came, he repeated his last offer.

"I want to move my cattle-breeding program here," he said. "The manager can live in the house, and we'll replace the outbuildings. And, of course, the fencing." For a moment he looked apologetic. "It would be perfect for what I need."

"I told you, the land isn't for sale," Sage said tiredly. He had been up all night with Comanche Princess's filly, Promise, who had suddenly become ill.

That morning, despite everything Sage had done, she had slipped away from him before the vet arrived. Sage was left with a heavy heart and the feeling that one more link with Carly, who had helped with Promise's delivery, had been irreparably severed.

After examining the body, the vet had assured Sage that his other horses were in no danger and had left right before Sim appeared in his tan-colored truck. He commiserated with Sage over the loss of the filly, then turned to peruse the horizon before speaking again.

"I must tell you," he said slowly, "that another piece of land has come to my attention. I originally thought it was not worth my interest, but the owner's situation has changed and he is willing to sell at a bargain price."

Sage wondered if Sim himself had maneuvered the situation change, then dismissed the idea as paranoia. Maybe this was the best way; Sim would revoke his offer and there would be no decision for Sage to make.

"This land is still better suited to what I want," Sim continued, "but I cannot wait much longer. I realize that you have given me no encouragement, but I must caution you that if you do not accept my offer soon, I will be forced to consider this other parcel."

Sage stared hard. As if he could read Sage's thoughts, the other man spoke again.

"Call the other rancher, if you like," he said. "You'll find that everything I have told you is the truth."

"I didn't mean to imply—" Sage began hotly.

The wealthy rancher shook his head. "Of course not. Any thorough businessman will double-check the facts. You gave no offense."

Before he drove away, Sim did leave the name and phone number of the other rancher with Sage, who confirmed the story, not only with him but also with the local real estate agent who had the listing.

All that was left was to decide.

Sage spent the next two days thinking of nothing else. When Pete questioned his preoccupation, he called Bernard Sim to inquire whether a job for the youngster could be added to the man's offer. Upon hearing Sage's recommendation, Sim agreed immediately. If Sage was looking for a reason to refuse, he needed to keep looking.

At night he sat on his favorite hill and held imaginary conversations with Mac. He dug his fingers into the dry soil, then let it fall back to the ground. It was not the land that had given his life substance and meaning, he realized eventually. It was his friendship with Mac that had made the running of Comanche Creek so rewarding.

Perhaps that was of the greatest importance—relationships with people, not possession of the land. Love, like the feeling he and Carly had shared, gave a man true purpose, not how many acres he owned.

Finally, when he was half-numb with lack of sleep, a plan began to form in Sage's tired mind.

"Good Lord, what are you doing here?" Rosa asked, wiping her hands on her apron.

Sage had been wondering the same thing all the way to the ranch. What right did he have to think that Carly might still love him?

"I'm here to see the boss," he began.

Before he could continue, he heard Mollie's piping voice from somewhere behind Rosa.

"Who's here?" she demanded, rushing down the stairs. "I saw a truck just like Sage's through my bedroom window."

Rosa turned aside to answer her, and Mollie's momentum propelled her right past the housekeeper and into Sage's waiting arms. Laughing, he scooped her up and swung her in the air.

"It *was* Sage's truck you saw!" he exclaimed, whirling her around before setting her back down. "How's my best girl been?"

Mollie hugged him with all the enthusiasm her little body contained. "Oh, Sage, I missed you like crazy!" she crowed. "Have you come back to stay with us?"

Sage's gaze met Rosa's over Mollie's shoulder. The older woman raised her brows in silent question, but Sage merely shrugged. If Carly wanted nothing to do with him, he didn't want to end up looking like a complete fool.

"For now I'm just visiting," he told Mollie. She released her hold and he straightened. "Is your sister around?"

Mollie frowned and shook her head. "She's gone."

His stomach dropped like an anchor. Had Carly gone back to Houston, after all? He looked at Rosa for an explanation.

"Carly, Ben and a new groom have gone to a sale," she told him. "I expect them back tomorrow, but Ben will be calling tonight. Want me to tell him that you're here?"

Sage answered without hesitation. "No, I'd rather you kept quiet about it. There's something I have to discuss with Carly, and I'd rather wait till she's back."

Rosa's expression was alive with curiosity, but she refrained from asking questions. "Best you stay the night," she said. "You can eat with us and bed down in the bunkhouse, if that's okay."

Sage doubted he would sleep. "Sounds good. Thanks."

Rosa encouraged him to come back and visit after he had taken a look around. He headed back down the front steps to move his truck and dump the duffel bag he had brought with him at the bunkhouse. Mollie went with him, chattering like an inquisitive squirrel.

The first thing Carly saw when she, Ben and the new groom, Jim Price, pulled past the house to unload the horses they had brought back with them was Sage's battered red pickup. Her stomach cramped and she bit her bottom lip, then she took a deep breath and told herself that it couldn't really be his. Sage had no reason to return to Rolling Gold.

"Looks like we've got company," Ben observed, taking a sidelong glance at Carly. "Oklahoma plates, too."

Carly hadn't noticed that. Ben stopped the truck and she pushed at him impatiently. "Let me out. I want to see what's going on."

"I just bet you do."

She whipped her gaze back to Ben's face, but his expression was bland, his grin innocent. She pushed at him again and he slid out of the seat, chuckling. By the time Carly had circled the other truck she had recovered some of her equilibrium.

"Maybe he's here to make me an offer for Sky Walker," she said casually, letting her gaze roam the area. "He mentioned an interest in him."

"Maybe," Ben agreed. "Jim, I'm going up to the house to say hi to Rosa. Start getting the horses unloaded and I'll be right back."

The groom nodded his agreement and walked toward the back of the trailer. Carly would have liked nothing better than to find Sage and confront him. Instead she forced herself to stay put. "I'll help him."

Ben put a detaining hand upon her arm.

"What is it?" she asked impatiently.

"Don't jump to conclusions," he said softly. "There's any number of reasons why he could be here."

"Oh?" She forced a smile. "I can only think of one, horse business. He's either buying, selling or breeding. This time he'd better have the stud fee." She shook off Ben's hand and made herself take a deep breath. "I'm okay," she said in a softer voice. "Don't worry about me."

Ben touched her cheek. "Okay," he said. "I'll be back in a few minutes."

Before Carly could take another step, she saw a movement by the new barn. When she looked up, her whole body froze.

It was Sage, and he looked even more attractive than she'd remembered, wearing tight jeans and a plaid shirt, his eyes shielded by the black Stetson. She began walking toward him, willing herself to act naturally.

"Hi," she said when they were only a few yards apart. "What brings you to Rolling Gold?"

Close up, his silver gaze was no longer hidden. It searched her face, then roamed over the rest of her and back again. Carly's face was hot. She felt thoroughly wilted and unattractive and wished she'd had time to freshen up after the long ride.

"How have you been?" Sage asked, instead of telling her why he had come.

Carly curved her lips into a casual smile, reminding herself to breathe. "I've been fine. And you?" She saw that he was thinner, his features sharper and his cheekbones more prominent. His hair was longer in the back and shaggy where it brushed his shoulders. When he stretched out a hand to shake hers, she saw a gleam of silver beneath his shirt cuff.

"I've been okay." He looked at her neck, but she knew he couldn't see the gold chain and horseshoe pendant she refused to take off. It was hidden beneath the collar of her shirt.

"I've been looking around," he said when she remained silent. "You've made some great improvements. The place looks terrific."

"Thanks. When did you get here?" The polite inanity of their conversation was driving her wild.

"Yesterday afternoon. Rosa put me up in the bunkhouse."

His reply shocked Carly. What could be so important to make him wait for her to come back?

To cover her sudden nervousness Carly said, "The horses we bought need to be unloaded. I guess you'll have to wait some more."

"I'll help you," Sage told her, his eyes lingering on hers before she managed to nod agreement. "I want to see them."

Carly took her time, settling the new mares and then keeping busy in the stable as long as she could after Sage finally wandered off to find Mollie. She knew that her coolness irritated him, but couldn't seem to help herself. Part of her wanted to know why he had come back, and another part to delay the news as long as possible. That way the tiny bit of her that still believed in miracles and happily ever after could pretend he had come back because of her.

Finally there was nothing left to do.

"Why don't you go on up to the house," Tony suggested. "You must be tired after that long drive. And you haven't even seen your sister or Rosa yet."

Carly was glad he didn't mention Sage. "Okay," she said, returning the tack she had been cleaning to its hook. "I guess you're right."

She was halfway to the house when Sage came to meet her. His face bore an expression of determination. "We have to talk," he said with the same single-minded arrogance she remembered so well. Then he glanced down at her wrinkled clothes. "Do you want to freshen up first, get something to eat?"

As if Carly could keep anything down. "Just let me change and run a brush through my hair," she said. "Then we can talk."

A slight smile relaxed his hard mouth. "Fine. Shall I meet you down by the creek?"

Her first thought was that the spot was too private, her second that privacy was something that no longer mattered to the two of them. "Fine," she echoed, deciding not to argue. "I won't be more than a few minutes."

"No hurry."

She noticed that his eyes blazed with impatience and for the first time felt a ray of hope. Sternly ordering herself to ignore it, she turned and walked slowly away without another word.

Sage thought he would go crazy waiting for her. Glancing again at the empty slope behind him, he bent to pick up another handful of stones, then skipped them one by one over the water. He had tried to read Carly's feelings in her face, but had failed completely. If she was happy to see him, she hid it well.

"So," she said a few moments later, surprising him, "here I am. Sorry I kept you waiting."

He turned to look at her. She had changed into a dark blue sundress that bared her delicate shoulders and turned her eyes to navy velvet. Her hair was loose and rippled around her face like molten gold. The scent of wildflowers drifted to him. At the thought that she might yet refuse his offer, his mouth went dry and he swallowed painfully.

"I guess you've been pretty busy since I left," he said, needing to fill the awkward silence.

At his comment, Carly began to tell him about all the improvements that had taken place. Her gaze darted to his, then danced away, as skittish as a foal that needed gentling. Her talk was rushed, as if she was afraid he might break in with something she didn't want to hear. After a few long moments Sage could stand no more.

He moved toward her and curled his hands over her bare shoulders, feeling her sudden tension. He marveled as always at the softness of her skin and the tempting warmth that flowed into him when he touched her. His body tightened painfully.

Her voice stilled and her eyes widened as she looked at him. "What is it?" Her voice was no more than a whisper.

It was time for the biggest gamble of his life. "You talk too much," he said softly. To his surprise she wrenched away, turning her back to him.

"Hey," he murmured, "I didn't mean anything bad." Cautiously he touched her arm. When she didn't flinch, he gently turned her around. To his utter surprise, her eyes were awash with tears. His heart rose to his throat and lodged there, beating like that of a calf cornered by coyotes.

When he reached up to cup her cheek lightly, she rubbed against his hand as if seeking more of his touch. A spark of hope warmed him and he leaned forward to kiss her. Immediately she straightened away from him.

"Why are you here?" she asked baldly, as if she couldn't bear not knowing for one more minute. "And how long are you staying this time?"

"As long as you'll have me." At her puzzled expression he dropped his bombshell. "I sold my ranch."

If he had told her he had sold his firstborn, she couldn't have looked more stunned. "I-I don't understand," she stammered.

"I had an offer I couldn't refuse. Now I'm looking for a good investment, and I thought that Rolling Gold would be the very best I could hope for." He waited in agony for her reaction.

"You sold your ranch?" she echoed. "But why?" She seemed to be barely breathing "It means everything to you."

"Not anymore," he murmured, wondering how much longer he could wait to kiss her. "My dreams are dust without you in them. I found that out the hard way. These last months away from you have been hell. *You're* the one who's given me gold fever. Not the palominos, not the land, but you. I want to buy into this operation, to form the partnership you mentioned before. I want a place in your life."

Carly stepped back, studying his face earnestly. "I would never consider selling part of Rolling Gold to someone outside the family," she said after a silence that stretched painfully. Her voice had turned cool.

Sage's heart plummeted. She had let him ramble on, and now she was avenging herself for his earlier rejection. If she didn't want his money, she sure as hell didn't want him. Swallowing the bitter bile of disappointment, he glanced away into the distance. He had the money now to start over elsewhere, but somehow the thought brought no comfort.

"I can't say that I blame you," he said, voice hoarse. "You have no reason to trust me." He raised his hand, letting his fingers touch a lock of her hair. "But I want you to know that I was wrong. About everything." He cleared his throat.

"I thought my land was the only thing worth having. I didn't trust my feelings for you, so I couldn't trust your feelings for me, either. But I want you to know that I love you." He didn't think he could continue.

Before him Carly began to smile, even though her eyes swam with tears. She laced her fingers with his. "Would you say that again, please? I've waited a long time to hear it."

"I love you," he repeated. "I'll always love you." He was hurting so badly that it was all he could do to remain upright and look down into her face.

For a moment Carly just savored the words, ones she had thought she would never hear from him. Then the strain on his face made her speak again.

"I told you," she repeated earnestly, "that I would never sell shares in Rolling Gold to someone who wasn't a part of my family. Do you understand that?" She had waited a long time for him and was no longer willing to settle for less than everything she wanted.

Sage hesitated, obviously puzzled. Then she saw his eyes widen and color stain his bronze cheeks. Carly felt an answering blush warm her own face. So much was riding on this that she was almost afraid to breathe.

The steely light in his eyes softened, warming to smoke, and the hard line of his mouth relaxed into a tentative grin. He moved closer, lifting her hand to stare at her palm. It was as if the mysteries of the universe were contained in the lines etched there.

"Does that mean," he asked hesitantly, "that someone like, say, a husband, might be allowed to become a partner?"

Her smile grew wider and tears pooled in the corners of her eyes. She didn't bother to wipe them away.

"A husband would make an excellent partner, with or without money," she said, voice husky. His brows began to pull together, so she added, hastily, "He could certainly buy into my fifty-one percent if he wanted to."

His brow cleared. "But you don't have a husband."

"No," she agreed. "I don't." Her heart was thumping so hard, she thought the vibrations must be plainly visible. She waited for him to speak.

"In that case I want to apply for the job," he said, eyes flashing. His hands gripped her bare shoulders, burning against her skin. "Will you marry me?"

Carly barely had time to answer with a fast yes before he pulled her into a powerful embrace.

"Thank God," he groaned when he finally lifted his mouth. "I thought I'd lost you, and all for a pile of dirt."

He lowered his head again, kissing her with a new possessiveness that she found she liked very much. It was a long time before he finally let her go. By then they were both short of breath.

"Tell me everything," she gasped. "Who bought your ranch? Where are your horses?" She hesitated, and a shaft of fear went through her. "Are you sure?" She gripped his hand, squeezing it hard.

He threw back his head and laughed. "What a woman! We have a wedding to plan and she wants to know where my horses are!"

His eyes glowed with silver fire, he scooped her up and spun her in a circle. "I left the horses with the neighbor who bought my property, okay? He may be the richest man in Oklahoma, but I don't know and I don't care. Now, do you have any idea how happy you've made me? Much happier than any piece of land ever could."

Carly touched her fingers to his cheek. "Do you have any idea how happy *I* am? You've come home, and we're going to run Rolling Gold together. You've given me everything I ever wanted. More than I dreamed even existed."

His expression sobered. "And I mean to spend my life making you happy," he said. "It's only fair after all you've given me. I know now what's important. Here with you is the only place I want to be. Together we'll raise the best palominos that anyone has ever seen."

He blinked, and Carly could see there were tears in his eyes. Her own eyes threatened to overflow with emotion.

"And maybe some children, too?" he added, a question in his voice.

"I'd love that. Let's go tell Mollie our news," she said, "and the others, too."

He curved an arm around her shoulders and looked lovingly into her face. "Sure, let's go. I don't care who knows. This time I gambled on gold, and I won the most important prize of all."

* * * * *

Silhouette Special Edition®

salutes

MOMENTS OF GLORY

from Lindsay McKenna

In a country torn with conflict, in a time of bitter passions, these brave men and women wage a war against all odds... and a timeless battle for honor, for fleeting moments of glory, for the promise of enduring love.

February: RIDE THE TIGER (#721) Survivor Dany Villard is wise to the love-'em-and-leave-'em ways of war, but wounded hero Gib Ramsey swears she's captured his heart... forever.

March: ONE MAN'S WAR (#727) The war raging inside brash and bold Captain Pete Mallory threatens to destroy him, until Tess Ramsey's tender love guides him toward peace.

April: OFF LIMITS (#733) Soft-spoken Marine Jim McKenzie saved Alexandra Vance's life in Vietnam; now he needs her love to save his honor....